THE LAST BARNES

Ruby Edye

Contents

CHAPTER 1

"Dad, why the hell are we moving six hours away?" Carter complained as the rest of us started packing. Connor and Cooper were in their rooms packing, at least I hoped they were.

"Because Carter, I got a new job and it's six hours away" Dad answered with a slightly raised voice as he was packing up the kitchen.

"Right before my junior year? Why'd you have to take the job? You had a perfectly good one here." Carter argued.

Dad glared at Carter. "This is a good opportunity for our family. You need a little bit of small town in you, all of us do. Trust me you'll make new friends. It's not the end of the world." Dad rolled his eyes and continued packing.

Carter growled in frustration. "I hate this"

"Go pack up your room, Cora and I can finish in here" he pointed down the hallway to the rooms. Carter rolled his eyes and sauntered away angrily.

Dad ran a hand through his hair and sighed. "I'm doing the right thing, right? You're not upset, are you?" He asked me.

I shook my head and walked over to him. I helped put the plates and the bowls in the boxes.

"Change is hard at first, messy in the middle, and gorgeous at the end. Mom told me that before she left. I will never forget it." I smiled. "Change is good for everyone and I think this change will be the most gorgeous one we've seen in a long time." I kissed his cheek and continued to pack up the kitchen with him.

We packed the kitchen in silence for a long time. It wasn't until we were almost done that Dad broke the silence. "Did you finish packing up your room, Coco?"

"Almost, I have a few things lying around but pretty much everything is in boxes."

He nodded. "Can you go check on the boys please? The movers come in two hours."

I nodded and made my way to the bedrooms. I knocked twice on Connor's door before I entered.

All his stuff was packed up in boxes. He was working on putting some clothes in a box.

"Hey Con, are you almost done?" I asked my oldest brother sweetly.

"Just the clothes, did you need my help?" He folded the shirt that was in his hands before he gave me his full attention.

I shook my head at him. "Nope, but the movers are going to be here in two hours. Dad told me to check in on y'all"

"Well I'm ready here. Cooper probably needs help though so I might head in there"

I nodded. "I'm about to go check on him."

I left his room and headed to Cooper's, who is just across the hall. I knocked before I let myself in. He had hardly had anything in the boxes.

"Coop" I whined. "You have two hours before the movers here to get your shit together."

"I don't know where to start, there's just so much stuff" he whined.

"Start on your clothes, that are pretty much all laying on the floor" I groaned. "Connor's coming in here to help after he's done with his room."

Without another word, I left. Cooper is definitely something else.

Carter was the one I was dreading the most. He hates the idea of moving.

I knocked and walked in.

"Go away Cora." He growled as I walked into the room.

"Two hours," was all I said before I left the room in annoyance.

I took a deep breath before heading to my room and packing up what's left of my room.

Four hours later our house was empty.

"Well boys we're off" Dad said and we got in our cars.

Dad was in his car. Connor and I were in his car.

Cooper and Carter were in Cooper's car.

"Are you excited, Coco?" Con asked as he backed out of our old driveway for the last time.

"Yeah, I actually can't wait to start at a new school this year, but I'm glad it's summer"

He chuckled from the driver's seat. "Yeah me too Coco"

I guess there is a perk of living with four boys. Having your you own room and bathroom is one of those perks.

Connor got his own room because he's the oldest. I got mine because I'm the only girl and the youngest. Cooper and Carter had to share, which Carter definitely wasn't too fond of. To be honest, Carter wasn't to fond of any of this moving thing.

We barely got all of our boxes and furniture in before we grew tired from the long drive.

"Hey Dad" I said sweetly as I could when I was this tired and hungry. I hugged him tight and kissed his cheek.

He looked at me with an 'I'm not buying it' expression. "What do you want?" He asked.

"Who said I wanted something?" I batted my eyelashes.

He gave me another look. "Sorry Coco, but I can tell when you're up to something" He laughed lightly.

I sighed. He obviously didn't fall for my sweet act. "I'm hungry and I want pizza"

"I think I saw a Pizzeria not to far from here. What do you say me, you, and the boys go get some?"

A smile spread across my face, showing my dimples. I jumped up in down in excitement.

"Boys, we're going to get pizza, get your asses down here!" Dad called out.

Cooper was the first one downstairs. I don't know how that kid eats as much as he does and stays fit, but I guess I was the same way.

Connor was the next one down. He was on his phone, but ready nonetheless.

"Carter didn't want to come. He locked himself in his room" Connor shrugged. "He said not to bother him and that he's not going to dinner"

Dad ran a hand through his hair and sighed. "All right" He turned to the three of us. "Let's go"

Cooper and I raced out of the house. Connor followed once he realized we were fighting over shotgun.

I ended up getting shotgun while the boys pouted in the back seat like children. Both of them are legally adults. Sometimes I honestly wonder if they got dropped on their heads as babies.

"Pirate's Cove Pizzeria" I read the sign as Dad pulled into the parking lot.

The whole pizzeria was pirate themed. All the servers were wearing pirate costumes.

"Ahoy me hearties, I'm red-beard Remi, how can I help you?" She was a redhead that looked around my age.

"Table for four Please" Dad said to Remi with a smile.

"Of course, just this way matey." We followed her to our table and she got our drink order.

"Oh the shiver me timbers looks pretty good" Dad said as he looked at the menu.

I shook my head at him. "Dad every time we go to a pizza place you always look at all the pizzas and try to pick a new one"

"And every time you end up picking cheese pizza" Connor finished for me.

Cooper put his arm around Dad. "So save us and yourself the trouble and just get a cheese pizza"

"I don't do that every time" He defended himself. He looked down at me. "Do I?" I nodded softly.

He looked at the menu. "Looks like that'll be the Jolly Roger. Are you all good with that?"

We all nodded in agreement.

"Perfect when, red-beard Remi gets back we can tell her" Dad smiled.

The three boys began to talk about football. All of us are very athletic, I don't chose to do any sports, but that doesn't mean I'm not athletic or out of shape. I work out with the boys all the time. I just haven't played any sports that have caught my interest yet and I don't know if I ever will.

"Ahoy again, what can I get started for you?" Remi asked.

"One large jolly roger, please" Dad answered.

"Avast me hearties!" a voice called out from the stage. All the little kids around squealed and ran up to the bottom of the stage. The voice was a man in a pirate costume. "I'm Cap'n Scott Braddock. They call me Black Eyes Braddock. Me ship was just taken over by a group of blimey scallywags. I need your help to take back me ship. Which one of you swashbucklers, are the bravest of them all?" He said in a pirate accent.

All the kids started jumping up and down yelling for the Cap'n to call them out.

"Aye, what about you lass? Are you brave enough to help get me ship back?"

The little girl nodded. She walked up on the stage. She picked out her sword.

"Aye, and what's your name little lass?"

"Suzie" She said.

"You shall be Suzie the Swindler. Are you, Suzie the Swindler, ready to take back me ship?"

"Aye Aye Cap'n!" She said and saluted him.

I laughed sweetly at her. She's so cute.

"Very good." The Cap'n smiled at her. "Avast matey, there they are up ahead" He pointed to two other guys dressed as pirates. They hopped down from the boat they were on.

The two other guys walked up to Suzie and the Cap'n. All the other kids looked at the scene in awe.

"Ah Yellow Teeth Pete, I should've known it was you and your scallywags were up to this"

Yellow Teeth Pete opened up his arms. "Aye, it is I, Yellow Teeth Pete and you're not going to get your ship back"

"This time I have my friend Suzie the Swindler" Cap'n pointed to the little girl.

"Argh" she said.

"Oh no not Suzie the Swindler. I hear she can tame the savage seas with one look and take one hundred men with the snap of a finger." The other men said frightfully.

This made Suzie smile brightly at the thought.

"I'm outta here" he wobbled in his boots. He went to run away but Pete grabbed his arm.

"Spike! We're pirates we don't run from a fight" Pete scolded.

"Oh right"

This made the little kids laugh.

"Charge!" Pete said and the four of them started fighting with the foam swords.

Yellow Teeth Pete and Spike went down.

"Yo-ho-ho! We have won my ship back!"

All the kids cheered, including Suzie. He bent down to Suzie's level.

"Thank you for helping me get my ship back, Matey." He pulled a gold coin out of his pocket. "Here's a gold coin for helping me"

He sent Suzie back into he crowd. All the other kids were jealous of her gold coin.

There was a loud noise to the side of the stage. Everyone looked where it was coming from. Pete dragged Spike off the stage while holding his side. Spike sent a little wave in our direction.

I followed his line of sight to see, Remi standing there watching him. She waved back at him with a small smile on her face.

Cap'n Scott clapped his hands and walked to the middle of the stage. "Join me in singing the Pirate Shanty in victory!" He said enthusiastically. Music played over the speakers and all The kids sang with Cap'n Scott as the curtains closed. The kids clapped as did the rest of the restaurant.

I joined in and smiled.

Remi set our pizza down in the middle of the table. "Is he your boyfriend?" I asked her.

"What? Bryce? No, he's just one of my friends. I've known him forever." Her cheeks reddened.

"Uh huh" I said smartly.

"He's not!" She protested and playfully hit my shoulder.

"Okay, okay" I put my hands up in mock surrender. "I'm Cora Barnes,"

"Remi, but you already knew that. Wait Barnes?" She turned to my dad. "Do you happened to be Coach Barnes?" She asked.

He nodded his head with a smile. "Yes that would be me" Dad said slowly.

"Small town word gets around fast," Remi explained. "Anyway, is there anything else I can get you guys? Refill on any drinks?"

I shook my head. "No I don' think so. Thank you, Remi."

"No problem," She said with a smile and walked off.

The rest of dinner the boys and I talked and joked around. The only thing missing is Carter. I wished he liked the idea of moving. I've been in this town for only a few hours and I already fell in love, I just wish he did too.

CHAPTER 2

It's been a few weeks since we got here and the house was almost completely unpacked. Remi and I exchanged numbers after seeing each other at the store. We've been talking for the past two weeks and it felt nice to have a friend here that isn't one of my brothers.

This week was the first week of football for the boys, which meant I got the house to myself most of the time. The boys were always at practice or just working out up at the fields with Dad.

It was extremely hot that week so I decided it would be best for me to stay home. I invited Remi over one day.

"So have you met any of the football boys yet?" She asked as we plopped down on my couch with two strawberry lemonades and a bowl of grapes. We faced each other. We were on separate sides of the coach.

I shook my head. "Surprisingly not, but I didn't want to go to any of the practices this week. It's been way too hot for me"

She nodded in understanding. "Amen to that sister. I'd rather hang out inside with my new bestie" She winked at me and clinked our glasses. We both spilled into laughter.

"So I've met every one of your brothers except Carter, why is that?"

I sighed. "Because Carter hates the idea of the move and is always at practice or in his room. There's no in between." I rested my head on the back of the couch. "Any way new topic of discussion. You and Bryce?" I wiggled my eyebrows at her.

Her face turned red. "There's nothing going on between us, I promise. I told you we've known each other basically our entire lives."

"Your mouth is saying one thing, but your face is saying another" I teased. She shoved my arm in protest, which caused the both of us to fall into a fit of laughter. I gasped as an idea popped into my head. "Let's go to the Pizzeria and see Bryce." I hit her arms repeatedly in excitement.

"No" she whined in protest. "He's not there" She lied.

I know it was a lie because her ears turned red and she broke eye contact with me.

"You're lying, your ears turned red"

She threw her hands up to her ears and growled in frustration. "You've known me for like a week, how could you possibly know that?" She almost seemed impressed but she was mostly frustrated.

I shrugged into a fit of laughter. "I'm god at observation I guess" I jumped up of my couch. "Let's go, Connor left his car for me in case I needed it." I grabbed his keys off the hook. "And I think I need it" I winked at her.

She rolled her eyes but reluctantly got up off the couch and followed me. I made sure all the lights were off and the door was locked before I headed to the car.

I drove to the Pizzeria and we walked in. I didn't see Bryce yet, but there's still hope.

"Oh hey Remi" The lady at the host stand said.

"Hey Ellie," Remi answered.

"Just the two of you?" Ellie asked. The two of us nodded in response.

"Go sit down, you know the rules" She nodded over to the tables.

Remi nodded and led me to a table.

"This better be in Bryce's section" I whispered to her as we sat down.

She rolled her eyes, but smiled. "Only for you, Cor"

I smiled sweetly at her.

A few seconds later, Bryce walked up with a smile on his face. "Hey Rem, and Cora, right?"

I nodded with a smile. "Yep, she talked about me?"

He laughed and hung his head a little bit. "That she has. What do you want to drink?"

"Lemonade" Remi and I answered at the same time before bursting into a fit of giggles.

"And I would just start a cheese pizza, because you know that's what I'm gonna get" Remi said.

We talked until Bryce came back. I tried to come up with a plan that would get them a date together.

"Hey do you guys want to watch a movie this week sometime? Oh wait I forgot, I'm busy at practice with my dad and brothers this week, but you two should totally still go without me. I promise I don't mind"

A sharp pain shot up my shin and I grabbed it in reflex. I smiled sweetly at Remi. Bryce chuckled at my attempt to set the two up.

"Actually, I think that's a great idea. What do you say Rem, do you want to go to the movies this week? It sucks that Cora can't go though" He smiled.

"Um sure" She smiled weakly.

"Your pizza's probably almost ready. Let me go check on that" He smiled and walked off.

Remi shot daggers across the table at me. "What was that?" She gestured to the direction of Bryce.

"What?" I shrugged with an innocent smile. "I got you a date" I batted my eyes.

She rolled her eyes, but I could see the smile forming on her face. "You are insufferable"

I blew a kiss across the table at her. She grabbed it and put it to her heart. We both laughed.

I know I've only known Remi for two weeks, but it feels like I've known her forever. She's so easy to talk to and joke around with. I think our personalities are similar and we just get each other.

"So how was practice this week?" I asked Connor as I sat on the couch with a bowl of chips. He wasn't on the team or anything. He's a freshman in college. He was just helping Dad coach.

"It was good." He dug into the chips.

We watched Friends, our favorite show to watch together. One episode later Dad and the other two boys came in with a bunch of grocery bags.

"Why did you get so much food? I thought you were shopping for dinner tonight" I asked.

They all looked at me.

"Wait, no one told you. Who was supposed to tell her?" Dad looked at the three boys. They all looked away awkwardly.

"Tell me what?" I stood in the middle of the four idiots standing in the kitchen.

"The whole team is coming for dinner tonight." Cooper said sheepishly.

"What?" I yelled in shock.

No one told me that thirty something guys were going to be in my house.

"It's a team bonding thing, especially since they got a new coach." Dad explained softly.

"Cool, I just wished someone told me"

They all started arguing whose job it was to tell me.

"Boys!" I yelled and they all looked at me. "Stop arguing."

I plopped back down on the couch and continued to watch Friends.

An hour and a half later the doorbell rang. All the boys were busy and Dad was cooking. Which left me to open the door.

I was wearing a gray hoodie, that used to be Connor's before I stole it, and a pair of running shorts. My hair was thrown into a messy bun and I wore my glasses.

I answered the door and revealed a tall teenage boy on the other side of the door. He stood at least six inches taller than my 5'7 height. His sun-streaked dirty blond hair flopped perfectly over his head. His light amber eyes showed a bit of confusion.

"Is this the right house?" He pouted ever so slightly in a confused manner.

"If you're here for the football thing, then yes. I'm Cora" I stepped to the side an gestured for him to come in.

"I'm Will. Are you Coach's daughter?" He asked as we walked into the house. He smiled and boy did he have a nice smile. His dimples showed on his cheeks.

I chuckled at the thought of Dad threatening the team about me. Dad and the boys are very protective over me.

"That's me" I smile and open my arms up slightly.

"Ay, Will. What's up my man?" Carter and him did a bro hug thing.

"Nothing much," he answered.

Thirty minutes later and there were like thirty guys in my house.

The boys were all conversing with their friends while I scrolled through Instagram on my phone. I took up the whole couch.

"Coco, come here!" Coop called from the kitchen area.

"Why?" I complained, not wanting to get up.

"Just come here would you, lazy ass"

I got up and walked over to him and a group of boys. "Call me a lazy ass again and I'll drop kick yours" I threatened. I get that from the boys.

The boys around him laughed.

"Anyway" he grabbed my arms and yanked me closer to him. "Guys, this is my sister Cora."

The reason he felt the need to introduce me to his friends was unknown. I waved awkwardly at the group of guys staring at me.

"Coco, this is Nick, Darren, Tommy, Sam, Cole, and you met Will."

"Hi," I turned to Cooper. "So am I free to go or do I have to pretend to care longer?"

The guys all laughed.

"Coop, stop tormenting your sister." Dad called as he brought the burger in from outside.

"Actually I think it's the other way around, Coach" Darren said which caused all the guys around him to laugh.

"I should've known," he sighed jokingly. "Coco, can I get your help over here?"

I walked over to the counter and helped him set up the line of sides and burger stuff.

About ten minutes later, all of the burger stuff was set out and Dad had to get the burgers off the grill.

"Food's ready!" he called. Boys came from all directions excited to get food.

Thankfully, I was close and I got to get closer to the front of the line. Will and I walked to the line at the same time.

"Oh sorry, you can go ahead of me." I said. He was a guest I wasn't. I can wait.

He stopped. "No ladies first" he stepped aside for me to go.

"Please, you're a guest and I live here, it's common courtesy."

"But you're the lady." He insisted.

"Fine, but I'm not entirely happy about it" I grumbled. I got my food and was happy again.

He chuckled. "You and your brothers seem pretty close." He started up a conversation as we walked to the couch together, or at least I walked to the couch and he followed.

"Yeah, well after our mom left, when I was around seven, we kinda just had each other. So I guess we've gotten closer since then. As long as I can remember, it's been just me and the boys. I like it that way though. It's probably the reason it's easier to talk to guys than girls." I shrugged.

I didn't have many friends outside of my brother's and Dad in Dallas. Now I have Remi and I guess Will.

"Oh I'm sorry." He said.

"Don't be" I waved him off. "It's been ten years I'm over it by now"

He stayed silent for a few seconds as we ate.

"So you're seventeen?" He asked.

I nodded. "I will be in two months."

We stayed silent for a few minutes while we ate our burgers. I may have been stuffing my face and I didn't care.

"I've never seen a girl eat like you do." He chuckled from beside me.

I shrugged. "I'm the youngest of four boys."

"You have another brother?" He asked.

I shook my head. "No I was counting my dad. He acts like the boys most of the time" I shook my head lightly and smiled. "I was raised by the four of them. There's just some things you pick up over the years"

"Ay, Will, we're going out back to play some ball, you in?" Carter called from the back door.

Will did his little head nod thing of acknowledgment. "I'll be out in a second" He called back.

Carter took that as an answer and walked outside.

"Do you wanna watch me destroy your brothers?" He turned to me.

I laughed. "Oh no I'm in on the game and you'll be the one I'm destroying" I smirked.

He shrugged. "Okay" He stood up and held his hand out for me to follow suit.

I walked out with Will and announced that I was playing. My brother's and Dad gave me a knowing smirk. All the other boys were a little concerned that I'd get hurt but were okay with it.

These boy won't know what hit them.

"Oh yeah that's how it's done!" I cheered as I made my fourth touchdown of the game. My brother's cheer and threw me on their shoulders.

"That's my favorite sister" Cooper cheered.

"She's your only sister you, doofus" Connor shook his head and congratulated me.

I looked around to see all the boys from the football team with a dumbfounded look on their faces. I smirked.

Will was the first to say something, "I gotta hand it to you, Cora, you did way better than any of us were expecting" he smiled.

"Damn straight! You were awesome!" The rest of the boys joined in and started cheering me on.

"Well not to brag or anything but I have been playing since I was in diapers" I wiped the fake dust of my shoulders and laughed.

He laughed too.

"Damn straight and she's better than half of the guys on the team" Cooper bragged.

Carter looked at him. "Yeah and you're one of them" He burned him.

Do you need some ice for that burn?

"Oh yeah?" Cooper challenged.

"Yeah" Carter countered.

Cooper tackled Carter and they began to wrestle. I couldn't help but laugh at my brothers. The boys crowded around and started picking a side.

I would say this is a little crazy, but this is completely normal. What can I say? I live with four immature guys and one of them is almost forty-five.

Chapter 3

I headed to the store to get a few groceries for dinner, after coming back from the strip mall. It was basically just a bunch of shops on a road.

I walked through the store. I grabbed some stuff specifically for me. I got candy and some snacks. As well as some cute stuff I saw for my room. I also got all the things I needed for dinner.

After I had all the stuff on dad's list, I went to checkout. I walked to a register that didn't have a line.

The girl running the register looked around my age maybe older. Her name tag read Sophie.

"I love your outfit," She complimented me. I was wearing a colorful striped cropped tank top and a pair of paper bag denim shorts.

"Thank you," I smiled as I put all my groceries on the conveyor belt. I paid for everything and headed to the car.

My goal when I got to my car was to get as many bags in the back as possible at the same time. I didn't feel like packing groceries for ten minutes before I left the parking lot.

My plan did not work. I picked up most of the bags and almost toppled over.

"Let me help you," A familiar voice said. That voice belonged to William Erickson.

He grabbed a few bags out of my hands and placed them in the back of my car.

"Thank you Will" I thanked him.

"It's no problem," he shrugged as he went back to get more groceries from the cart and put them into the car.

"You don't have to do that," I said in protest as he continued to put all my groceries in the back of my car.

"Don't worry Cora. It's fine. What kind of athlete would I be if I didn't help out the coach's daughter?" he said. I couldn't tell if he was joking or being serious.

I nodded my head in an over exaggerated motion. "So, that's what this is all about? Saving the coach's daughter in her times of need, so she would go tell her father and you'd get on his good side" I joked.

He threw up his hands in surrender. "Ah, you got me. That was my goal all along" He joked back. We both broke out into a laugh. "No, but really it was hardly anything."

"I appreciate it, thank you. Now if you don't mind I have to get the groceries home for dinner"

"I've got to go too. See you later Cora" he smiled.

"Bye Will" I waved as he walked towards the store.

"Okay Dad, I got everything you asked for and a little bit extra. I bought a few snacks and things for my room, but I can pay you back, don't worry." I said as I saw him in the kitchen awaiting my arrival.

He shrugged me off, "No worries Coco, you don't have to"

I guess that's a perk of being the youngest and only daughter.

"Okay, do you want some help with dinner?" I asked sweetly. If he want's to pay for my snacks, he's got to at least let me help cook dinner.

"Um sure sweetie, but you don't have to."

I shook my head. "No, I want to"

"Can you start on the salad, and I'll cut the pork?"

I nodded and began to dice the tomatoes I bought.

The boys came in a few minutes later sweaty and gross from their run. Cooper tried to come over and hug me.

"You better take a shower before coming within five feet of me. " I put my hand out to stop him. Which of course only caused him to come closer. "I will seriously chop your arms off, if I'm tempted or maybe just for fun" I warned intimidatingly.

His smile dropped, and his face paled. He dropped his arms to his side and basically ran upstairs. The other two laughed and teased him on the way to take their showers.

"One of you can use my bathroom, but if you do anything else than take a shower I know where you sleep!" I called upstairs.

Dad laughed and shook his head at me. "I love it when they're scared of you. I can't tell if I've done something right or very wrong as a father" He laughed.

"Trust me it's something right." I kissed his cheek and hugged him from the side.

He took the plate of seasoned pork chops and took them outside to the grill. I started on the mac and cheese. It wouldn't take that long to cook.

Twenty minutes later we were all sitting at the dinning room table talking about our day.

The boys had a day off from practice, so most of them stayed home and played video games.

"How was your day full of shopping Coco?" Cooper asked.

"It was fine, I got a few things for my room and some clothes." I shrugged. I looked over at the bags of my stuff still on the counter as well as all my bags of clothes on the couch. I really needed to put those in my room. Normally they didn't care for a whole haul on what I get when I go shopping.

"Thanks for letting me use your car Connor" I thanked him.

He nodded as a you're welcome because his face was stuffed with food.

"I did run into Will at the grocery store though"

"Oh really?" Carter asked.

I nodded and chewed what was in my mouth. "Yeah he helped get the bags into the car. We didn't really talk, both of us had to go" I explained.

"Speaking of Will, we're going to his house for dinner tomorrow night. His parents want to welcome us to the town."

"That's really nice of them" I said.

"Oh yeah, we get to see Will's crib" Carter pumped his fist in the air.

I turned to Dad. "What about you Dad, how was your day?" I asked.

He explained his day for us. Not much happened on the day off for him or the boys. They all did their daily workout but other than that I don't think any of them left the house.

My phone dinged, and I picked it up in reflex. We tried not to be on our phones at the table. It wasn't a rule. It's more like a goal we set for ourselves to be more connected to the family and not our phones.

It was Remi.

At the movies with Bryce!! Kind of nervous.

I smiled at the text and replied.

Good luck! Don't be nervous it's just a friendly outing ;)

"Cora" Dad warned. I looked up at him and all the boys staring at me.

"Sorry it's Remi, she's on a date" I put my phone in my back pocket, so it's less of a distraction.

We finished eating dinner, and it was Carter's and Cooper's turn to wash the dishes and clean up the kitchen.

The rest of us headed up to our respective rooms. I watched as few episode of The Big Bang Theory.

My phone rang, and I paused the show to see Remi's contact picture on the screen. I answered immediately in excitement.

"AHHHHH!!" She screamed on the other side of the phone.

"Tell. Me. Everything." I squealed. "Wait do you think you could sleepover I if I asked?"

"I could ask my mom"

"Okay, call me when you know"

A few minutes later she called back and told me her mom said yes. I told her I'd ask my dad and call her back.

I jogged downstairs to where Dad was most likely sitting on the couch watching TV.

"Hey Dad" I jumped on the couch next to him. "Can Remi spend the night? You met her, and she's really nice. Plus she's already been to the house."

"Of course she can Coco" He laughed.

"Yes! I'm going to go tell her" I jumped up and ran to my phone to tell her.

She told me she'd be here soon. I put up all my clothes that have been sitting on my bed ever since I brought them in here after dinner. I also put up the decorations I bought and got the candy out.

A few minutes of tidying up my room I heard the doorbell ring. I ran downstairs to find Carter opening the door.

"Are you Coco's friend?" Carter asked.

"Remi!" I squealed excitedly.

"Cora!" She pushed past Carter to get to me. She enveloped me in a hug immediately. The initial force almost knocked me over, but I kept my balance and wrapped my arms around her while laughing.

"Gosh Rem, you make it seem like you haven't seen me in forever." I laughed and we broke apart.

"It feels like it,"

"You look cute" I looked her up and down. She wore a sage green cropped tank to and a pair of ripped denim shorts with black converse.

She smirked and flipped her hair over her shoulder. " I know, but I have so much to tell you"

I smiled at her. "I can't wait"

Carter walked by us and rolled his eyes. "Dorks" He mumbled, but he had a small smile. I could swear I saw his cheeks have a tint of pink on them.

Hmm.

"Let's go to my room" I said and dragged her upstairs.

I basically threw her on my bed and demanded every little detail of the date and she did not disappoint.

"He walked me out to my car after the movie was over and we just talked for a little bit and got to know each other a little bit more. We've known each other for most of our lives, but it felt different. It's surprising how much I learned about him tonight. When we said goodbye, I hugged him. He kissed my cheek before leaving." she ended. The smile on her face was so cute. I literally couldn't help but fangirl.

"Awww that's so cute!" I squealed.

"AHHH I know!"

I heard a phone buzz and I looked at mine. The screen was black which meant it wasn't mine.

Next thing I know, Remi was squealing and threw her phone at my pillow.

"What happened?"

She pointed at her phone with a huge smile across her face. I grabbed it in confusion and saw that Bryce texted her.

"I hope you had a good time tonight. I'm sorry it was a lame excuse for a first date. I look forward to going on another one if that's okay with you." I read aloud. "You have to answer him" I threw the phone back at her.

"What do I say? What do I say?" She freaked out. She threw the phone back at me. "You answer I can't"

I let out a chuckle. "Just tell him that you had a good time, it wasn't lame, and you would like to go out again" I handed her her phone back to her.

She typed out something and showed it to me for approval. I nodded with a smiled at her nervous demeanor. For the weeks I have known her, she's never been this nervous before.

She pressed the send button and threw it back at my pillow.

I laughed and grabbed the phone. He texted back.

Glad you thought so I'll see you tomorrow

Goodnight Remi

"What does it say? Wait don't tell me. Nope just tell me, I can take it. Ugh just give me the phone." She reached over and snatched the phone out of my hand. I couldn't help but laugh at her bipolar state right now.

"Remi this boy. I think you got yourself a good one"

Her cheeks turned red as the looked at her phone and heard me. "Ugh I hate you" She smiled at me.

"Good because I can't stand you and I've been waiting for the right time to tell you" I joked.

She took a deep breath of relief. "Thank God, I thought I would have to pretend to like you the entire night. I can just leave now" She got up and I dragged her back on the bed with me.

We both busted out into laughter. Tears came to my eyes and I held my stomach because it hurt so much.

The rest of the night we talked about the guys on the football team, the guys from our favorite tv shows and movies, and the guys from our favorite books. It was just a bunch of guy talk.

CHAPTER 4

Let's just say I was a little bit nervous about having dinner with Will and his family. I don't know why. I don't have a problem meeting new people or anything. I've never had a problem meeting my friend's parents or having dinner with another family. It's something about it being Will's family that I can't quite understand.

Remi left for work and I was left alone at the house while the boys had practice. I didn't really feel like going out. Most of the day I sat on the couch and watched reruns of my favorite tv shows.

I looked at my phone. Dad texted me.

practice done soon be home in about an hour.

don't forget about dinner at Will's.

Love you.

I answered him.

Copy that boss see you soon love you

He replied with a thumbs up. The boys would be home in an hour and then we'd get ready for dinner. I decided that I wanted to curl my hair and since that takes forever I started then.

I put last minute touches to my hair when I heard the boys come in.

"Cora?" Dad called out.

"I'm in my bathroom" I called back.

I heard footsteps come up the stairs and to my bathroom. There was a soft knock on the door before it was opened. Dad leaned against the doorframe.

"Hey Coco, oh you curled your hair?" He sounded kind of shocked.

I shrugged. "Felt like it" I sprayed my hair with a little bit of hairspray so it would stay.

I hugged Dad. I could smell the sweat from the sun on him.

"No offense Dad but I think you need to take a shower before we go to the Erickson's." I joked and waved my hand on front of my nose.

He smiled and pushed me away. "I will. We leave in a little over an hour."

I nodded in response. He left, most likely to go take a shower. I walked into my room to go pick out an outfit.

It took my a few minutes but I finally found something cute. It was a lavender tank top with a ruffled hem and went just below my belly button. I paired it with a pair of ripped light wash denim shorts and my favorite pair of light tan sandals. I layered a couple gold necklaces and put on a few rings.

Finally, it was time for my makeup. I used concealer, blush, mascara, and a little bit of natural eyeshadow for my makeup. I didn't want to put on too much, plus it was cute.

A little bit of last minute touch up and I was ready. It was almost six. The dinner started at six thirty.

Dad was the first one downstairs. "Boys let's go! We're going to be late"

They all came down the stairs at the same time. Cooper was still trying to fix his hair, Cater let his hair roam free and Connor looked completely ready.

"Okay" dad clapped his hands and gestured towards the door. "Let's go"

We all piled into Dad's car, which hasn't happened in a while. I sat up front with all the leg room and the three boys crammed themselves in the back seat.

A few minutes later we pulled up to a nice looking house. It was two stories and had brown siding.

I knocked on the door as the boys stood behind me. A lady that looked to be in her thirties opened the door and smiled at us. Her hand rested on her noticeable baby bump. Her hair was raven black and curled. It was opposite from Will's blonde hair.

"Hi, you must be the Barnes's. I'm Karla welcome to our home. Will your wife not be joining us?" She asked my dad.

"Oh um my wife and I are divorced, it's just me and the kids" He answered politely.

Karla covered her mouth with her hand. "I'm sorry I had no idea"

Dad gave her a reassuring smile. "It's no big deal really"

"Please come in" She stepped to the side and the boys piled into the house. They introduced themselves as the walked in. I was the last one to enter.

"You must be Cora" she smiled at me.

"Yes ma'am" I answered.

"I've heard so much about you from Will and none of that ma'am stuff call me Karla."

I nodded in answer. "How far along are you?" I asked.

"Six months, he's due in August." She smiled adoringly at her stomach.

"Congratulations" I smiled and followed the same path the boys walked.

"Thank you" She smiled and closed the door behind me.

Their house had a homey feel to it. You could tell that this house was full of love the second you walked through the door.

"Kenzie, Come down and greet the guests" Karla called up the stairs.

A girl, who looked to be around thirteen, came down the stairs wearing a red crop top with 36 written across it, light wash denim shorts and a black and white flannel wrapped around her waist. She wore white hightop converse and gold jewelry with it. Her hair was black like her mother's and thrown into a low messy bun with a backwards hat.

"I'm Kenzie" She said as she walked up to me with a smile.

"I'm Cora, it's nice to meet you. How old are you?" I asked.

"I'm thirteen, I'll be in seventh grade in the fall. Are you a senior, like Will?"

I shook my head. "No, I'm a junior"

We walked into the living room, where all the boys are.

"Hey guys, I'm Kenzie"

"Cooper" he smiled with a wave.

"Connor" he smiled.

"Carter" he half waved, but didn't bother looking up from his phone.

The boys took their turns sharing their names.

Will walked down and all the boys stood up and did their weird bro-hug things. "Hey Cora, It's nice to see you again" He smiled at me. I love his smile, somehow it always seems to brighten my day.

"You too" I smiled at him.

"Dinner's ready!" A middle-aged man came in holding a plate of what looked like chicken, but I couldn't tell as he took the plate into the kitchen.

"Kids, table" Karla pointed to the dining room.

Kenzie and Will obediently walked into the dining room to set the table. Karla stood up from her place on the couch with the help of Connor.

"Thank you Connor" she patted his arm. We followed Karla into their dining room.

We all took our spots. I sat in between Connor and Will. On the left of Will, was Carter. Dad sat at the head of the table on Connor's side and Mr. Erickson on the other. Cooper sat to Dad's right and across from Connor. Karla was sitting to her husband's left and Kenzie sat next to her.

"Thank you guys for coming. I hope you like it here in Greenhill." Will's dad, whose name I have yet to learn, said.

"Thank you, Michael, for having us. We really appreciate y'all welcoming us to the town." Dad answered.

"Ken, please no hats at the table" Karla pleaded. Kenzie sighed but took her hat off anyway.

The food was passed around the table and everyone got their fair share of food. The boys were encouraged to eat as much as they liked. Conversations were flying from all directions. It defi-nitely a quiet dinner, but that's what I liked about the Erickson's.

They were all so kind and easy to talk to, no wonder Will is such a good kid and as far as I could tell Kenzie.

"So Cora, do you play any sports?" Karla asked.

"Well I've always been a very athletic person, but I haven't really found a sport that I love yet, besides football. I love working out with the boys though"

"Well that's nice, at least you don't mind trying. That's the most important thing." She smiled at me.

Questions were thrown about college to the boys and I ate my food.

"Maybe you should come work out with us one day" Will whispered to me.

"I thought about going to football practice this week and working out with y'all." I answered. I really did love working out with the football team, whether it was lifting, drills, or conditioning. I think my favorite part was watching the looks on the boys' faces when I'm beating them at their own sport as a girl.

"You should, I'd like to see how 'athletic' you are. Every time I've seen you, you've been stuffing your face with food and watching tv on the couch. I bet you couldn't last through one of our practices."

I smirked, knowing full well that I could last through one of my father's practices plus more. "Oh yeah Erickson, do you wanna put money where your mouth is. Twenty dollars says I can last through one of your practices."

"I'll take that bet Barnes" He smirked.

Someone cleared their throat and Will and I pulled our faces away from each other. I didn't notice how close out faces had become. I tried to hide my blush and Will just sat back in his chair and looked at Carter expectantly.

"I asked about coming to our house tomorrow after practice." Carter repeated.

"Oh yeah of course, if it's okay with you guys" Will asked his parents.

They both nodded in agreement.

"How long?" Kenzie asked. "You promised you'd take Shelby to get snow cones tomorrow, remember?" She groaned.

"No worries I can take you and Shel before I go to Carter's. I promise I didn't forget about you Kenz."

This brought a smile to her face and she went back to eating her food.

Dinner was over and we really didn't want to leave. I got to know so much about Will and his family just over this dinner, not to mention we talked for a while after.

"Do you guys want to stay and watch a movie or something?" Will asked.

We looked at Dad for an answer. "Sure if it's okay with Karla and Michael" He nodded.

Karla smile politely. "Of course, y'all are welcome anytime." Michael walked over to her and wrapped his hands around her and kissing her head before kissing her belly.

"Thank you Karla" I thanked her. "Bye Dad" I kissed his cheek.

"To the game room" Will said and started to walk down the hall.

"Am I invited?" Kenzie asked.

"You're always invited" Will picked her up and threw her over his shoulder with ease, which caused her to bust in a fit of laughter.

I loved how he included his sister even though there's a five year age gap. It seemed to make her smile. He really is the best brother.

He carried her down the hall and opened a door. The boys and I followed behind. Behind the door was a set of stairs, most likely leading to a basement turned game room.

Will threw her on the couch before he jump on top of her.

"Will" She said from under him and tried to push his back off of her. "I can't breathe" She kept trying to push him off to no avail.

"Do you guys hear anything because there's this annoying buzzing in my ear?" Will joked. The boys laughed but did nothing to help poor Kenzie.

I sneaked up to the couch casually. "You know what Will, I do hear something." I said with an evil smirk. I tried to tickle his sides but it didn't work.

He shrugged. "Sorry Cor, I'm just not ticklish"

"Try his feet" Kenzie said.

Before I could even try to tickle his feet, he threw himself off the couch, and Kenzie, and huddled up defensively protecting his feet. The boys all busted into laughter and I high fived Kenzie. She sat up on the couch and I took the spot next to her.

"You are officially my favorite" She smiled and ugged me, to which I hugged her back.

After a few minutes, we settled down and chose a movie to watch. We chose The Game Plan.

CHAPTER 5

"So are you ready to lose twenty dollars today, Cora?" Will asked as he walked up to me and the boys stretching before practice.

My three brothers gave me confused looks. "What's he talking about Coco?" Connor asked.

"We made a bet. He thinks I can't make it through a three hour football practice." I shrugged.

They all gave me knowing looks and I begged them to go along with it with my eyes.

"Good luck Coco" the boys pretended they didn't know I could beat more than half of the guys on this team.

"Yeah you're going to need it." Carter joined in.

"What are you talk-" Cooper started in confusion, but was cut off by Connor smacking him in the stomach.

"See?" Will motioned to my brothers. "Even they don't think you can do it"

Dad's whistle blew and we all huddled up around him.

"As some of you might have noticed my daughter will be joining us in our workout today." He announced to the football team.

"I'm out of shape but don't go easy on me. I like competition." I told the team.

They all busted into conversation. Some of them were checking me out, gross. Others felt bad for me because I was a girl and was going to get beat at everything. Most didn't think I'd make it through half the practice.

Dad blew his whistle again "Stretching lines, go. Oh I almost forgot, if I catch one more of y'all looking at my daughter's ass y'all will regret it." He yelled.

A group of freshman boys tried to look anywhere but me. I tried to stifle my laughter.

I stretched in a line next to Connor and Will.

"Ready to give up yet, Barnes?" Will smirked from beside me.

"Never gonna give up, Erickson" I smirked back. He has no idea what I'm capable of.

After a half hour of stretching and warm ups, we started a two mile run. Some guys started off pretty close to a sprint, idiots.

It was pretty easy. I passed at least ten guys in the first lap. My plan was to catch up to Will and my brothers, who were in the front. I knew I had time and didn't need to tire myself out this early.

The second lap I passed maybe another ten guys and they did not look happy when I passed them, neither did my dad. I know he was happy that I'm showing them up, but also these are his players and they need to be in shape for the season.

The next three laps I passed most of the guys and I was close behind Will and my brothers as well as Nick and Tommy. I already passed the rest of my brothers group of friends, although they weren't far behind me and could easily catch up in the next two laps.

The last two laps I picked up my speed and passed Nick and Tommy. I sprinted the last two hundred meters and finished just behind Will and my brothers.

We all took a few deep breaths. Will turned to me with shock and a smile stuck on his face.

"Out of shape my ass" He grumbled. "If that was you out of shape, I would like to see you in shape Barnes." He smirked at me.

I took a step and almost immediately fell. Thankfully Will was there to catch me.

"Are you getting clumsy on me, Cora?" He let out a small laugh.

I could see the boys giving me worried looks. I gave them a discreet, reassuring nod.

"My legs must be a little bit tired from running" I lied.

"Coco, are you okay? How's your knee? It's not hurting is it?" Dad asked frantically as he looked at me with wide eyes. He must've seen my little fall.

"Dad, I'm fine. I promise. My legs are just a little bit tired." I smiled to prove that I was perfectly fine.

He nodded and went to yell at the boys more. He looked back at us, or more specifically me, a few times with a worried look.

"What's wrong with your knee?" Will asked curiously.

"I tore my ACL my freshmen playing soccer and he's been worried about it ever since. That's when I stopped playing sports and just worked out after I healed." I explained.

The truth is my knee is a little sore and I should be wearing my knee brace, but I couldn't find it after we moved and I decided to go without it. It was over a year ago, I don't need it anymore.

As more guys finished their two mile, I could feel a bunch of them glaring at me or looking at me in shock. I smirked knowing that I'm totally going to win this bet.

"Ready to just give me the twenty dollars now and give up?" I asked Will.

"That was just one hour. I still got two hours left to win this thing."

I shrugged. "Your loss, Erickson"

"That's what you think, Barnes" He smiled.

Dad blew his whistle a few minutes after the last players finished. "Weight room" he called and half the team groaned. "What's that? You want to run even more" Dad said.

The half that groaned freaked out a little and frantically said no repeatedly.

Dad laughed. "Yeah that's what I thought"

We all made our way to the weight room together. Once we got there, I could tell this place was going to be crowded. There was a lot more boys and I than there were weight racks.

"Four to a rack, squat and bench, go"

The players broke into their separate groups. All the racks were full with four and I was left with no one.

"Dad?" I asked.

He pointed to the rack with my brothers and Will. "With them." I nodded.

"Looks like I'm over here with the big dogs" I joked as I walked over to them.

"Are you sure you can handle it over here with the big dogs?" Will asked, going with my joke.

I smirked at him. "Did I or did I not beat ninety-eight percent of your team in the two mile?"

He put his hands up in defense. "You got me there, but lifting and running are two different things. They don't go hand in hand. I promise not to underestimate you though." He smiled.

It was no secret that I don't lift as much as the boys do, it's science. They're all a lot stronger than I am, but I'm comfortable around my brothers and I'm pretty sure Will won't be staring at my ass the entire time. He might end up dead in the end if he tries.

For the next hour, I surprised Will with my amazing lifting skills. I'm stronger than I look. My arms weren't as strong as the boys' for obvious reasons. The only difference is that I don't need really strong arms to throw a football or anything.

Dad blew the whistle again and we went back to the football field for drills. Dad had a tires set up and a quick foot ladder as well as some cones. We separated into sections. I ended up with Will, Cooper, Cole, and a few other boys, whose names I don't know.

Dad explained what we were doing and we started. He yelled at the freshmen a lot and most of the football team. I could hear things being said about me throughout the workout. Stuff about me being a stuck up bitch and a turn off.

"Are you going to say that to my face like a real man, or are you going to hide behind your whispers?" I yelled at the guy who said that.

"And what are you gonna do about it, Princess? Call your daddy and brothers for help." The guy asked condescendingly.

My blood boiled. No one gets to call me princess and a stuck up bitch without any consequences. "Oh no, they know full well I can take care of myself." I smirked.

"Oh I'm so scared" he said sarcastically and threw his hands up in the air.

Without a second thought, I balled my fist up and punched the guy on his cheek.

"Bitch!" He screamed and held his cheek in pain.

"You might want to think twice about who you insult behind their backs, because my bite is worse than my bark"

If people weren't looking at me before, then they definitely were now.

"What is going on here?" Dad yelled.

"Your daughter just punched me in the face" The boy complained.

Dad looked at me with a shocked expression and awaited an explanation. He knew I wouldn't make such a violent choice without reason. I threatened a lot and I definitely could back it up, but it's always jokingly with my brothers.

I shrugged. "He called my a stuck up bitch and insulted me and my strength, making fun of you and the boys in the process." I said nonchalantly. The boys might be overprotective over me but I'm overprotective over my family.

Dad looked around at the other guys and they nodded their heads in agreement with my statement.

"You go to the locker room and get dressed you're done for the day and after practice you can meet me in my office." he pointed at the locker room. The boy held his face and walked away with a scowl in my direction.

Dad turned to me. "You know punching people is not the answer to your problems, but I am proud of you for sticking up for yourself and your family. Do you need some ice for that hand though?"

I shook my head. "I'll be fine for the rest of practice."

"You're still going to finish practice?" He asked. "Of course you are, why would I ask you and your stubborn ass?" He rolled his eyes playfully at me. "The rest of you back to your drills!" he yelled and blew his whistle.

I like to push myself past my limits in everything I do. If I know I can do better, I simply try until I can't get any better. It's one on the things I love about sports. You can never stop improving.

I wouldn't be lying if I said I think the freshmen were a little scared of me now. They stood a little bit further in the distance than everyone else and with a scared eyes.

"Cool down lap and break out on Will" Dad called before he made his way back to the locker rooms.

We ran a cool down lap. Everyone else stopped after one. I still had a lot of stuff to clear out of my head. I decided I would take a mile.

"What is she doing?" Some guy asked.

"She, my friend, is not finished" Carter patted the guy on the back.

I heard the boys break out and footsteps behind me. Within as second, Will was beside me running at my pace.

"Didn't get enough at practice?" he asked.

"I needed to clear my head." I corrected him.

We ran the third lap together. As we rounded the first curve on the fourth lap, Will spoke up. "Wanna race last 100?" He asked.

I didn't answer until we got to the last 100 and I started sprinting.

"Hey!" Will exclaimed from behind me.

I finished and Will was a couple steps behind me.

"You cheated, that wasn't fair" he pouted.

I reached up and pinched his cheek. "Poor baby"

He grabbed my hand that had a noticeable bruise across my knuckles.

"You need ice" he said.

I shook my head in protest.

"No, you need the swelling to go down. Come on" He nodded his head to the locker rooms.

Will walked me into the training room. I sat on the training table as he put ice into a bag.

"I gotta hand it to you, Cora. I didn't expect you to make it through the practice. You're a lot tougher than you look." He smiled and walked over to me.

He grabbed my hand and gently placed the bag of ice on my hand. I winced at the cold as it touched my hand.

"How's it feel?" he asked.

"I told you it doesn't hurt"

He shook his head with a smile. "Not that. I meant being twenty dollars richer, because I sure as hell didn't win this bet. You've grabbed my attention, Barnes, and I'm not very quick to let go." He whispered the last part in my ear.

CHAPTER 6

Will dropped me off at my house because the boys left without me and I didn't want to wait on Dad to get out of his office. I noticed the boys cars were still gone, which meant they most likely went to get food. I hoped they bring me back something.

"Thank you Will" I smiled as him and got out of his truck.

"It's not problem Cora really. I'll see you later though, right?" He asked.

I nodded. "I'm pretty sure all the boys are coming. I invited Remi over too, but she won't be here until after her shift"

"Gotcha" He smiled. "Bye Cora"

"Bye" I gave him a small wave and walked up to my front door.

I immediately went upstairs and got into the shower, washing off the sweat and grime as well as the stress of the day. I stayed in the shower until the water ran cold.

Ha, looks like the boys will have cold showers, sucks to be them.

I dried off my body and changed into a fresh pair of clothes. I threw my hair up into my towel and headed downstairs. I could smell the fast food from downstairs.

I walked down stairs to see five more bodies than normal. "I didn't know you guys were here already" I said.

"Wow Coco, you and Daniels today" Nick said. The boys started calling me Coco since my brothers do it. They know it annoys me so naturally they have to do it.

All the other boys joined in and told me how much he deserved it and that it was a good punch.

I laughed at the boys as they crowded around me.

"Lesson number one, Don't make my sister mad" Carter said and wrapped his arm around my shoulder.

I shrugged. "He deserved it"

"We know, he's the biggest dick on the team. He thinks he owns people and girls. It's honestly disgusting. I'm glad you put him in his place" Darren explained.

I jumped up on the counter and smiled. "Glad to be of service" I did a fake bow. "Did you get me a burger?" I asked Connor.

He pointed to the bag on the counter and I took it.

"Pickles?" I asked worriedly.

"No, we ordered it without." He answered.

I took a few bites and swallowed. My throat started itching after a few seconds and I could feel it starting to swell. I ripped open my burger to see a half eaten pickle and two other ones.

"Connor?" I said and showed him my burger.

I could feel my throat closing up and it got harder to breathe.

"Oh shit!" Carter yelled and the three of them boys looked around frantically for the EpiPens.

"Shit, shit, shit" Connor mumbled, they ransacked the drawers in the kitchen, while I'm sitting here dying.

"What's going on?" Will asked worriedly.

He had a worried look on his face as he walked up to me. His hands were on either side of my legs. My breathing had become really rugged. The boys around had confused and worried faces.

"She's having an allergic reaction and we can't find the EpiPens" Carter yelled.

"Found it!" Cooper yelled and threw it at Will. "Stab her in the leg with it"

Will took the cap off and stabbed me in the leg.

It took a few minutes but my breathing was back to normal. I glared at the boys for ordering me a burger with pickles on it.

"You three could've killed me!" I yelled.

"Sorry Coco we told them no pickles. We had no idea" Connor apologized.

I sighed and looked at the three of them. They all had scared and relieved looks on their faces. They could've lost me and they would've blamed themselves. "It's okay, it wasn't your fault."

After they were completely sure that I was okay, I practically forced them to hang out with their friends. I turned to Will who was looking into my eyes with worry.

"Are you sure you're okay, Cora?" He asked seriously.

I nodded silently. "I promise" I whispered.

"How many times am I going to have to take care of you in one day, Barnes?"

I shrugged. "As many times as I let you, Erickson." His perfect smiled spread across his face.

"That's better" I poked his dimples.

"What do you like when I smile?"

I shrugged and said nonchalantly, "You have a nice smile and you were far too worried before"

He looked at me like I grew three heads or something. "You almost just died, I think I have a right to be worried about you, Cora."

I groaned and threw my head back. "Don't call me that."

"Call you what? Cora? I hate to break to break it to you, but that was the name that was given to you." He laughed. "What do you want me to call you?"

"I don't know just not Coco. It's a family thing and you haven't earned that right, at least not yet."

"Okay" He pondered for a second. "I'll have to think about it but I will find another nickname."

"Will!" The boys called and Will turned to them. "Tell Coop that the stealers won the superbowl in '06 not the seahawks"

Will walked into the living room and began arguing with the boys.

Through all the commotion I could hardly hear the doorbell ring. I opened the door to see my best friend.

"Rem!" I squealed and hugged her.

"What did I miss?" She asked.

"I almost died, but it's okay we had an EpiPen." She gave me a confused and concerned look. "I'm severely allergic to pickles and the stupid burger place put pickles on my burger and I didn't realize until too late" I explained.

All the boys watched as Remi walked into the house. They were practically drooling over her. My redheaded best friend was hot as hell and definitely worth too much for these guys. These guys are mainly dicks, from what I've seen of them so far, except for maybe Darren, he seems like the sweetest guy. She has Bryce so it really didn't matter.

"Sorry guys I'm out of your league" She smiled and waved before she looked at me. With that one look we both busted into laughter.

For the rest of the night, the boys fought a lot. There was a lot of wrestling and arguing. Remi and I had the time of our lives and for that I was glad.

Everyone went home except for Will and Remi. We sat around the fire in the backyard. Will and I sat on a bench and Carter and Remi on another and Cooper and Connor on the last one.

"Ah I will forever love summer nights like these" I sat back with a smile. I heard the crackling of the fire and you could actually see the stars. In Dallas, you could hardly see any due to light pollution, but out here they were visible for anyone to see.

"I agree with you there, Marshmallow" Will said.

I gave him a confused look. "Marshmallow?"

"You said you didn't want me to call you Cora or Coco, so Marshmallow it is. It goes with Coco and I think it's cute"

I thought over it for a second. It had a nice ring to it, especially when Will said it. "Yeah I like it"

"I'm glad, but even if you didn't I probably would've still called you it." He laughed and I playfully elbowed him in the side.

I looked around and everyone was enjoying themselves. Cooper and Connor were in yet another argument about football. Remi and Carter were talking about star constellations.

"So what really happened with Daniels?" He asked. "I doubt he just called you a stuck up bitch."

I looked at my hands. "Well he did add a little bit more to the conversation. He called me a turn off because I was strong and better than him in all the things we were doing. That's exactly how my last relationship ended and I guess he just reminded me of my ex and he did imply that I need my brothers to fight my battles for me."

"What happened with your last relationship?" He wondered.

"Well I was on the girls soccer team freshman year and he was on the boys, he was a sophomore. Sometimes our coach's would combine practices and we would all go up against each other. We got put against each other and I won. He was pissed and called me a turnoff and broke up with me. It was my first relationship and I was devastated. It was his mistake to join football the next year though." I laughed.

"I'm sorry that happened to you. That guy was a dick."

"Yeah but it was my freshman year and I couldn't see the guy was an absolute douche." I shrugged. It happened so long ago. I've grown so much since then.

"Yeah well it happens to the best of us" He shrugged. "I'll admit that I don't have the best track record of relationships either."

I fake gasped quietly. "Was the William Erickson, star football player and all around good guy, a player?" I asked dramatically and put my hand over my heart.

He shrugged going along with my joke. "Nah, I'm just joking. I've only had a couple but the last one is what makes my record not the best."

"What happened?" I asked curiously.

"That's a story for another time"

We played board games for hours. It was past eleven and Will and Remi decided to spend the night. They didn't have anything to do tomorrow and their parents were both okay with it.

"Okay, I think me and Remi are hitting the hay. See you losers tomorrow." I said as I started to walk inside and stopped when I remembered something. "Oh and if any of you try to prank us or something you won't be able to reproduce after tomorrow." I gave them a sweet smile before heading up to my room with Remi.

"So my bestie is badass" Remi laughed as she reached.

"Hell yeah I am" I smirked. "I really don't want to put up with their shit tonight so I threatened them." I shrugged with a small smile.

We both got ready for bed. I let her borrow some clothes and an extra toothbrush I had lying around. ***"Good morning all" I grumbled as I was met with the smiling faces of my brothers, Will, and Dad.

"Where's Remi?" Dad asked.

I pointed up to my room. "Sleeping. P.S. that girl is a monster in her sleep. She wouldn't wake up even in an earthquake." I shook my head at my best friend.

"Morning dad" I kissed his cheek and took my seat to eat with everyone.

Dad made eggs, bacon and toast. It smelled delicious.

We talked for the majority of breakfast. We learned new things about Will and even his family. It was a good time.

Towards the end of breakfast Remi came marching down the stairs.

"Morning sleepy head." I teased as she sat right next to me.

She growled in correspondence.

"Okay kiddos I've got to run some errands, so I hope you have a nice day. I'll see you at dinner. Connor it's your night to cook so just text me what your making and I'll run by the store."

Connor nodded as he stuffed bacon in his mouth.

"Boys don't ruin my house. Cora please keep an eye on the boys, you're in charge. And don't forget to do the dishes"

The three all shouted in protest.

"But I'm the oldest and most responsible" Connor argued.

We all gave him a knowing look.

"The oldest" he corrected himself. He looked around at all of us. "Ugh fine" he sighed in defeat.

Will and Rem watched the whole exchange with amusement evident on their faces.

Dad patted around himself, looking for his keys.

"On the hook" I reminded him.

"Yes right. This is why you're my favorite" he kissed my head and grabbed his keys off the hook by the door.

"I love you all, yes even you Will and Rem" he called as he left the house and locked the door.

"Did he just-" Remi started.

"Admit Coco was his favorite?" Carter finished for her.

"Yes yes he did." Connor answered.

Coop slung an arm around me. "Don't worry, we all know it" he smiled goofily.

I shoved his arm off of me and grabbed a Remi's hand. "We're taking the loft, have fun doing the dishes losers"

I threw up a peace sign with my free hand before I dragged Remi to the loft.

Chapter 7

My phone buzzed and the screen showed Will's contact picture. "Hey, Marshmallow," He said as soon as I picked up the phone.

"Hey, what's the occasion?" I asked. He doesn't normally call me out of the blue, or in general. We normally text or he's hanging out here with me and the boys.

"Why does there have to be an occasion to call my favorite female Barnes?" He asked.

"We all know I'm your favorite Barnes in general." I smirked into the phone.

I laid on my bed.

"That may be true, but don't tell your brother's they might get a little bit offended" He laughed and I joined him. "So there might be a reason for my call" He said slowly.

"Called it. What's up?"

"Can you come over? Kenzie said she needs girl talk immediately."

I sat up at Kenzie's name. We really clicked when we hung out after dinner. She's a really cool kid and she loves sports. It's so cute when her and Will bicker and fight. She's such a goofball.

"I'm on my way I'll be there in five." I said happily.

"Cor, it takes like ten minutes to get to my house from yours" Will said with a laugh.

"Yeah, yeah" I said and hung up the phone.

I slipped on my vans and headed out. The boys, besides Carter who was probably hiding in his room, were in the loft area right outside my room. "I'm going to Will's. Con, I'm taking your car" I saluted them and headed downstairs.

I grabbed my wallet and Connor's keys. "Bye Dad, I'm going to Will's" I said and shut the door.

I most likely just left all the boys in a state of confusion. Will and I weren't best friends. Sure we hung out with each other when he came over for the boys, but he was more of the boys' friend than mine.

It took me around seven minutes to get to Will's and Kenzie was waiting on the porch for me.

I got out of the car and she ran into my arms.

"Hey kiddo, I heard there was an emergency." I hugged her tightly. She wore a distressed rolling stones cropped tank top and a pair of denim shorts with a black beanie.

"Yeah, let's go to my room" She grabbed my wrist and lead me upstairs to her room.

I sat on her bed and she jumped on her bean bag chair.

"What's up?"

She groaned and covered her face. "I need girl advice. I might have a crush on this guy"

I perked up. "Tell me more"

"Well he's a seventh grader like me. His name is Grayson and he's really cute. He has brown hair and blue eyes. He really likes sports. He plays basketball and maybe football. He's really nice and he has a two year year old brother and he absolutely adores him." She gushed about this guy.

It was moment like these that made me wish I had a younger sister. I don't get to have girl talks with someone younger than me. The boys try to have girl talk with me and it ends up being an awkward, overprotective mess.

"He sounds adorable. Do you ever talk to this guy?"

"Yeah we sat next to each other in science last year and were science partners. I think that's were the crush started. Then he asked if my friends and his friends want to hang out, this weekend. I think we're going bowling."

"Well did you say yes?" I asked.

"Of course I did and I texted Shebly and Anna. They still haven't responded, but I think he's bringing Bennett, Archer, Jake, and Theo. Mom said I could go. I need advice. How do I get him to like me?" she asked timidly.

I walked over and sat on the floor to be closer to her level.

"Kenz, you don't need to make him like you. Just be yourself and if he doesn't like you then it's his loss. He lost a pretty amazing girl. With that being said, if he does ask you to hang out again, I will give you some flirting tips. Just remember to be yourself and don't try to be someone you're not. I juust happen to know you're a pretty cool girl."

She reached over an hugged me. "Thank you Cora, I don't know what'd I do without you"

"You'd probably be hating your life when you ask Will for girl advice." I laughed.

"Trust me, I wasn't THAT desprate." She joked.

We laughed and talked about stuff for her to wear and all the outfit possibilities.

"Do you think you could take me?" Kenzie asked over the phone."Will is at practice and too protective and Dad is busy. I don't want Mom to have to get out of the house if she doesn't need to"

"I would love to and I know how brothers can be. I have three of them. Trust me they don't get much better, but they are truly the best supporters."

"Thank you Cora. I think we have to leave in thirty minutes, so can you be here by then?"

"Of course, I'll see you soon"

We hung up the phone and I got somewhat presentable, before I left.

She had on a cropped black and white stripped tank top and a black baseball jersey with a pair of white denim shorts. She wore a backwards red baseball hat and her white converse.

"Cute" I said as she got into Connor's car.

"Thanks" She had minimal makeup, mascara and blush, on.

"You ready?" I asked. She definitely didn't seem nervous, but I remember my first date. I was driving myself crazy and the boys didn't help much.

"Ready as ever," she smiled and I drove off.

I saw Kenzie meet up with one girl and a couple boys. Seconds later I saw Remi walk by hand by hand with Bryce.

I immediately pulled out my phone and dialed her number.

"Remi!" I screamed in her ear.

"Ow, what do you want?" She laughed.

"Are you on a date with Bryce?" I smirked.

I could see her look around. "How'd you-. Oh I see you." She hung up the phone and said something to Bryce before heading my way.

I got out of the car and hugged her.

"So date?" I asked.

"Yeah number two" she said and held up a two with her fingers. "What are you doing here? Will? The boys? All of the above?"

I shook my head. "Actually I'm here dropping Kenzie off for her date hangout thing."

"Kenzie, Will's sister?"

I nodded. "If you see her, spy a little bit for me please."

"Promise. We need a girls night tonight."

"I agree. You wouldn't mind if Kenzie came, right? She needs all the big sisters she can get."

"Of course I don't. I love that little girl. She's been in my sister's grade since their third grade year."

I hugged her. "Thank you. I'll have to run it by Karla first, but maybe a sleepover at mine."

"Well I know for a fact I would love that." She hugged me. "I have a date to get to. I'll spill at the deets later and I promise to watch over Kenzie like a guardian angel" She joked.

I waved bye and she went off on her date.

I drove back home. I contacted Karla.

"Hey Karla,"

"Is everything okay? Is Kenize okay?"

I laugh lightly at her motherly worries. "No, actually I was calling to ask if Kenzie could spend the night I my house. It would just be me and my friend, Remi. Of course this is if Kenzie would want to"

I heard a breath of relief on the other side of phone. "Of course she can. She talks highly of you and I've known Remi for a while. I trust you, Cora and your brothers."

"Okay, perfect. I'll drive by later for her to pick up her stuff if that's okay."

"That's perfectly fine Cora. I hope the three of you have a great time tonight. Will's going over tomorrow. I think he should be able to grab her then."

"That's perfect, thank you for letting her come"

"Thank you for inviting he Cora, most people your age don't want to be hanging out with a thirteen year old. I know it'll make Kenzie happy."

I smiled at the thought. Kenzie is already like a little sister to me and it makes me happy to know that I make her happy. "It's nothing, really. I like hanging out with her."

"I have to go, Cora, but I guess I will see you later. We really need to have dinner again sometime soon. I'll have Micheal coordinate that with you dad."

"Bye, Karla. I hope you have a great night"

"You too dear, bye now" She said before she hung up the phone.

I plopped on the couch. The boys were at practice and the house was quiet. It was a rare occurrence in this house. It only happened when the boys were gone. I headed up to my room and grew tired as I made it to my room. I did stay up later then normal last night. Before I culd protest my eyes closed and I drifted to sleep.

I woke to the sound of my name being called. I opened my eyes and saw Kenzie staring at me.

"What how'd you get here?" I mumbled and sat up.

"I brought her" Remi smiled as she came into the room with snacks. "The boys told me you fell asleep and since I was already there I picked her up."

"Thank you"

"No problem" She shrugged and set the snacks down on my dresser.

"We have a lot of girl talk to catch up on" I wiggled my eyebrows at the two girls and we all three burst into a fit of giggles.

We all sat on my bed and listened to Kenzie talk about her date.

"Okay okay so tell me about him. His name is Grayson?" Remi asked Kenzie.

"Yeah. He was my lab partner last year and we went to each other's houses a couple times to work on projects. He has brown hair and blue eyes. He's so kind to everyone. He always holds the door for the people behind him, especially when it's a girl. He's polite to everyone. He's not a jerk around his friends. He loves to joke around and make people laugh." She gushed abut Grayson to Remi.

"He sounds amazing." Remi smiled.

"He really is." Her face lit up as if she remembered something. "Oh and guess what he told me?"

I looked at her happily. I loved seeing her this excited. "What?"

"He said he can't wait to hang out with me again" She squealed.

I remember when I had my first crush. I felt this exact same way, giddy and excited. The only difference was my first crush ended up being a jerk. I had a feeling Grayson wasn't the same. I think I'm going to be seeing a lot more of him.

Remi squealed with Kenzie.

"Enough about me. I want to know about your date" She wiggled her eyebrows at Remi.

"It wasn't anything special. It was a normal second date. I've known him since we were kids, but I feel like I really got to know him tonight. He did ask me to be his girlfriend though" She said calmly.

Kenzie and I looked at her in shock.

"Nothing special huh?" Kenzie asked.

I hit Remi on the side of her head with my pillow. "That's special!" I shrieked.

"I know, I'm freaking out right now" Remi squealed.

The next thing I know I'm being hit with a pillow. Kenzie looked at me guiltily. I hit her back and we all started hitting each other with pillows.

I hit Remi and she fell off of the bed and hit the floor. I was laughing so hard I was crying. Remi and Kenzie were falling into each other.

"Ow" I laughed.

"That was hilarious!" Kenzie laughed.

"I'm sorry"

The laughter would die down and the second we looked at each other it got ten times funnier.

The laughter died down and my stomach was hurting and I was out of breath. The rest of the night we watched classic 2000s movies like Legally Blonde and The Notebook. I think we fell asleep around two am.

CHAPTER 8

S unday was a normal day in the Barnes household. It was one of the few days of the week that the boys didn't have football practice.

"What are you kids doing today?" Dad asked Coop, Con, and I as we sat on the couch watching Last Man Standing.

I shrugged. "This was pretty much my plan." I gestured to how we were now.

"I'm going to the store and running errands. I won't be back for a while. Y'all should get out of the house. Go to the park. Go shopping. Do something." He urged us. "I'm out of here. I love all of y'all. Try and take Carter too."

He waved as he left the house.

"What do you say about football in the park?" Connor asked the two of us.

"Hell yes, I'm in" Coop and I said at the same time. "That's creepy" we said again.

"Ugh shut up!" I growled.

Connor was laughing his ass off as was Cooper. I rolled my eyes and headed to my room.

I changed out of my hoodie and leggings and into a pair of running shorts and a tank top. I threw my hair up into a high pony and I was ready.

Cooper and Connor were trying to get out of his room and come with us. I looked at Connor with a questioning look to which he shook his head.

"Come on Carter, you should get out of the house." I urged.

"Leave me alone. I don't want to go." He growled at me.

"Why not? You've been a grump ever since we got here unless you're around your friends. You need some sunshine. Get adjusted to the place."

"I told you I don't want to go Cora. Now leave me the hell alone" he snapped.

I growled in frustration. "Fine be a jackass, but you can't mope around all the freaking time. It's childish and stupid." I yelled and stormed away.

The boys followed me silently. Connor grabbed his keys off the hook and the three of us went outside. I hopped into the front seat and slammed my door in anger.

Connor and Cooper got in the car slowly. I took a deep breath to calm myself down.

"Coco?" Coop asked softly.

I turned to him and Connor. Their faces showed concern. I never really blew up at my brothers. I've always had a pretty good relationship with them. There have been sibling fights but it was over something stupid and ended quickly.

"I'm sorry guys." I apologized and ran a hand down my face. "He's been a jerk recently and it got to me."

"It's okay. We understand." Connor said as he started the car, but made it move to back out of the driveway. He looked over at me with another concern look.

I put a smile on my face and looked at my brothers. "Let's go to the park" I smiled and Connor pulled out of the drive way.

We played our favorite music and all of my worries about Carter just washed away.

The town wasn't that big. They had a Main Street with most everything on it. The store was at the end of the road. The school was to the left of Main Street as well as the football field. The park wasn't far from the school.

I haven't had much of a chance to explore the town. It was small and a little run down, but it was a great town.

We arrived at the park and walked to the little clearing. Good thing there weren't any kids practicing football or soccer. We started playing football, even though it was unfair because it was two on one.

We played for a while until some guy came up to us. He looked like a teenager. Most likely a junior or senior.

He smiled at us. "Hey do you mind if I join in?" He asked.

His smile wasn't as cute as Will's.

"Yeah sure man" Con answered. "I'm Connor, that's Cooper, and our little sister Cora"

"I think I've grown out of little sister by now" I grumbled with my arms crossed.

Cooper slung his arm over my shoulders. "You'll always be our little sister"

"And you'll always be a pain in my ass" I shot back.

Guy who has yet to name himself laughed at our exchange. "I'm Jonah by the way. Are y'all just visiting for the summer or did you move here?"

"We just moved here from Dallas. Our dad got a job as football coach at Greenhill High." I answered.

He nodded. The boys we're getting antsy so we started the game. It was Jonah and I on a team again Cooper and Carter. We played our own version between two touch and tackle. Mainly because of me because the boys think I'm made of glass. Jonah kept up surprisingly well.

I felt a pang of pain hit my knee and I stopped. "I'm going to take a water break really quick." I called out to the guys.

"You good?" Jonah asked.

"I'm fine, just a little tired." I hobbled over to my water and sat against a tree.

"Cora Maeve Barnes don't you even lie to me right now. Does your knee hurt?" Connor asked me seriously.

"No I'm fine"

He gave me a stern look.

"It's just sore" I lied. My knee hurt a lot more than I let on.

"You and your stubborn ass." He rolled his eyes. "Where the hell's your knee brace?"

I shrugged. "Home? I think it's hidden somewhere in a box or something."

"Yeah you're done for the day." He stood up and looked to Cooper and Jonah, who were throwing around the football. "Sorry guys we're leaving." He called out to them.

"What? Why?" Coop pouted.

"Cora's hurting." He pointed over at me. "Don't give me that look Cora. I've known you your entire life, I can tell when you're hurting."

I rolled my eyes, but I stood up and got my stuff together.

"Sorry Jonah my brother are a bit dramatic and overprotective, but it was nice playing football with you" I said.

He waved me off. He pulled out his phone. "Nah you're good my mom wants me home anyway." He smiled. "Bye guys, it was good meeting y'all" he waved and we all waved back and said bye.

"He was nice" Cooper said.

"Yeah he was" Connor and I agreed.

We made our way back to Connor's car.

"Snow Cones!" Coop yelled. "Can we please get them? Please!"

"Do we really need them, Coop?" Connor groaned.

I turned to Connor and gave him my puppy dog eyes. A little trick I learned years ago. The boys hardly ever say no to my puppy dog eyes.

He rolled his eyes, but a smile crept on his face. "Fine. You two are children" he mumbled under his breath.

Coop and I ran to get in line while Con followed behind us.

"What can I get you?" The lady asked with a smile.

"Can I get the cotton candy in a medium?" I asked politely.

"And I'll have the blue raspberry also a medium." Cooper said.

I turned to Connor. "So you want one Con?"

"Small birthday cake, please" he told the lady.

"$8.50 is the total and I'll get those snow cones right out for you." She said with a smile.

Connor handed her a ten dollar bill. "Keep the change" he told her.

Our snow cones were done and the lady wished us a good day. Coop and I did a happy dance as we ate our snow cones.

"Children, literal children" Connor rolled his eyes. He couldn't help but smile though.

We drove home with music playing as we screamed along to the lyrics. We all had smiles on our faces as we sang our favorite songs together.

Instead of growing straight home, we drove around town. We rolled the windows down and felt the wind on our sweaty faces. My stomach growled and I turned down the music much to Cooper's dismay.

"Hey!" He yelled in protest.

"I'm hungry" I told Connor.

"We'll go to the burger place. It's right up here" Connor pointed up the road.

"Is this the one that almost killed me?" I asked.

He nodded as we pulled into the parking lot.

We all walked it and it smelled amazing.

"Hi welcome in. What can I get for you today?" The guy behind the counter said.

"Can I have the bacon cheeseburger with fries and a medium drink please?" Connor asked.

"Make that two." Cooper said.

The man looked at me in anticipation. "And for you?" He asked.

"Chilly cheese fries and a medium drink, please and thank you." I smiled.

"Is that all for you today?" He asked.

I looked at the boys and nodded. "That's all"

"$23.84 is your total" he said.

I handed him my card despite the boys' protest. The guys asked for a name for the order and I gave him my last name. He gave us out cups and we filled them up ourselves.

Connor was grumbling about how I paid for lunch.

"You bought snow cones" I argued.

"Is there a problem with treating my sibling with food?" He asked as he plopped down at a booth.

"It is if I want to too" I stuck my tongue out at him.

I heard the bell above the door ring and instinctively I looked up to see who it was. Will and Kenzie walked through the door.

"Hey guys!" Cooper called.

Will and Kenzie both looked over here and waved. Will silently gestured to the counter indicating that he was going to order.

Kenzie told him something before walking over here to hug me.

"Hey Kenz" I hugged her.

"Hey Cor. Guess what?" She said.

Her smile was from ear to ear. Her eyes lit up in a certain way. "What?"

"Grayson asked me out on a real date." She squealed.

"That's great news. I told you being yourself would pay off." I nudged her shoulder with mine. "Does Will know?" I asked.

"Does Will know what?" He asked as he walked up to our table.

He took a seat with Connor on the other side.

"About my date with Grayson." She said.

Will grumbled something I couldn't hear, but apparently Kenzie did and she punched his arm. Will jutted out his bottom lip and rubbed the spot she punch.

"Do you guys see how much I'm abused?" He joked.

"You deserve it" Kenzie said as she took the seat next to me and flipped her hair sassily.

We all laughed.

"Anyway what are you guys doing here?" Will asked.

"We we're at the park playing some football and got hungry." I explained.

"Yeah we had to leave because someone's a stubborn ass and won't wear her knee brace like she's supposed to. You have to ice that when you get home" Connor ordered sternly.

I rolled my eyes, "Yes dad."

"What are y'all here for?" Cooper asked Will.

"Came from the mall" he pointed across the street where the mall was located.

I turned to Kenzie. "Oh did you get anything cute?" I asked.

"I got some more flannels and denim shorts. Nothing much." She shrugged.

"Order for Barnes" the guy called.

"Is that yours?" Will asked. I nodded. "I'll get it"

"Thank you!" I called out.

Will came back with our tray. He put it in the middle of our table. The boys grabbed their burgers and I got my chilly cheese fries.

"Chilly cheese fries?" Will asked.

"I almost died last time I ate a burger from here, not chancing that again. At least not now."

Kenzie gave me a questioning look.

"I'm severely allergic to pickles and last time we ordered without pickles and they still put them on. It was really my fault. I should've checked before I bit it." I shrugged.

"Wow, that's crazy" Kenzie said.

The guy called for Will's and he got up and got it for him and Kenz. As we ate, we talked and joked around.

CHAPTER 9

I sat on the couch stuffing my face with Doritos and watching reruns of Friends.

"Cora, do you know where the beach towels are?" Carter called from upstairs.

"Did you check the cabinets where they always are?" I yelled back.

"No" a few seconds of silence. "Found them!"

I shook my head and laughed. He definitely is something else.

"Wait, why do you need beach towels?" I hopped up off the couch for what felt like first time today.

The boys were all running around in their swimsuits.

"We're going to the lake with the guys. It's just Nick, Darren, Cole, Will, Sam and Tommy" he said. "and us of course." He added as an afterthought.

Connor walked into the living room and put on his shirt. "Do you wanna come? I think the boat holds like ten and we're taking Cole's jet ski"

I looked down at my outfit. My booty shorts and hoodie were covered in Dorito dust and my hair was thrown up into a really messy bun.

"How much time do I have?" I asked. I was really skeptical that my hair would come out of the ratty mess.

"We'll give you fifteen minutes"

I rushed upstairs and found a bathing suit in my top drawer. It was a white wrap around bikini top and the bottoms were white with tropical leaves covering them. I threw on one of my dad's old college shirts and a pair of comfortable shorts.

I went to my bathroom and almost cried when I saw my hair. I shrugged and started brushing through it.

It took me less than ten minutes and I had time to double french braid my hair. I slid on a pair of flip flops and grabbed all my lake things. You know the usual towel, sunscreen, tanning lotion, a water bottle and sunglasses.

Miraculously, I finished in less than fifteen minutes and ushered the boys out to the cars. Connor and I took Connor's car and the other two took Cooper's car.

The lake was about an hour away, but it didn't seem that long when I was jamming to music with Connor.

When we got there Cole and Darren were unloading the jet ski and the rest were getting the boat into the water.

"Sorry we're late, Cora decided she wanted to come." Connor said walking up to the guys and bro hugging all of them.

"You're the one who invited me dumbass and gave me fifteen minutes to get ready. You're lucky I look this cute" I flipped my hair behind my shoulder, causing all the guys to laugh.

"The boat's ready" Nick called and we all piled on. Nick drove us out to the middle of the lake.

The boys threw on some music and started acting like a bunch of wild banshees. Most of them jumped off the back of the boat into the water. I was left on the boat with Will, Connor, and Tommy.

Connor looked at me worriedly. He was almost asking if it was okay for him to leave me. I gave him a reassuring nod.

"Let's go man" Tommy smacked Connor lightly in the chest. Connor ripped off his shirt and jumped in with the rest of the boys.

I ripped off my shirt and sprayed myself with sunscreen. I noticed Will staring from the corner of my eye. I smirked to myself.

"Are you not going in the water?" I asked Will as I took a seat in the sun. It was a great day to crack open an ice cold beer and tan in the sun. I slipped on my sunglasses.

"Nah, not right now at least." He shrugged and took a seat next to me. "Thought I'd keep you company."

"You don't have to go have fun with your friends. I'll be okay" I gestured out to the water.

Even though I couldn't see his face, I could feel him smirking in my direction. "And who says I'm not right here."

I left the conversation at that.

"Did we bring any beer?" I asked.

"This is Nick's boat of course there's beer" He laughed.

"Could you grab me one?" I asked.

He stood up and walked to a cooler. I heard some movement before he walked back over to me. He handed me an already opened bottle of beer.

"Thanks" I said before taking a sip.

The boys were out messing around in the water. I was so glad the boys made such good friends. I was kind of worried they wouldn't, especially Carter. I, on the other hand, had nothing to worry about. I sit on the couch most of the time and I know my brothers will always be there for me. If I didn't make friends, I knew I had them.

"DID YOU CRACK A COLD ONE WITHOUT ME?" Nick asked, clearly offended.

"You know it" I called back with a smile.

I was enjoying the sun as I sipped my beer. This was the life. Will left a little while ago to join in a game of football. I swear anytime they're not practicing they're playing or talking about football.

"Cora, you should come in." Sam called from the water.

"Yeah, you've been tanning since we got here" Coop whined. "Enjoy the water"

I sighed and stood up. I took off my shorts and I could almost feel the stares from the other guys.

"Dude your sister is hot as fu-" Cole didn't get to finish his sentence because he got hit in the head with a football by none other than Connor and smacked in the back of the head by Carter, not to mention the deadly glare coming from Cooper.

"I was just saying" He mumbled.

I laughed at my brothers's over protectiveness and jumped into the water with the boys.

We swam around and messed around for the longest time. The boys took turns on the jet ski. We all got back on the boat for snacks and beer, since I already had one I didn't get one right then. The boys talked and argued about football and we had a great time.

"Who's next?" Cole asked as he pulled up on the jet ski.

"I'm down" Will stood up and put on a life vest. "Anyone want to come with?"

"I will" I stood up and put on a life vest.

Will sat on the front wanting to drive.

"That's cute. Move" I jammed my thumb back.

Will cocked an eyebrow at me and tilted his head in confusion.

"You think you're driving." I answered his unasked question. "And you think wrong. Move." I repeated.

All the guys laughed.

"I wanna drive it. I was the one who said it in the first place." Will complained.

"Well I said move so" I crossed my arms and looked at him.

"Just give it up man, she's not gonna give up" Carter suggested.

The other two nodded in agreement.

"Lesson number two about Coco. She's a stubborn ass." Cooper said.

"Anything she wants she gets and she won't stop until she does." Conner chimed in.

"Should I be writing these down?" Tommy joked.

Will sighed and scooted back as I hopped on the front with a smile. Once Will was safely attached to me I took off like a shot. I drove around fast and made sharp turns. I could hear little screams from Will every time I made another sharp turn.

"You drive like a mad woman" He yelled at me.

"It's more fun this way" I yelled back.

After a few more sharp turns and Will screaming later, we decided to head back to the boat. The boys saw us coming and met us at the side of the boat.

"You're welcome to drive now." I smirked and got off of the jet ski. I took a seat in the sun. "Can you hand me a beer?" I asked.

Sam popped one open and handed it to me.

"Thanks" I raised the bottle to him before taking a sip.

"So Cora, do you have a boyfriend?" Darren asked. "Ow" He exclaimed after being hit by all three brothers.

"Don't even think about it?" Carter growled out.

Darren put his hands up in defense. "It's not for me. My girl, Summer, heard about you and was curious. She asked me to ask you."

They let him off the hook and continued their conversations.

I laughed lightly. "Just for the record I am single, but where is Summer? Why isn't she here?" I asked.

"She lives with her Dad during the Summer. She should be back the week before school starts" He explained. "You two would get along well, I think" He said.

"Tell me about her"

A smile took over his face as he talked about his girlfriend. His face lit up like a kid in the candy store. I could tell by the way he talked about her and the look in his eyes that he was in love with this girl.

"Can I see a picture of her?" I asked.

He pulled out his phone and showed me a picture of them together. She had beautiful chestnut skin and mid-length curly brown hair and the most beautiful brown eyes. The smiles on both of their faces were as wide as ever. You could tell the two really loved each other.

"She's beautiful" I said and handed the phone back to him.

"Yeah she is" He smiled proudly.

"How long have you been together?" I asked and took a sip of my beer.

"Two years now. We started dating at the end of our sophomore year."

"Cute" I awed at him.

He began talking with the boys about football again. I joined in and we all joked around and had a fun time. The music was playing and the boys were all singing and dancing. As it got late, we packed up. We all needed to be home. We were out almost all day long. Plus the drive home is an hour away.

We hooked up the boat to Nick's truck and packed up the other cars.

"Bye guys, I'll see you at practice tomorrow" Carter said. They all said their goodbyes.

"Marshmallow, will I see you at practice tomorrow?" Will asked.

I shrugged. "I thought about it, most likely" I answered.

"Then I guess I'll see you tomorrow" he smiled.

"Bye Will" I waved at him as I walked away.

The boys and I walked to the cars. Connor and I got into his and buckled up.

"Marshmallow?" He questioned.

"I told him I didn't want him calling me Coco ad that's the nickname he came up with."

We played music on our way back. The lake tired me out more than I thought it would. My eyes closed and I drifted to sleep.

I was been shook awake. "Coco we're home" Connor whispered.

I got up and got all my stuff before walking into the house.

"Wow honey, you take lake hair don't care to a whole other level" Dad laughed as I walked by him in the living room.

"Haha very funny" I rolled my eyes. "I'm taking a shower then a nap. If anyone decides to wake me up and it's not for food, just remember I know where you sleep" I fake smiled and headed up stairs.

The next day I decided to go to practice with the boys. Not to work out. I just wanted to watch and chill. It was the boys' play day. The just went over plays and practiced them. They do it two times a week and the other day is conditioning and drills. The day I came last time.

I waved at Will from the stands. He waved back with a smile.

"No wave for me?" Coop asked as he feigned hurt.

"Nah, I see you too much" I laughed.

He pouted and walked away.

After practice, Dad blew the whistle and everyone gathered up. They broke out and went their separate ways.

The same guy I punched came up to me by the bleachers. I didn't remember his name though.

"Hey Cora" he said as he stood next to me.

"Hey" I said coldy.

"Do you want to hang out after practice? I know we started off on the wrong foot, but it's a chance for me to apologize and make everything better." He explained.

I looked over at the boys, Will was among them. He looked over at me and waved.

"I actually already have plans, maybe next time" I smiled.

It was a sweet gesture, but I'm not really sure I want to talk about it. I hardly know the guy and he brought up some unpleasant memories.

"Be careful around Will, he's a player and the last time he had a girlfriend he caused her to commit." He said blatantly.

"What? How?" I yelled out in shock.

He shrugged. "I don't know, I just heard about it, just be careful okay" He actually sounded concerned.

I nodded silently.

"Owen stop flirting with my daughter and hit the showers" Dad yelled from the field. My cheeks burned red.

"You got it coach" Owen yelled back and ran off without another word.

Next thing I knew, Will jogged up to me.

"What was that about?" He asked with a smile. A smile that I've grown fond of these past few weeks. "Just know that anything Owen says is pretty much going to be a lie, especially if it's about me. He hates me."

At this point, I don't know who to believe. I've known Will for longer and he seems so sweet. If what Owen says is true, I have to stay away. On the other hand, Owen could be lying.

What do I do?

Chapter 10

We sat around our house doing nothing yet again. This had become something of a cycle on the days the boys didn't have practice. We sat around for the first bit of the day and got bored. Then we decided to do something.

Unfortunately for us, we haven't had anything come to mind.

A sudden memory came to me.

"Do you guys remember when Connor almost fell off the roof?" I laughed.

The boys joined in my laughter.

"Yeah we were all sitting down like Dad told us to and Connor just had to get up and start running around" Cooper remembered.

"Yeah and dad yelled at him and he freaked out. If dad wasn't there to catch him, he would've ended up on the pavement" Carter finished the memory for all of us.

True we laugh about it now, but back then that shit was scary. It was only a few weeks after Mom left. It was Dad's first horrifying thing that she wasn't there for.

Connor crossed his arms. "I was only eight. Plus I wasn't the only one who did stupid shit. There so many times Coop or Carter did stupider shit than that." He pouted.

"Aww" I pinched his cheeks. "Is baby Con all upset cuz he was stupid?"

He swatted my hand out of his face. "At least I wasn't the one who decided to have a flour fight and a water gun fight in the kitchen" he countered to Cooper.

Coop put his hands up in defense. "In my defense, it was Carter who started the flour fight. It was just my idea to spray him back with a water gun."

"Remember when we threatened that fifth grader who had a big crush on Cora?" Carter brought up.

I didn't remember this.

The boys laughed. "Yeah we made him cry." Connor said.

"What? Who did you make cry?" I ordered.

"Adrien Head?" Connor said like he wasn't quite sure.

"Dri Dri?" I asked.

He had a crush on me since we were in second grade. It wasn't until fifth grade that he gave up. I kept telling him that I didn't want to have a boyfriend and that I had three brothers. I never realized that they were the reason he stopped trying.

"Oh I remember that!" Coop said excitedly. "Didn't he move once he got to middle school?"

I nodded. "Yeah he wrote me one last letter. I wonder where he's at now."

"Hey why have we thought of a million and one stupid shit we did, but none for Cora?" Carter asked his brothers.

"Because I'm the perfect child" I flipped my hair over my shoulder.

Connor scoffed. "Yeah right, you did so much shit. You just always got away with it."

Carter and Cooper agreed.

"I guess that's how it is being Dad's favorite." I smirked at my brothers.

Carter's phone started ringing and he answered.

"Hey what's up man" he answered.

"Oh yeah. Sounds good. Yeah well be right over. See y'a there man"

We all gave him a confused looked.

"We're going to Sam's for a pool party. So get ready" he said.

We all went to our rooms to get dressed.

I put on a white bikini top with thin black stripes and high waisted light maroon bottoms. I threw on a over sized shirt and grabbed my bag with things left over from the lake.

"Ready" I called as the boys were running around like chickens with their heads cut off.

I rolled my eyes and headed down stairs. I filled up my water bottle, though I'm sure they'll have drinks there.

It took another couple minutes for the boys to be ready.

I remembered that Will was most likely going to be there and what Owen said about him.

"Cora, let's go" Connor called and broke me out of my thoughts.

I put on a smile and headed out the door with my brothers.

We drove over to Sam's. Several of the boys were already there. The door was open and we didn't see anybody. We walked through the house.

"Hey I'm Wanda Dawson, Sam's aunt. You can call me Wanda." She smiled. She couldn't have been over twenty-five. I would say twenty-two or three.

"Hey Wanda. I'm Cora and these are my brothers Connor, Cooper, and Carter. How are you?" I asked politely.

"I'm good, Cora. How are you?"

"Good" I smiled.

"There's food and drinks outside. Most of the boys are already out there." The boys disappeared to the backyard but I didn't feel like going just yet.

Two little kids came running out of the back of the house. They squealed and ran from a guy, who looked closer twenty-five.

"Aaron, Aubrey. Get back here." He called out to them. I noticed the girl only had half her swimsuit on and the boy had only his shorts on.

"Aubrey Josephine Dawson! Put your shirt on right now, we have guests!"

She stopped running as did the boy, Aaron. She put her head down. "Sorry mommy" she said sweetly.

She ran back to her the guy I assumed was her Dad. Aaron followed them back to the back of the house.

"I'm sorry about that" Wanda smiled sheepishly at me.

"You're fine" I waved her off. "I'm going to head back to the backyard now"

"Okay sweetie have a good time"

"I will thank you"

I waved to her and walked to the backyard.

I walked into a backyard full of guys. There were a couple people I didn't know.

"Oh my gosh you must be Cora" a girl came up to me. I recognized her as Summer, Darren's girlfriend.

"Yeah, you're Summer right?"

She nodded with a big smile. "I'm so excited I'm not one of the only girls that come to these things"

"Don't worry I almost always do."

"Babe!" Darren whined.

"Coming" she rolled her eyes. "He's a bit clingy when he doesn't get his cuddles." She laughed and went to him.

I little hand pulled on my shirt. I looked down to see the little girl from the house, Aubrey.

"Hi" I said and squatted down to her level.

"Hi. Can you help me swim? I'm scared" she said.

I smiled at her sweetly. "Of course I can" I stood up and she grabbed my hand. The little boy was already in swimming with the boys.

I picked Aubrey up and walked into the water. She looked over at her brother jealously.

"He can swim good, but I can't. I don't like it. I wish I could swim like that. He's only two minutes older" she cried out.

"It's okay Aubrey. One day you're going to find something that you do better than him."

Her face lit up at my statement like she couldn't believe what I was saying. "Really?" She asked hopefully.

I nodded. "Yep. Do you see those three boys over there?" I asked. She nodded vigorously. "Those are my brothers. I was sad that I couldn't play football as good as them but then I found out that I could play soccer better than all of them"

"Really?" She asked as her eyes went wide.

"Yeah"

"Wow. I wanna be like you. Do you think I could play soccer?"

My heart swelled at her words. She was just so cute.

"Maybe. You'd have to talk to your mom first though." I laughed.

"Hey Marshmallow!" Will called as we walked out from the house.

I smiled and waved at him. I still didn't know what to think about what Owen told me. I decided I would stay as far a possible from him for today.

"Marshmallow? I thought your name was Cora" Aubrey put a finger on her chin in confusion.

"It is. Marshmallow is a nickname that Will gave me."

"Will's nice."

I nodded in agreement.

She gasped loudly. "Are you his girlfriend?" She asked.

I laughed at what her brain made up. "No we're just friends"

"Samuel Elijah Pitts" Summer shouted in frustration.

"Uh oh, he's in trouble." Aubrey whispered beside me.

"Sum, I'm sorry. I didn't mean to." He tried his hardest not to laugh at her.

She growled and rolled her eyes. "You are insufferable"

We spent hours at Sam's house. Aubrey told me that Sam is her cousin and something bad happened to his mommy and that his dad went to jail a long time ago. She also said that he's like her brother and she loves him so much.

Aubrey went to go eat lunch and the boys were now playing football in the pool.

"Hey Cor, you in?" Will asked as he tossed the football in the air and caught it.

"I'm good, actually I'm getting a little hungry. So I'll go eat" I made up an excuse and left the pool.

I ate and talked to Summer the rest of the time. I stayed away from Will, unless I had to then I basically ignored him. I felt bad but it's what's best until I find out the truth.

"We need to talk," Will said, busting into my room. I had just gotten home from Sam's house and taken a shower.

"What the hell, Will? You can't just barge into someone's room like that" I yelled as I put my hand over my racing heart. I quickly put my blanket over my bare legs.

"Sorry to scare you, but like I said we need to talk"

"You ignored me at the pool party, the entire time. What's wrong?" He asked.

I looked away from him. I didn't know what to say.

"Nothing's wrong. Please get out of my room" I begged him.

He shook his head lightly. "I'm not leaving until I find out what's wrong with you."

"You hardly know me, why do you care?" I snapped defensively. I don't want to bring up what Owen said. If its true, I don't want to upset him.

"Because Cora. We were friends and you started to ignore me. I want to know why."

"Because of Owen. He told me you're a player."

He nodded and sat at the end of my bed. He left plenty room between me and him. "I've had a few girlfriends but you already knew that. I don't think that's why you're ignoring me."

He's right that's not why. I looked down and my cheeks reddened.

"He also told me you were the reason you last girlfriend committed suicide." I said quietly and still didn't look up.

He was too calm. He didn't jump up in shock or anything. I looked at him. His head was in his hands and his eyes were glossed over.

"Will?" I questioned and moved to sit right next to him. The sides of our legs were touching, but I ignored it. "I'm sorry. I crossed the line" I shook my head.

"No, no, it's okay. I get where you're coming from" he took a deep breath before continuing. "My last girlfriend, Samantha, did kill herself but it wasn't because of me. We started dating in sophomore year. It wasn't long but we'd grown attached to each other. It was that same year and her father lost his job and became an alcoholic and because of this her Mom left her and her father. Her father blamed her for it and he uh he started to um hit her."

I looked at him intently. I put a hand on his arm. "Will you don't have-"

He shook his head at me signaling he was okay.

"I was her escape for a long time. She always called me her light. Then one day, in the middle of junior year, she called me. I was at the doctor and I couldn't answer. They um they uh found her at the bottom of her apartment building. I listened to her voicemail all three minutes of it. It was her note to me. She told me she loved me and that she was sorry she couldn't be here for graduation. She told me to move on and graduate with a smile on my face for her."

This time it was my turn to comfort Will. "I'm sorry Will, that must've been really tough on you."

"It's just sometimes I think that I could've helped her. I could've gotten her away from her dad. She was so excited to graduate and go to college. In the end, it wasn't enough to keep her here."

I gave him one of my best hugs. He deserved it.

I let go and looked down at my hands ashamed. I feel terrible.

"I'm so sorry, I shouldn't have assumed the worst. Owen told me and my brain was telling me to stay away from you. I didn't want to get hurt again. I've been through a lot in the past ten years and as much as I hate to admit it it still bothers me. I really liked you and I didn't want what Owen said to be the truth" I rambled.

He put a had on my shoulder and lifted up my chin."It's fine, we're all good now" he smiled. Something about that dazzling smile made all my worries go away.

"Yeah" I smiled lightly.

CHAPTER 11

"**H**ey Nick" I smiled as I walked into his house.

"Hey Coco, there are drinks and a giant nacho ring out back." The boys followed behind me and they all bro-hugged as they walked by.

"Thank you" I said and made my way out to the backyard. I could hear everyone talking and music playing.

I walked out back and pretty much everyone greeted me.

"Hey I'm Amber, Nick's mom" An older lady introduced herself to me.

"I'm Cora, Randy's daughter. Thank you for agreeing to have this at your house this week"

She waved me off. "It's nothing really, I love doing things for my son and his friends. I like putting myself to work."

"Amber!" a middle aged man called. I assumed that was her husband.

"Coming, Dyl!" She called back. "I gotta go sweetie, have a great time"

"Thank you" I smiled and she walked away.

I saw the boys all mingling with their friends. Dad was talking with Amber and her husband.

"Hey marshmallow," Will said and slung his arm around my shoulder.

"Hey Will," I laughed.

"How is my favorite Barnes?"

"Well he's right over there, why don't you go ask?" I pointed over to Carter.

He looked down at me with his amber eyes and perfect smile. "Ha ha, Cora. I meant you."

He looked around before leaning down by my ear. "Just don't tell Carter that." He backed away from my ear with his finger attached to his lips.

I couldn't help but let out a smile and a laugh.

"You're a dork" I laughed and hit his chest.

"But am I at least your favorite dork?' He asked with puppy dog eyes.

I put my finger to my chin and pretended to be in deep thought. "I don't know, I do love Cooper a lot, but as long as you keep it between us. Yes, you're my favorite dork"

He pumped his fist in the air victoriously. I rolled my eyes at his behavior. Will and I have gotten pretty close after her told me about Samantha. I loved hanging out with him and the boys. They just made everything ten times better.

My stomach growled, signaling that it wanted some food. "Let's eat!" I grabbed his wrist and pulled him to the giant nacho ring buffet. A few of the boys followed including the boys and their friends.

I piled my plate with food and they say teenage guys eat a lot. Clearly they haven't seen a teenage girl raised by four guys eat.

"Yo, Tyler there's no way she's going to be able to finish that." Some guy said to his friend.

Connor slapped the guy on the shoulder. "Clearly you don't know our sister, Austin." He smirked.

A smirk spread across my face. "You wanna put money where your mouth is, Austin?" I asked, using the name my brother just used.

"What are you saying, you wanna bet if you're gonna eat all of that or not?" He asked in shock.

I nodded. "Not only that, I bet I can beat anyone here in a contest. You choose."

Austin looked around and picked Cooper. Cooper is one of the best foodies I know, behind me of course. If I had any competition here, it would be him.

"Hell yeah, I'm in!" Cooper agreed and people began to bet who was gonna win. We all put five dollars in the bet. Austin and I were against each other directly, everyone else will get an even split. Even my dad was in on it and he got elected the judge. He promised not to be biased because we were both his children.

Dad walked around and explained the rules. We both had the same amount of food and whoever finished first won. We had to be completely done and everything swallowed for it to count. It was a simple competition. Cooper and I stared each other down when Dad was explaining the rules.

"Get ready, get set, go!" He called.

We both started eating the nachos like maniacs. All the guys around us were cheering us on and Dad was laughing at the situation.

A few minutes later, both plates were almost completely empty. The only difference was I was still eating a little bit faster than Cooper. He looked like he was about to give up.

I chewed and swallowed my last chip. I put my hands up and opened my mouth to show that I was done. I was declared the winner and everyone that bet on me started cheering.

I walked up to Austin with a smirk on my face.

"Wha- How-" Austin was speechless.

I opened up my hand for the five dollar bill. He reluctantly pulled out his wallet and handed me five dollars.

"Honestly, I'm shocked. I bet you had all the guys chasing you, back in Dallas."

I shook my head with a laugh. "That's kind of hard when you have three older brothers and a Dad who can snap anyone like a twig."

"Yeah, that makes sense." he laughed.

"I tried to warn you, you don't know my sister" Con shrugged and went to eat his own food.

"Lesson number three, this girl can eat" Coop joked.

I looked around, but I couldn't find Will or Carter anywhere. They probably went inside for a minute.

I walked up to my dad, who had a proud smile on his face. He hugged me. "Great job Coco. I love when you show these guys up."

"I love doing it"

"You're definitely your father's daughter." He laughed.

Carter and Will came from the side of the house yelling and throwing water balloons everywhere. They had buckets scattered across the year and everyone had a free for all.

I turned to a water balloon being thrown into my face. I opened my eyes to see the culprit. Connor stood in front of me and gave me a sheepish smile. He waved at me with one hand and scratched the back of his neck with the other.

"Connor Mitchell Barnes" I growled. "You have five seconds left to live, use them wisely." I threatened.

"Oh shit" He mumbled and ran away from me.

I chased him all around the backyard. I grabbed a few water balloons from a bucket and backed him into a corner. "Coco, coco" He put his hands up. "Let's be rational about this." He tried to negotiate.

I was having fun with this. An evil smirk spread across my face. "Oh brother, since when have I ever been rational?" I said before I chunked the three water balloons at him, which he tried to dodge and failed miserably.

I grabbed more water balloons and began throwing them at random guys. I hit Will with at least three and all the others I used on random guys from the team.

Laughter, broken water balloons, betrayal, wet t-shirts, and many smiling faces later and all the water balloons were gone.

"Well that was fun," Will laughed and threw and arm over my shoulders.

"Yeah it was" I laughed.

He crashed one last water balloon on my head. I pushed him off of me laughing and he was too.

At least I didn't wear the white shirt.

Summer had to go home for the rest of the summer, but she promised to be back before school starts. Darren wasn't the happiest. He was pouty almost the entire time at Nick's.

After we finished at Nick's house we decided to go home. Will of course was invited. Ever since our talk I feel a lot closer to him than I was before.

"Let's get ice cream!" I said excitedly.

Will chuckled and smiled over at me. "I'm down."

"Hell yeah, ice cream!" Coop yelled and the boys rolled their eyes at his childish behavior.

"We'll follow you Will." Carter said and hopped in the drivers seat. I guess Connor or Cooper didn't feel like driving.

"I'll come with you" I smiled and hopped in the passenger seat of his truck.

I buckled up and Will drove off.

"I have to warn you. This is the best ice cream you'll ever taste in your life." Will said.

"Is that so?" I smirked.

"That is so." He laughed.

We pulled into the parking lot of the so called best ice cream place I'll ever taste in my life. The boys pulled in seconds later.

We all got in and ordered our ice cream. Will got strawberry, I got chocolate chip cookie dough, Connor got chocolate, Carter got vanilla, and Cooper got rainbow.

"Are they all together?" The lady asked.

"No separate" I answered.

"I'm buying hers" Will chimed in.

I looked at him and tried to argue. Before I could get my money out to pay for the ice cream, Will gave the lady the money for both of our ice creams.

"You didn't have to do that" I protested as we made our way to the table with the boys.

"I wanted to. Plus you were the reason that I'm at least five dollars richer." He shrugged.

I looked at him. "So you bet on me this time?" I asked.

He laughed. "I've learned not to underestimate you,"

"It's a good lesson to learn" I said and sat next to Connor while Will sat next to Carter.

"What's a good lesson to learn?" Carter asked.

"Not to underestimate your sister. I learned that the hard way." He laughed.

We all laughed with him with the memory of him losing our bet flooded through our minds.

We talked about all the childhood memories for both of us. Will talked about his second grade wife moving away. I talked about Adrian and how the boys scared the kid away. We had some good times in our childhood. We all bonded over the stupid things we did as children.

Connor looked at his phone. It was nearly six and the boys had to go home for something. I didn't feel like going home just yet.

"Dad said he doesn't need you, but there's no way for you to come back home. You'd have to go home before you stay here" Connor explained.

I guess I really hadn't thought about that. I sighed in defeat.

"I'll take you wherever you want. I don't have to be home for a while." Will offered.

"Are you sure?" I asked.

"Yeah man she can be a bit much" Carter joked and I pushed him. He laughed. "I'm sure"

My brothers reluctantly let me go. I don't know why. It's not like he hasn't driven me anywhere before. Hell, he even drove me here.

We all went out to our cars. Will opened the passenger door for me as I got in his truck.

"So," He started as he buckled up his seat belt. "Where are we off to?" he looked over at me and asked.

I shrugged. "I don't know. I just don't want to go home right now."

"How about we go to the store and look around or something?" He suggested.

I nodded in agreement. "That sounds fun" I said.

Once we got to the store, we walked around and had some fun. We didn't really know what to do. We walked around aimlessly and made fun of things and made jokes.

We passed by the Halloween section and I spotted a pink and glittery cowgirl hat that had fake blonde braids on the sides. I picked it up and walked behind Will. I put it on his head. He freaked out for a second before he realized it was me.

"What did you put on me?" He laughed and took the hat off to look at it. "A cowgirl hat? I have a real one of these at home, you know."

"Well keep this one on" I took it out of is hands and put it back on his head. "It's cute"

"Okay but only if you put this on" He put a viking helmet on my head.

"Fine then" I laughed.

We stayed on the kid aisles and messed with the kid toys. Will tried to ride a toddler bike, that was easily ten times too small for him, and failed miserably. It took all I could not to die right there on the spot. Tears came out of my eyes I was laughing so hard.

A plan formulated in my mind.

"I have to go to the bathroom." I said once I sobered up.

"Do you want me to go over there with you and wait outside?" He got up and put the bike where it's supposed to go.

"Nah," I waved him off. "I got it. You can just chill around here" I said before I took off and turned the corner. Instead of going to the bathroom, I lied in wait for Will to walk down the aisle.

It took a few minutes, but he finally walked down the aisle. As he was about to walk the other direction, I grabbed his arm and made a loud noise.

He jumped up in fear and turned around with a glare to see me. An evil smirk spread across his face.

"Cora, you're gonna get it now" He tickled my sides and I squealed in protest. He picked me up and threw me over his shoulder. My viking hat fell off my head, but I caught it before it had the chance to hit the ground.

"No Will, I'm sorry" I said as I laughed so hard. "Please I'm sorry." I squealed.

I heard someone clear their throat behind us. Will turned to face them to where I couldn't see who it was and they had a clear view of my ass.

"Mr. Erickson, is this how we behave in public?" An old authoritative voice said.

Will was silent as he sat me down right in front of him. I turned around and I was so close to Will that my body was pretty much up against his.

He cleared his throat. "Um sorry, Mrs. Atkins" he apologized.

I looked up at him in shock. He doesn't need to apologize for being a teenager and having fun while he can.

"Excuse me, Mrs. Atkins, is it? Yeah so please explain to me why you're so bothered by the behavior of two teenagers who essentially have no association with you?" I asked sassily.

The lady was taken aback by my outspoken statement. "Who are you to question me young lady? I am your elder; therefore, you should be respectful and polite."

"I'll be polite and respect you once you respect me and my friend. We are just here enjoying our summer as teenagers and have fun because childhood doesn't last forever, something of which I'm pretty sure you know. We were not bothering you before so please don't bother us." I snapped.

She cleared her throat once more. "If I were you Mr. Erickson, I would be careful about the company I keep." She said simply before walking away.

Will and I looked at each other before busting into laughter.

"Wow no one has ever talked to her like that before. That was ballsy Barnes. I would say I'm shocked but I've expected this from you by now" He laughed.

"Let's get out of here" I suggested.

We bought our hats and left the store. It was getting late so Will took me home.

"Thanks for that Will, It was really fun."

"Anytime, Cora" He smiled.

I started to walk off but I remembered something and turned around. "Oh and Will, I want to see that real cowboy hat sometime" I said before retreating to my house.

Chapter 12

"Yes that's great news, thank you Coach Andrews. My boys will be excited. Our field at three? Yeah, thanks again Coach. See you at three."

I looked at Dad curiously. It was a practice day, but it didn't start until one. The boys went to grab breakfast with the group. I didn't feel like going and I thought they need some time away from me. I know they're all nice, but sometimes I feel like I'm the brother's little sister that has to come.

This left Dad and I alone for breakfast. Not that I minded, I loved our father daughter time.

"What was that about?" I questioned.

"We have a game today at three. I haven't told the boys yet. I was going to tell them at practice. I've been trying to find a game for them to play before school starts. Thankfully someone in the next town over agreed to play with us." He explained.

"That's cool"

"Yes you can be on the sidelines with your old man" He answered my question before I even got the chance to ask.

"How are people gonna know about the game if the boys don't find out until one?" I asked.

"I have my ways, Coco, I have my ways." He said creepily before he got out of the counter stool to put his cereal bowl in the sink.

I rolled my eyes playfully at him.

"I'm glad they get a game though. They're going to be so happy"

"Yeah I know" He basically squealed and cleared his throat. "I've got to go work on some plays and stuff." He said before practically skipping to his room.

I laughed at the retreating figure of my father and finished my cereal. I jogged up to my room and grabbed my phone. I made sure to let Remi know that there was a game at three.

I sat and watch Friends until i t was almost time to leave for the boy's 'practice'. Then I decided to get ready. I put on a coral halter crop top and a light wash of ripped denim jeans and my favorite pair of tan sandals. I put my hair in a half up half down messy bun and a pair of sunglasses. I put on my blush and mascara and I was ready after adding some perfume.

I hopped out to the cars with a mile on my face.

"Why are you smiling so much?" Carter asked in his grumpy mood as per usual.

"Um I'm just happy I get to see Will" I said almost too quickly.

I can't let them know they have a game.

"Oh someone had a crush" Coop mocked from the back seat. I turned around a punched him in the arm.

"I don't. He just my friend."

"That you see literally almost every day" Carter said. "Plus he's my best friend, you couldn't have him even if you wanted him"

I don't know why, but when Carter said that I felt a small twang of hurt in my heart. Why couldn't I date Will if I wanted to?

The other boys agreed.

Them too?

We pulled up to the football field and got out. Dad directed the boys to wait for him on the field. It was my job to direct others to do the same.

"Hey snowflake" Will said as he came up to me.

"Snowflake?" I questioned.

He shrugged like he didn't even know where it came from. "Rolled off the tip of the tongue. Wanna hang out after practice?"

I shrugged. "I don't know, but I have a feeling you'll want to hang out with your team. I might hang around just in case though."

"Okay." He didn't think much of it. "Ready for practice?" He asked me.

I nodded. He picked me up and threw me over his shoulder causing an involuntary squeal to escape my lips.

"Will, put me down" I squealed. "The whole team is going to be staring at my ass" I groaned.

"Eh, not with me and your family here to stop them" he said nonchalantly.

He set me down on the field with everyone else. A confused furrow settled in his brows. "Why isn't anyone stretching?" He asked Carter.

"Dad said to wait here" he shrugged.

I like that I know and they don't know.

"Is everyone here?" Dad asked as he came out with the laundry bag.

"Coach, those are game jerseys" Darren pointed out as he tried to be polite.

"Oh I must've grabbed the wrong bag." He acted as if a light bulb went off in his head. "Oh wait no I didn't because I scheduled a game today."

The team went crazy with excitement.

"With who?" Sam asked.

"The East Conbridge Eagles. The game starts at three. Text friends and family and whoever else you can get to come watch. I want those stands full" he pointed to the home stands, which were absolutely huge.

"Meet back here in thirty minutes so we can go over stuff before the game actually starts."

"Break it out, Will"

"Bloodhounds on three," Will started. "one, two, three, blood-hounds" they all finished together.

"You knew about this, didn't you?" Will, Carter, Cooper, and Connor cornered me.

"That's why you were so smiley this morning" Cooper accused.

I nodded. "Dad made the arrangements when y'all went to breakfast." I explained.

Will went of to text his parents and my brothers and I stayed out her and tossed the ball around.

The bus for the other team drove by and stopped in front of the locker rooms. They all hopped out and looked over at us.

I recognized Jonah from the park. I waved politely. He waved back with a smile.

"Are you waving at Franklin?" Will asked disgusted.

"Jonah? Yeah I met him the other day when we played football in the park. Is something wrong with him? He seemed pretty nice."

"Please Cora take my advice and don't talk to him. He's bad news and a total asshole."

Not like I was planning on talking to him ever again. I don't know the guy.

"Okay" I said softly. The boys got called to start warm up.

"Cora!" Kenzie screamed and jumped into my arms. She wore a black old band tank top, ripped denim shorts, and a red and black flannel he ties around her waist. Paired with her white converse.

"Kenz!" I hugged her and spun her around.

"You need to come over more. I missed you. I have to tell you about my date with Grayson" she squealed.

"Oh" I perked up. "How was it?"

She proceeded to tell all about her date. It was so cute.

"Oh and he asked me to be his girlfriend" she squealed excitedly. "I said yes of course. He's actually coming to the game." Her smile was a mile wide.

"That's great" I smiled. "Beware I'm going to be down here for the whole game, but Remi will be up there. Be very careful, she might tease you" I only half joked.

We talked for a little while longer before we went up in the stands to see Karla and Micheal.

"Hey Cora" Karla called.

"Hi Karla" I said as I walked up the stairs. I sat next to her and gave her a hug. "Hey Micheal" I said.

He waved at me kindly.

"How's the baby?" I asked and set my hand on her bump.

"Good. We have a doctor's appointment to find out the gender tomorrow actually."

I smiled at her. I know Will was pretty excited to find out. "So late? Aren't you supposed to find out around four months?" I asked.

She nodded. "At first we didn't want to know and keep it a surprise for everyone, but as we thought about it we wanted to know the gender of our child. The only one who knows right now is our doctor, my sister, and Michael's mom."

"Are you having a party?" I asked.

"Yeah, has Will not said anything? You and your family are invited. It's Tuesday at our house at four."

"I will be sure to tell the boys" I smiled.

The game was going to start soon and I headed back down to the field. I hopped next to my dad and Connor.

"Coach K" one of the guys from the other team called and walked right by me. I didn't miss the flirty wink he sent my way before he walked away.

The game started and the boys were pretty much bouncing off the walls with excitement.

"It's gonna be a good game" Dad smiled at his team as they took to the field.

By the end of the first half, we were leading by a touchdown. I decided to up to see Remi and Kenzie.

"Cora!" Remi practically tackled me when she saw me. I hadn't seen her in a week because she was on vacation with her family. I kinda missed her and her crazy attitude.

"Remi!" I laughed and hugged her back. "Gosh I missed you" I squeezed her tight.

"I know, me too" She laughed.

"Is your boy toy here?" I asked as we walked up to sit with Kenzie and her boyfriend.

She shook her head. "Football is not his thing. He doesn't understand nor is he going to try or pretend to." She shrugged.

He didn't even come to hang out with her. If my boyfriend was gone for a week, I would take every opportunity to hang out with him when he got back. I pushed the thought out of my head as we reached Kenzie.

"Hey Kenz" I smirked at her. "Who's this?" I asked.

Obviously, I knew who it was. I wanted to tease Kenzie a little bit.

Her face was already on its way to becoming a tomato.

"This is my boyfriend Grayson," She introduced him with an eye roll. "Gray, this is mine and Will's friend Cora and her best friend, Remi." She smiled at her boyfriend.

"Nice to meet you Cora" He smiled at me.

"You too, Grayson." I smiled back. "You were right Kenz, he is cute and nice" I said in a loud whisper so he could hear me.

He smiled at her when her face turned bright red.

My job was accomplished.

"Cora!" A new voice squealed and Aubrey ran up to me.

"Hey girl" I smiled as she jumped on my lap.

"Did you hear?" She asked.

I shook my head at her. "Hear what?" I asked.

"My mommy's going to have a baby!" She squealed happily.

"Yay! I'm so happy for you. You're going to be a big sister"

"Yeah and and guess what?" Her face lit up with happiness and excitement.

"What?" I laughed.

"Mommy signed me up for soccer! I'm going to be just like you" She squealed.

I looked at her with wide eyes. I didn't actually expect her to want to play soccer like I did. "Wow that's really cool"

"Wait you play soccer?" Kenzie asked me. "I do too"

"Well I used to play. I got injured my freshman year and I just stopped playing." I answered. "I could give you pointers though if you want"

"That would be great. I have tryouts just before school starts" She smiled at me.

Halftime was almost over but I decided to stay in the stands for the second half.

"Hey, Aubrey, where's your momma sitting?" Karla asked the little girl in my lap with a smile.

Aubrey pointed down a couple rows and Karla went to talk to her.

The game started and Aubrey left with Aaron to play with some of their friends.

Remi was sort of confused and Kenzie and I had to explain what happened. Grayson and Kenzie were so cute together. I swear I've never seen this child smile as big as she did when he was around. He made her laugh several times throughout the game. I couldn't help but smile at them.

I looked away from them once the timeout was over and watched the game. It was tied at the beginning of the fourth quarter and we had the ball.

Will called for the snap and the ball connected with his hands. Neither receivers were open and he had no choice but to run the ball. He got tackled just a couple yards past the line of scrimmage. The refs didn't agree and called it a sack.

"What the hell? He was in front of the line of scrimmage!" I yelled.

I got a couple of death glares from the parents of young children. I also had some people agreeing with me, mostly the dad and students.

After a few minutes, the refs agreed that it was in fact in front of the line of scrimmage, which gave us a first down. Our entire stands clapped.

The game was over and we won. I walked to the field to hug my brothers and Dad.

Carter was the first I saw and I ran and jumped into his arms. He spun me around making me laugh. Will just smiled over at us.

"You did great bubba" I smiled. Cooper came up to us and I hugged him. Dad and Connor followed not long after. I hugged both of them and Will after them.

"What no hug for me?" Nick joked as him and the rest of the boys walked up to us.

I rolled my yes but hugged him and the boys anyway.

"You go shower, pizza on me" Dad laughed. The boy all ran to the locker room. "I have to go do some coach things really quick."

"Okay" I said as he kissed my head and walked off. I was left alone.

Remi had to leave for work and the Erickson's left already. I decided to head to the boys' cars and wait on them.

I scrolled through my phone as I leaned against the car.

"So you and Erickson, huh?" A voice asked from beside me. It was Jonah.

I jumped and put a hand to my heart. "Jeez Jonah you scared the hell out of me" I took a deep breath.

He chuckled. "Sorry I didn't mean to. So are you and Erickson a thing?" He asked.

"No, he's my brothers's best friend. Why do you care?"

"Just wondering." He shrugged. "Now I know you have better standards than Erickson"

I looked at him in shock and disgust. "Do not talk about him like that. If anything, that boy is too good for me. I guess I failed to mention that not only is he my brothers's best friend but also one of mine. He is and forever will be a better guy than you" I snapped.

He can't talk about my friends like that and get away with it.

He put his hands out in defense. "Sorry. I guess you're not the kind of girl I thought you were."

"And you're not the guy"

He walked to his bus without another word.

"Asshole" I muttered. Will was right.

"Who's an asshole?" Cooper asked. The guys walked up with him.

"Jonah" I muttered.

I went to open the back door of Connor's car.

"Hey Coco, I told some of the guys they could ride with me. There's room in Coop's car or you could go with Will" Connor said apologetically. "I'm sorry. I know post game jams"

Post game jams are jam sessions with Connor and I. After every game as Connor and I drive home or to eat we jam out and sing to our post game jam playlist. it was one of my favorite traditions.

"It's fine Con, ride with your friends, I'll just go with Will" I assured him.

He gave me an incredulous look.

"I promise" I smiled. "You just better not bail out next time"

"You know I won't, cross my heart" He crossed his heart dramatically and turned to his car with his friends.

I walked with Will to his truck and he opened the door for me.
We went to the pizzeria and had a fun dinner. It was an experience
that I'll never forget.

CHAPTER 13

"Did you guys hear the fair was in town? It's not to far from here." I said as I plopped on the beanbag next to Darren and Tommy with a bowl of freshly made popcorn. All the boys were at my house and we were sitting in the loft watching movies. It was a little cramped for ten people, but it worked.

"Where'd you get popcorn from?" Tommy whined as he tried to steal a piece, but I moved it away from him.

"My kitchen you nitwit, get your own" I smacked his hand and shoved a few more pieces in my mouth.

The boys laughed when me crossed his arms and pouted.

"The fair does sound fun though" Con said.

"I know right"

"I say we go tomorrow. I'm too tired right now." Coop groaned.

I rolled my eyes at him. "C'mon Coop a three hour practice isn't that bad" I teased.

The boys all groaned. "How would you feel after that practice we had today? All you did was run and ab workouts" Nick said.

I thought about it for a minute. Dad really did put them through the ringer today. I'm actually not sure if I could have done it. Dad definitely wouldn't have let me because of my knee. "I think you guys are a bunch of sissys." I shrugged. I knew I would be just like they are now after that workout but they don't have to know that.

"So fair tomorrow?" Darren asked.

All the boy and I nodded in agreement.

"Great, I'll ask my mom" He said.

"Tori's in town this week but I'm sure I can go" Said Nick.

I looked around. "Good so we're all in agreement, tomorrow."

"Meet at Riley's at noon and we'll leave from there" Con said we all came to an agreement. For the rest of the time we talked and joked around. I beat the boys' asses in Call f Duty.

"Let's go" I called out to the boys. They woke up late as always and were rushing out of the house. I invited Remi too and she's gonna meet us there a little bit later.

I checked my outfit one last time. I wore a yellow cropped champion shirt and a pair of denim shorts and my white high top converses.

"We're coming." Con called as he, followed by the other two, came walking down the stairs.

We made our way to Riley's. Riley's Kitchen is the burger place that nearly killed me, but everyone called it Riley's.

Connor was taking his with Cooper and Nick. I was going in Will's truck with Carter. Darren and Sam were going with each other. Tommy and Cole were taking Cole's car.

We met up at the diner and went to the cars that we decided to go in after we got a little bit of ice cream. I don't know why we didn't just take two or three cars, but I guess this is the way it worked out in the end.

"You guys ready?" Will buckled his seat belt in the drivers seat. Carter took the front seat. Which left me in the back seat.

"Yep" I smiled.

"Go man"

Will back out of Riley's parking lot and we started our hour-ish drive to the fair.

We sung to some music on the radio but for the most part it was a quiet ride.

"What are three things you can't live without? Materially I mean. You obviously can't live with food and water" Will asked.

"Football, the sun, I don't look this tan without it, and probably pasta." Carter answered.

"Okay football's obvious. The sun, really? Hate to break it to you bro but you're not all that hot" Will joked.

Carter playfully smacked him in the arm.

"Pasta?" Will questioned.

"Whoa, don't go there Will, that boy is obsessed with his pasta" I joked from the back.

Will glanced at me with a smile as the boys laughed.

Carter just shrugged. "It's true man"

"What about you Cor?" Will asked.

"Hot showers, Dad's burgers, and lazy days"

"Everyday is a lazy day with you Coco" Carter joked.

I laughed but punched Carter in the arm harder than I originally meant to. He whined and rubbed his arm with a pout on his face.

"Oops my arm slipped" I smiled sweetly at him. Will laughed at us.

"I don't disagree with you though. I would literally kill for his burgers"

I shrugged. "Then maybe you should come over again sometime for dinner. Oh and bring Kenz"

He shook his head with a smile forming on his face. "I swear you liked her more than me or even your own siblings" He laughed.

"Maybe" I said sweetly.

When we got there it looked pretty busy, but it was a huge place so I kind of expected it. We went to the ticket booth and paid the lady working.

We walked around for a little bit and checked things out before deciding what to do first.The group split up before long because some of the boys saw something they wanted to do.

"Oh let's go on the ferris wheel" I smacked Carter's arm about a million times.

"Okay, okay" he put his hands on mine to stop the smacking and chuckled at my excitement.

I grabbed his and Will's hands and dragged them to the ferris wheel line. Thankfully for us it wasn't excruciatingly long. Connor and Cooper followed behind us laughing.

We had to wait maybe ten minutes to go up there. There were six people to a cart. The five of us piled in.

"Are you okay with adding an extra to your group?" The guy working the ferris wheel asked.

I looked at the boys and they didn't seem opposed to the idea.

"Yeah that's fine." I shrugged.

"Can I have one more for this group?" The guy asked. The first six people looked at each other and shook their heads.

One girl spoke up and agreed to go with us.

I ended up sitting m in between Will and Carter. Will was on the end and sitting next to Carter was Cooper, then Connor, then the girl.

"Hey guys" she smiled. "I'm Selena, but most people call me Lena"

"I'm Cora. This one sitting on my left is Will and right is my brothers, Carter, Cooper, and Connor" I introduced them.

"Nice to meet you" Will smiled at her.

"Hi," Cooper waved.

"Hey," Carter said nonchalantly.

Connor just waved at her.

The ferris wheel started going and Selena just grabbed onto Connor's arm.

"Oh I'm sorry" she let go of Connor's arm with a sheepish smile and red stained her face.

"Nah you're good. Are you scared of heights?" He asked.

She shook her head. "No, I'm scared of ferris wheels that can be moved in a day. Who knows someone could've forgotten something and we could all fall to our deaths, but I really love the view from the top of the ferris wheel" She held onto Connor's arm.

He chuckled and put his arm around her to comfort her as she held his other hand.

"Did you come with your friends?" Will asked as the ferris wheel stopped about half way.

She shook her head. "My family. My mom, dad, and little brother, Jake." We stayed silent for a few seconds before Selena spoke up. "How old are you guys?" She asked.

"I'm going to be seventeen at the end of next month" I answered.

"Eighteen" Will answered.

"Same here," Cooper said.

"I'm seventeen"

"I'm nineteen. I just graduated and the others are juniors and seniors. What about you?" He smiled at her.

"I'll be eighteen at the beginning of September and I'm a senior in high school."

We all smiled and talked about ourselves. She went to our rival school in football. Of course we didn't put that against her. She was really cool.

We finally reached the top. Lena got excited and took a picture of the skyline. Then we all squished together to get a picture on my phone. Lena felt like she was interrupting at first but we assured her it was completely fine.

It wasn't long when we reached the bottom. We all exchanged numbers and socials with Lena.

"Bye Lena, we should hang out sometime." Connor said.

"I can hang with you right now if you want," she smiled.

"We don't want to keep you from hanging out with your family." I interjected.

She waved me off. "It's fine. This is a common occurrence. We always hang out. I'd just have to let them know." She shrugged.

"Just to warn you, we have five other boys in our group," Cooper said.

"I'm used to it, all my cousins are boys and I have four older brothers. Plus Jake" she shrugged.

I thought it was just her and Jake.

"Let me go tell my parents real quick." She walked away for a few minutes and came back to us.

"Let's go find the gang" Cooper joked and we walked to find the rest of our friends.

We found them by the bumper cars. They were waiting on Cole and Tommy to get out.

"Hey guys" Sam said as they watched us approach them. "Who's this?"

"This is Selena, we just met her in the ferris wheel" I answered. "She's pretty cool. So don't scare her away."

"I'm Sam, this is Darren and Nick" he introduced him and his friends.

"Hey" she waved.

We talked for a few more minutes. Then Tommy walked out with Cole right behind him.

"Jake was a-" Lena stopped mid sentence as she saw Tommy and Cole.

Cole stopped in his tracks when he saw Lena, standing there. He looked at her with wide eyes and he almost looked relieved.

"Oh thank god you're okay" he crashed his body into her as he hugged her tight.

She stood as stiff as a board. "Okay is a bit of an overstatement."

He backed away and held her at arm's length.

"I'm sorry, for everything. I was terrible and you definitely didn't deserve that." He caressed her face.

"You left me there and something bad happened. I trusted you and you broke that trust, Cole. It's been four months. Four months and you've not said one thing to me since that night. Not a single word. Cousins aren't supposed to do that to each other, especially us. We were like siblings." I could see the tears brim her eyes.

Wait, they're cousins?

"I know I know and I should've called or texted or something. You know I was in a tough spot. Do you know how many times I fucking wanted to call and make sure you were okay? Every fucking second of every fucking day."

All of us looked at each other in confusion. No one knew what was happening. Not even Nick or Tommy, who were his best friends.

She took a deep breath before looking into his eyes. "You know what, let's just forget about it for today. We'll talk later. I want to have fun right now and your presence sure as hell isn't going to change that."

"Okay as long as you promise to actually talk later." He agreed.

Lena turned to me and the boys. She wiped a few stray tears and smiled. "Let's have some fun"

We all looked at both of them with confused faces. They both assured us everything was okay and we went on to the rest of the fun things at the fair.

"Oh my gosh the swings. This is one of my favorite rides. Who wants to come with?" I smiled.

Lena back away. "No no no there's no way in hell you're getting me to go on that thing. You could literally fly off at any moment."

"You're a big baby. Anyone else?"

No one volunteered and my brothers went of to get food. I looked at Will with puppy dogs eyes. Suddenly, Tommy gasped and pointed to a game stand.

"Look, I wanna win a goldfish" He pointed and dragged Nick away with him.

Darren and Sam went off doing who knows what. Which left Lena, Cole, Will, and me.

"Alright snowflake, I'll go" Will gave in.

"Let's go, let's go, let's go" I squealed and ran to the line.

He shook his head and followed me.

"You are something different Cora Barnes" He laughed as I jumped up and down waiting in line.

Chapter 14

"**K**arla" I smiled as she opened the door.

"Hey Cora" she hugged me. "Hi boys. Everyone is out back. Fair warning there are a lot of people."

"Ah we're used to the crazy" Dad shrugged and hugged Karla.

She laughed a little. Her dress was white and flowed perfectly over her bump and down to her mid calf.

The boys were all wearing pink of some sort. They all thought it was going to be a girl, or at least that's what they wanted.

Connor found a light pink t-shirt he wore with denim shorts and Adidas. Carter wore a more coral-pink t-shirt and black shorts with sneakers. Cooper wore a bright pink shirt with matching socks and black shorts. Dad just had a pink shirt and golfer shorts.

I, on the other hand, thought it'd be a boy. I wore a baby blue cropped tank top with white stripes on it. I paired it with a pair of denim shorts and of course my converse.

We walked to the backyard which was filled with a lot of people I didn't know. I looked around for the few faces of the people I did know.

"Cora!" Kenzie called and ran over to hug me.

"Hey Kenz" I hugged her back.

The backyard was decorated in a blue and pink barbeque theme. "It's so cute out here"

"I helped set it up with Aunt Kyndal and Poppy. The fruit bar is over there and the drinks are in the kitchen. Dad is cooking the burgers and hot dogs."

"Hey Snowflake" Will gave me his best smile and threw an arm over my shoulder, pulling me in for a hug. He wore a blue shirt with jeans. "Don't you like what I did to the place?" He joked.

"You?" Scoffed Kenz. "All you did was help Uncle Tristan bring out the tables" She accused.

He bent down to where his eyes were even with hers. "Are you sure about that, Ken?" He narrowed his eyes challengingly.

"You know it, William" She smirked as she used his first name. In one motion, he swooped her over his shoulders where she was laying against his back upside down and he was holding on to her feet.

I stood back and watch the scene unfold in front of me with amusement.

"Tri, Tri, please help me" She pleaded to a man as he walked by her. He looked like he was in his thirties and definitely Michael's younger brother.

He laughed and walked over to me.

"What'd she do this time?" He asked.

"She called out Will on his BS" I laughed.

He nodded and watched for a few seconds. "William, let your sister go" He helped Kenzie up.

"Thanks Tri" Kenzie hugged him.

He high-fived her and put her on his shoulders and walked away.

"Did you just rat me out?" Will pouted.

I shrugged as I bit my lip trying my hardest not to crack a smile. "Maybe"

He sighed. "I thought we were friends, Snowflake, I thought we were friends" He feigned hurt as he put his hand over his heart. "I'm hurt" He pouted.

We both busted out laughing.

"Where are my brothers?" I asked as I sobered up.

"I think they're casting their vote" He pointed to the "voting" table.

"Oh let's go" I clapped and grabbed his hand before pulling him away to the table.

I put my vote in for boy and I spent the day with the boys.

Will introduced us to his family. We met, his aunts and uncles from his dad's side and a few from his mom's side. The boys ran off to get some fruit and something to drink. Will took me to meet his grandma.

"This is my grandma. We call her Poppy." He introduced me to an old lady sitting in one of the chairs on the patio. He hugged her and leaned down to her level. "Poppy, this is Cora Barnes."

I reach out my hand for her shake. She grabbed and she held it.

"Is this the girl you told me about?" She asked him.

I could see Will blush a little bit. "Yes, Poppy, this is the girl. She's Coach's daughter and Carter's little sister."

"She's just as beautiful as you say" She smiles at me as she pats my hand.

My face heats up a little bit as I push a piece of hair behind my ear with my free hand. "It's nice to meet you ma'am" I smiled politely.

"Oh please don't call me ma'am. You can just call me Poppy, everyone else does." She said.

"Sorry, Poppy" I corrected myself. Will started talking to his uncle or cousin or someone.

"Oh dear you are just the cutest thing. All nice and beautiful. You probably have boys lined up at your door wanting you."

I shook my head. "Oh I really don't. All the guys that had a chance turned out to be bad."

Her face lit up. "Ah William here is a good boy and such a gentleman too."

I couldn't help but laugh a little at her sudden statement. "I'll definitely put that in to consideration" I smiled.

Will looked back over at me and took me away. "You'll put me into consideration huh?" He smirked at me.

"Shut up" I shoved him while laughing.

"What? I think it's cute." He laughed.

"Well you know what, William? I'm thirsty." I held out my hand for him to take.

He sighed and grabbed my hand. "Well I guess, we'll have to do something about that"

He lead me to the kitchen. He insisted that he write my name on the cup and everything. He poured me a cup of sweet tea and handed it to me with a smile. The word snowflake was written across the cup in his handwriting.

"Snowflake, really?" I looked at him with a raised eyebrow.

He took a long drink from his lemonade. "Yes, really. I told you I liked that nickname."

"Better than Marshmallow?"

He nodded. "Better than Marshmallow" He confirmed.

I laughed and nudged him lightly.

"Burgers are ready!" Micheal called from outside. Will and I went outside and several people already had food and parents had plates for their children. Will and I got in line and got all the food we wanted.

"Do you want pickles?" Will joked.

"Get that shit way from me Erickson" I warned in a half joking tone.

He laughed and put some on his burger.

"Do you not like pickles?" Will's aunt Kyndal asked me.

"I'm severely allergic if I eat one. I almost died the last time I accidentally ate one" I explained. "Will was actually the one who gave me my shot"

"Thank God he was there to help."

"Yeah." I finished putting my stuff on my plate and I followed Will.

"Where do you want to sit? We can sit inside? Or stay out here?"

I shrugged and looked around. I didn't really care where we sat. I could see my brothers in line getting their food and I knew we had to sit somewhere where they would be with us.

"Oh I have and idea. Can you hold this? I'll be right back." He handed me his plate and ran off into the house.

He came back a couple minutes later with blankets in his arms.

"We can have a picnic" He laid down the blankets in the grass and sat down on them.

I handed him his plate and sat down next to him.

"Hey pretty lady" Some guy said as he took a seat next to me. He was around our age and I assumed he was Will's cousin.

"Back off Liam" Will growled.

"Look we're having a picnic!" Coop said and rushed over to us excitedly. The other two followed behind casually, talking to each other.

They saw the guy, Liam, sitting there and sat down. They saw the guy and just like me they probably assumed it was Will's cousin.

"Or what? Is she your girl or something?" Liam pushed.

"She is my girl and I said back off" Will repeated himself.

The five of us looked at him. I was confused, my brothers looked angry, and Liam almost proud of him. Liam just stood up and walked away.

"What?" Connor said.

"The" Cooper continued.

"Hell" Carter glared at his best friend.

Out of all of them Carter has always been the most protective over me and boys. I think it was because we were always in the same grade. Will is a different level of protection. Will is his best friend and little sister and best friend don't go together.

"I was about to ask the same thing." I said.

They looked at me in confusion. "Wait you mean, you didn't even know what he was talking about?" Coop looked shocked.

"So you're not together?" Con asked me.

"No" I answered.

We all looked Will for an answer.

"Look guys, that was my cousin, Liam. He's a player and a terrible guy. He's Mom's nephew, technically we're only related by marriage.

We've been competing since we were kids. If I didn't say that she was my girlfriend, even you guys or your dad couldn't scare the guy away. She would've probably been flirted with nonstop all night even if she rejected him. His definition of flirting is definitely not appropriate or vocal."

"Wait, Karla isn't your real mom?" Cooper asked completely confused.

We all looked at Cooper.

"You didn't know that?" I asked the nitwit.

He shook his head.

Will just laughed and shook his head. "No dude Karla's my step-mom and Kenzie's my step-sister. My dad and real mom got divorced when I was like four."

I love how even though Karla isn't his biological mom will treats her as such. The fact that Karla helped raise him for most of his life makes her his mom, not his mom that he hasn't seen since he was four.

"Anyway thanks for you know keeping our sister away from him" Carter said.

"No problem man, I got her back" He clapped Carter on the back.

We just talked while we ate. There were stupid arguments and fun jokes being thrown around. It was a great time. Kenzie came and sat with us at some point with a watermelon.

"Wait you're telling me that I've been here the entire time and I didn't know there was watermelon?" I asked in disbelief. How dare they hide something like that.

"It's right over there" Kenzie pointed to the table filled with fruits.

I jumped up immediately and ran to that table. There was a three tiered tray thing filled with watermelon. I grabbed two pieces and went back to the boys.

"Who's the other one for?" Will asked.

"Her" my brothers answered at the same time.

"They're both for me of you want some get off your lazy ass and get some" I held over them protectively.

"Okay everyone! The ballots are closed and thanks to Tristan and Kyndal the votes are all counted." Michael announced. Karla stood next to him holding her bump with a smile on her face. "The team with the most votes was Team Girl"

All of the people who voted for team girl clapped and cheered.

Kyndal and Tristan brought out a giant balloon and two confetti cannons. Will and Kenzie got up and took the confetti cannons. Micheal took the balloon and they were both handed a pin to pop it with.

"Oh gosh I'm so nervous" Karla said. "I can't, I can't" She freaked out a bit. Her smile was already a mile wide.

"On Three" Micheal said.

Kenzie and Will were standing behind them with the cannons ready to go. Some people were filming. Most were just enjoying the moment.

"One, two, three" They counted together and popped the balloon. Kenzie and will popped the cannons.

Blue confetti came from the balloon and a blue powder settled over the family.

"It's a boy!" Karla screamed. She jumped up and down and hugged her husband. They were both crying with joy. Will hugged his sister. Will's face lit up with complete happiness. I knew he wanted a brother so bad. He hugged his dad, then Karla.

"I'm gonna be an uncle!" Tristan yelled.

"You are an uncle!" Micheal yelled back.

"I'm gonna be an uncle again!" He corrected himself.

Everyone just laughed then started to congratulate the couple and the family. It wasn't long after that it was time for us to go. The boys decided to stay with Will and play video games in the basement.

"Bye Kenz" I hugged Kenzie.

"Bye Cora" She hugged me back.

I hugged Karla and Micheal and congratulated them on the baby boy.

"Are you sure you have to go?" Will pouted.

"Yes, Will, I told you I have stuff to do today. I'll see you tomorrow, okay?"

"Promise?"

I nodded. "I might have helped dad plan the practice and I might be coming to watch you suffer"

He looked at me wide eyes and his jaw dropped. "I hate you"

"You love me" I smiled and flipped my hair over my shoulder.

He pulled me in for a hug. "Bye snowflake"

"Bye Erickson"

CHAPTER 15

"So wait what's wrong? I thought you really liked Bryce." I asked Remi.

She sighed and flopped down on the couch. "I don't know. He's a great guy. He calls me at least once a day sometimes twice. He buys me flowers and takes me out on dates. He's nice and sweet. I don't know why but I just don't feel the same. I feel distant"

"Well sometimes you just fall out with a person. It's perfectly natural."

"Am I going insane? This guy is literally every girls dream. Good looking, kind, and the perfect gentleman. It's like he's trying too hard and it's hard for me to keep feelings for him. Time just seems to drag on around him." She ranted and put her head in her hands.

I sat down next to her a rubbed her back. "You are not insane. Maybe he's just not the right guy for you. One day you will find one. It just might not be Bryce."

"It's not that, Cora. I've known the guy pretty much my entire life. He's doing everything right and I don't want to be the girl who breaks him." She admitted.

"Then tell him that"

"It's not that simple" She groaned and stood up again.

"Why can't it be? I'm sure he'll understand Rem. Have you met the guy? There's not a single thing that can make him angry or upset."

"That's the problem. I almost want him to be angry at me. I want him to blame everything on me."

I gave her a questionable look. "Rem, why?"

She threw her hands up in exasperation. "I don't know. I guess it's easier for me to think he's angry at me, than for me to think I hurt him"

"Remi, I think you just need to talk to him. Tell him how you feel or just break up with the guy. I know that's not really what you want but it might be what needs to happen" I stood up to stand next to her.

"Yeah I know" She sighed.

"Oh some real deep girl shit is going on in here" Carter said as he walked into the kitchen.

I growled in frustration. "Carter Maverick Barnes"

"Cora Maeve Barnes" He copied me.

We just stood there across the counter and glared at each other.

"Jeez you guys are acting like you're in some old western movie" Remi broke the silence and hopped up on the counter next to me.

I looked up at her with a smile and rolled my eyes playfully at her comment.

"Ha you broke eye contact, I win" He turned around to the cabinets and started pulling stuff out.

"And I thought Coop was childish"

He pulled out cereal and milk. He made himself a bowl of cereal before stuffing a huge spoonful in his mouth.

"Cereal?" Remi asked. "It's like two o'clock"

He shoved another bite in his mouth and shrugged. "Any time is cereal time"

She laughed at him. "I'll take your word for it, I've never had it after breakfast."

"Do you want a bowl?" He asked.

She looked at me as if she was asking my permission if she could have one. I shrugged. "Go for it."

She hopped off the counter and walked around it next to Carter. He handed her a bowl and she began eating the cereal.

"Great now I want cereal" I said and made myself a bowl.

Dad walked in the front door. "What are you doing having a cereal party?" He laughed as he walked over to us. "Oh hey Remi" he waved at her.

"Wow Dad. Favorite daughter over here feeling very ignored" I waved at him.

He rolled his eyes and walked over to me. He wrapped his arms around me dramatically. "I'm so sorry. I promise I didn't forget about you." He dramatized.

I rolled my eyes playfully and pushed him off of me.

"Anyway I have a dinner tonight with Karla and Michael. We're going somewhere in the town over. So you kids are left alone. You can call Will and Kenzie over, but nobody else. You could also go over there. I think Kenzie wanted to do some soccer drills with you, Coco."

I nodded. We'll probably just go over to Will's and chill all night.

"Remi don't worry you can stay" he chuckled at her taken aback face. She was offended that she couldn't come over.

"Don't worry Mr. B I knew I was invited all along" she waved him off.

We all laughed. "All right well I'm going to go for a run then get in the shower."

"Love you dad" I called after him as he headed up to his room to change.

"Love you too Coco" he called back.

Remi and I stayed in the kitchen after we finished our cereal. Carter just stormed off to his room.

He had been doing so much better in terms of getting angry and upset over nothing. Once he got some friends and could use football as an outlet he was fine.

"Well I actually have to go now. I just got called into work. Hailey called in sick and I'm her back up." She hugged me bye.

"Love you" she blew me a kiss.

"Love you too" I blew her one back and giggled.

"Bye boys" she called up to Cooper and Connor who were playing call of duty in the loft.

"Bye Rem" they called back in sync.

"Bye Remi" Carter called from his locked door.

I watched Friends as I waited for time to pass by. I was going to Will's later with the boys to help Kenz with some drills before she does something with Grayson and some friends.

"Coco let's go" Carter called impatiently at my door after he knocked for the fiftieth time.

"I'm coming, I'm coming" I called back.

"Cooper and Connor already left and you're the only one not ready. Let's go"

I came out of my room with everything I needed for tonight. It was just my charger and chapstick and little stuff like that. "Don't get your panties in a twist, I'm ready."

"Great. Let's go." He grumbled and made his way downstairs. I followed him to Cooper's car.

"What crawled up your ass and died?" I mumbled under my breath. Carter glared at me but turned his head straight at the garage door.

The entire ride to Will's was quiet. Carter kept his eyes intently on the road the whole time. I just scrolled through Pinterest until we got to the house.

Kenzie was already outside kicking the ball around and juggling it. I hopped out of the car and joined her.

Once I scored on her, she hugged me.

"Hey Kenz" I smiled and hugged her back.

"It's been too long."

"It's been three days Ken" Will walked out.

"Three days is too long. You need to invite her over more." She stuck her tongue out at her brother.

I laughed at the exchange.

"But then you would steal her from me. Why would I do that?" He pouted.

"Because you love your little sister" she smiled sweetly at him.

"That I do, sis, that I do" he smiled and went back into the house with the boys.

I turned to her. "Do you want to do drills or just play one on one?" I asked.

"Can we just play one on one? I don't really feel like doing drills right now."

"Yeah I agree with you." I laughed. "Drills suck."

We kicked around the ball for a while, but we didn't do much.

"So what's new in the world of Kenzie?" I asked as I made a pathetic attempt at a goal.

She shrugged. "Not much. Mom's getting ready for the baby. Grayson and I have been dating for almost a month. He's scared of Will and his mom is picking me up soon." She laughed at the thought of her boyfriend being scared of her brother.

"Sounds fun, what are you doing?"

"Going to the mall, might go watch a movie" She shrugged as she pushed the ball passed me and scored a point.

"God you guys suck" Will called from the top of the porch.

"Yeah well if we suck so bad, why don't you come down here and show us how it's done." I challenged.

"Okay it's on, you chose teams. Pick one of us."

Kenzie shook her head. "Oh no bro it's four of you against us two." She smirked.

The boys all came down here in hopes of beating us. Their hopes were wrong.

They tried but couldn't even control the ball. It was so easy to take it from them and score. They surrendered right before a black Tahoe pulled into Will's driveway.

"That's Gray. See you boys later. Bye Cora"

Grayson hopped out of the car and met Kenzie in the grass. He gave her a hug which she gladly returned.

Grayson waved awkwardly at the four boys and me standing in the yard. "Hey boys. Hi Will" he swallowed hard when he saw Will staring at him.

"Bye guys we have to go now" Kenzie grabbed Graysons hand and started to drag him away.

"Wait I wanna talk to him" Will took a step but I stopped him.

I smacked him in the chest. "Leave the poor kid alone." I said to him. "Don't worry Grayson, he's joking. You kids have fun." I waved them bye.

"Back before nine" Will called out to Kenzie.

I turned to Will, who could hardly contain his laughter. "Did you see the look on his face?" He laughed.

"William Erickson!" I chastised. "That poor kid. He looked like a ghost" I let out a little laugh against my better judgment.

The boys were already inside undoubtably raiding the kitchen. We followed them inside and made our way down to the basement. I plopped down on the couch as did Will.

The boys found controllers and started to play video games. Will laid his head down in my lap and closed his eyes.

"Are you tired or something?" I joked.

"A little bit" he mumbled.

I absentmindedly began messing with his hair as I watched the boys play their video game. When I stopped, he grabbed my hand and put it back on his head.

"Don't stop" he whispered.

"Okay" I replied.

Carter had won at Call of Duty and they grew bored almost instantly.

"What else can we do?" Cooper pouted.

"Well I heard there's a party at Clay's house tonight. If we wanna go to that. I'm not sure if it's your scene or not." Will shrugged.

"I want to go, but I have to change first. There's no way I'm going to a party dressed like this" I gestured to my outfit.

I looked at the boys for confirmation. I think it sounds fun, but they're usually the ones to decide. Dad doesn't like us around too much alcohol, but he trusts us in a situation like this one.

Coop shrugged. "Sounds fun to me."

I looked to Carter and he nodded.

Connor was thinking. He was the one to make the decision. He was the oldest; therefore, he was the final vote.

"As long as we have a DD and we're responsible drinkers, it's good with me." He shrugged.

I threw my arms around him. "Thank you."

Cooper agreed to be the DD and we drove to our house to get ready.

I put on light denim shorts with light pink embroidered flowers and a light pink cropped tank top to match the flowers. I wore my white air forces. I braided the top half of my hair into two braids. I did minimal makeup just blush, mascara, and a little bit of lipgloss.

"Okay I'm ready" I hopped downstairs in my cute outfit, that I was really proud of.

"Finally you took long enough" Coop groaned as he stood up from the couch.

"I took less than fifteen minutes." I rolled my eyes at him. I looked in the living room to see Connor and Will. "Carter's not even in here yet" I pointed out.

"I know" Coop whined and flopped dramatically back on the couch.

I sat next to Will as I waited for Carter.

"You look pretty" he smiled down at me.

"Thank you" I blushed.

Carter walked down a few seconds later and we all went to the car.

I got stuck between Carter and Will in the back because their legs were too long to sit in the middle. Connor was sitting the the front with Cooper obviously driving.

Chapter 16

The party was in pretty much full swing by the time we pulled up. The music was blasting and people were dancing. You could smell the alcohol in the air. It was different then most parties I've been to or thrown.

At the parties we've thrown, we usually hang around a bonfire and have an ice cold beer. There are times where we'll have a shot of tequila or something, but there's hardly ever this much alcohol.

"Ay Will!" Some guy calls out obviously drunk and still had a drink in his hand.

"Hey Clay" he did a bro hug with him. "These are my boys Connor, Cooper, and Carter and their sister, Cora."

He looked me up and down. The boys didn't notice it but Will did. He smacked Clay in the chest. I smiled slightly at Will.

Clay left with some other guy on promise of some beer pong.

"Cora, make sure you're around one of us four at all times" Carter ordered.

"We don't want you getting lost or hurt." Connor said.

I stare at my brothers in disbelief. "First of all, I'm almost seventeen and I can take care of myself. Second of all, I'm not dumb enough to go off by myself and I came with y'all why would I leave you."

"Guys she makes a fair point" Will shrugged.

"Thank you." I finally have someone on my side against the boys. "Let's just go and have some fun, okay?"

We walked more into the house and everyone was dancing up against each other in the cramped in the living room made dance floor. I don't ever see myself coming in here tonight and grinding up on someone. It's way out of my comfort zone.

"Ay yo Darren" Coop called out to Darren as he passed us in the hallway next to the kitchen.

Darren turned around to the sound of his name and smile when he saw our small group. He said something to the boys he was hinging with and walked over to us.

"Hey guys, what's up?" He asked. He was a noticeably tipsy but he wasn't drunk.

"Is Sam here?" Coop asked, loudly due to the blasting music in the room over.

I swear those two are usually attached at the hip. There's hardly been a time when I haven't seen the two of them together.

"Nah, he had to babysit the twins while Wanda and Zach went to a party celebrating the pregnancy. I think I saw Cole here and maybe Nick." He shrugged.

The song that was currently playing ended and a new song took over the speakers. Darren's face lit up with excitement and he looked at Cooper. "Dude this is my favorite song" He grabbed Cooper and took him to the cramped dance floor.

I laughed and turned to the remaining bit of our group. "Let's go to the back, maybe it's quieter." I yelled over the music. They all nodded in agreement and we found our way to the backyard.

As I suspected, the backyard was much calmer. There was music playing but it wasn't blasting like it was in the house and people weren't going crazy dancing. It was mainly people talking in groups with drinks in their hands. There was a game of beer pong going on back here, but that was pretty much it.

We found a picnic table and sat there. I sat on the opposite side of Will and Carter sat on the right. Connor sat next to me on the opposite side of the other two.

"Alright, I'm in need of a drink, anyone want anything?" Connor asked.

"Corona" I said.

"I'm good with whatever" Carter shrugged.

He looked at Will expectantly. She shook his head and put his hands up. "I'm good for now, man"

Connor nodded before he headed back into the house to get the drinks. The boys broke into conversation about something. I looked into the sky. It wasn't quite dark yet but the sun has almost completely set. The stars had just come out to play. I loved looking at the sky. It was beautiful almost all of the time.

Connor came back almost ten minutes later with two drinks in hand. Someone followed behind him with more drinks in their hands. It wasn't until they came closer that I saw who it was.

"Look who I found" Connor said as he set the drinks down on the table.

"Lena!" I squealed and hopped up to hug her.

She set the drinks down on the table before wrapping her arms around me.

"Hey Cora and boys" She waved at the other two.

"Hey Lena" They waved at her.

I pulled her down to sit next to me and Connor at on the other side of her.

"So we haven't seen you in a while, how's life?" I asked her. None of us really know what happened in the past between her and Cole or if they made up after the fair.

"It's been good I suppose. I'm trying to get transferred over to your school, but I'm having a difficult time convincing my parents. They don't really know all the details of what happened so they're curious as to why I want to move." She explained.

We don't know all the details either. All I know is that four months ago Cole left her stranded and something bad happened. She was in the hospital for two days. I assumed she was at a party or something and someone from that school hurt her.

"Oh well I really hope you convince them. I would be able to see you more often." Connor nudged his shoulder. She blushed a little bit at his statement.

"Yeah, me too because then we could go to the same school and maybe even have some classes together." I hugged her happily.

We had so much fun at the fair with her the other day and I would love to become better friends with her.

I gasped when I realized something. "I never got your number at the fair"

She gasped at my words and pulled out her phone. She opened her contacts and made a new one before handing me her phone. I did the same thing on mine and gave it to her. We both put our contact information in. We took a picture together to have as a contact picture.

The rest of the night went pretty well. I didn't have another drink which is more than I can say for the boys. They've already had a couple as well as Lena. Will had maybe one drink the whole night.

A slow song came on in the back and Connor took Lena to dance. Some girl asked Carter and her accepted. Will held his hand out to me.

"Wanna dance? I can't have you being the only one not dancing, now can I?" he asked softly.

I nodded. "Of course" I smiled and took his hand. He pulled me away from the picnic table that we claimed as our own since the beginning of the night.

He held me close to him as we swayed to the rhythm of the music. He spun me out and back in at the perfect time in the music.

"Wow you're quite the dancer, Will" I smiled as her spun me back in.

"You're not so bad yourself, snowflake" He smiled.

I looked up at the sky for a second and got distracted. The stars shined bright in the sky next to the crescent moon. I stopped dancing as I looked at the beautiful sight above me.

"I'm sorry" I apologized to Will. "The sky is just so beautiful right now."

My hands were still in his as he took a step closer to me and whispered in my ear. "Follow me"

He gently lead me back through the house and up the stairs.

"Where are we going?" I asked.

"You'll see" he smiled at me.

He led me into someones bedroom. I looked at him questioning-ly. What the hell is going on here?

He must've seen my panic stricken face. "Trust me okay?"

I kept my hand in his as he led me to a window. He opened the window and walked out onto the roof. I stopped at the window. I was weary to climb out of it.

"Hey, it's okay. I've done this a million times" His voice calmed me and made me feel safe.

I climbed through the window and followed Will a couple feet before he sat down. I took his hand and used him to help me sit down.

I looked up at the sky, which I could see much better from here.

"Wow" I said in awe as I looked up at the clear sky.

Will laid back against the roof while I stayed sitting up. I admired the stars in the sky. They were absolutely breathtaking from up here. After a while I laid back on Will's chest.

"It's beautiful, isn't it?" I asked quietly.

"Yes it is" He answered.

I turned my head took look at him and he was already looking down at me. A blush formed on my face as I turned back around away from his gaze. We sat in silence for a few more minutes.

"What did you mean by you've done this a million times? Are you and Clay good friends?" I asked curiously.

He shrugged as much as her could with me laying on his chest. "We were really good friends in middle school. We used to come out on the roof sometimes. It was our place of peace. We kind of just grew out of our friendship as the years went on. I joined football and he didn't."

I nodded in understanding. It happens to even the best of friends. Sometimes you just grow out out of relationships.

"Yeah I get that"

We laid there for a few more minutes. The minutes passed but they felt like seconds. I heard my phone buzz and I reluctantly looked at my phone, which pulled me out of the moment I was in. I sat up and read the text message.

"It's Carter" I informed Will. "He wants to know where we went."

Will sat up too. He sighed and ran a hand through his golden locks. "Yeah we should get back"

He went to stand up, but I grabbed him arm. He looked down at me questioningly.

"Thank you, Will" I said genuinely.

His face softened into a sweet smile. "You're welcome, snowflake"

He stood up and helped me crawl back through the window.

"I have to go to the bathroom. Do you know where it is?"

He climbed through the window after me. "Yeah, its the first door to the left after you walk out of the room." He answered me. "I'll wait right outside, okay?" He asked.

I nodded and followed his directions to the bathroom. Thankfully, there wasn't anyone in there. I turned around and locked the door before I did my business and washed my hands. I walked out and true to his word Will stood there waiting on me.

"The boys are waiting." He said.

I took his outreached hand and he led me back through the crowd of people and back to the boys. We reached the backyard and Connor was still talking with Lena. She was laughing at something he said. Carter was sitting at the picnic table with Coop and Darren. Nick and Cole have seemed to join the group as well.

"Hey guys" I said as Will and I approached the table. My hand was still in his.

Carter glared at our connected hands but I didn't care.

"Where have you guys been?" Nick asked. His words were slurred and he was working on yet another drink.

"I had to go to the bathroom and Will showed me where it was. What are you guys doing?" I changed the conversation.

"We're trying to figure out a way to get them home." Carter groaned. "They're all wasted and they don't have a DD"

I shrugged. "Call them an uber"

"None of us have any money. I'm just going to drive them to our house. Cooper will take the rest of you home and I'll drive everyone else" He stood up and grabbed someone's keys of the table.

I grabbed his wrist to stop him. "You can't drive, Carter. You've had too much to drink."

He ripped his arm out of my grip. "I'll be fine Cora. I haven't had that much." He argued.

"You know Dad's rule. Even if you had one sip of alcohol, you aren't allowed to get in the drivers seat. You could get seriously hurt or even killed, Carter."

"Cora, stop. I'll be fine" He argued back.

I grabbed the keys out of his hand. "I haven't had as much as you. I hardly had anything and that was hours ago."

"Cora no" Cooper interjected. "You can't drive"

I turned to cooper with a questioning look. "So you're completely fine with Carter driving right now, but not me, who had one drink at least two hours ago?" I questioned.

"She's right bro. She drank the least out of all of us, besides Cooper. The only other option is to leave them here." Will came to my rescue. "Carter you're in no shape to drive right now."

Carter growled in frustration. He knew that we were right. "Okay, Will go with her and help her with the boys. Connor with come with us and maybe Lena too"

We all nodded in agreement and got everyone out to the cars and on the way to our house. Dad was about to be pissed.

Chapter 17

"What the hell?" Dad asked at the front door as we dragged in a bunch of drunk football players. Will and I were the most sober out of everyone that had a drink.

Connor tried to bring in a laughing Lena.

"Oh hey coach" Nick slurred as Cooper helped him stumble in.

Dad saw me get out of the car and help Darren get into the house. Cole was able to walk by himself but he was stumbling everywhere. Will was standing there to help him up every time he fell over. Carter walked in. He probably looked worse than he actually was. Connor look sober but his words were slurred.

Cooper, Will, and I successfully got all the boys to the living room. Darren took over the couch. Cole and Nick were sprawled out across the floor. Carter made his way up to his room, groaning.

"I repeat, what the hell?" Dad said as he shut the front door and looked at the three of us for an explanation.

I explained that we decided to go to a party but Cooper volunteered to be the DD. Then we saw the boys, who were way too drunk to drive themselves. So when we came home Cooper and I were the ones driving.

"That explains all that, but why did you bring them here?" He asked as he gestured to the bodies laying around our living room.

I shrugged. "I didn't know where else to take them. It was simpler to bring all of them here than try to take them all home. We were going to text the parents to tell them that they're safe."

"Okay and you didn't have anything to drink right? That's why you were the one to drive, right?"

I looked down at my feet in shame. "Not exactly." I said quietly.

"What?" He yelled. "Cora, you know the rule. I allow you to go out a drink, which is more than I can say for most parents because I know I trust you to make responsible decisions. I have one rule for you and you broke it."

"I know and I'm sorry. I had to stop Carter from driving. You see how he is right now. I had one beer earlier in the night and was the second most sober one there, Dad. I know it wasn't the most responsible decision, but it was the most responsible option I had." I explained. I tried not to yell, but my voice got louder as spoke.

He sighed and ran a hand down his face. "Okay I understand why you made the decision you did, but you're grounded for the next week, because you broke that rule"

I let out a breath of relief. "Thank you"

"Let's get these people sobered up and in bed. Will and Cooper Gatorade and animal crackers. Cora get clothes for them, who's that girl by the way?"

"That's Lena, we met her at the fair" I laughed.

I walked upstairs and grabbed clothes from all the boys rooms for the boys and my room for Lena. Thankfully all the boys were relatively the same size so it was easy to get clothes for them. I grabbed a pair of sweats and a t-shirt for each of the boys.

By the time I got back downstairs, the boys had started to feed everyone. I threw the sweats and t-shirts at Cooper and Will. I grabbed Len and dragged her up to my room. I changed her into a tank top and a pair of pajama shorts.

She was basically asleep by the time I finished changing her, so I laid her on my bed and put her under the covers. I made my way down stairs to see the boys' progress. They all successfully changed the boys into different clothes and put their clothes in the washer.

Nick and Cole refused to get off the floor so they left them their with a couple pillows and blankets. Darren was fine on the couch and they gave him a pillow and blanket. Cooper got Connor upstairs and into bed. He asked about Lena several times before he went though. We assumed Carter was already in bed.

I hopped up on the counter in exhaustion. Getting a bunch of drunk people sober and ready for bed is a lot of work.

"Are you good?" Will asked as he hopped up with me. He was wearing grey sweatpants and was shirtless.

I nodded and laid my head on his shoulder. His bare skin was warm against my face. "Yeah, I'm just tired." I answered. "Where's your shirt?" I asked without thinking.

"None of your brother's shirts fit my shoulders so I went without one. You should probably get to bed. Go change and get to sleep."

"I'm too tired to move" I groaned.

He hopped off he counter, leaving me with nothing to rest my head on. He stood in front of me and lifted me off of the counter.

He lead me up the stairs and pushed me towards my room while he went in the direction of carter's room.

"Goodnight, Snowflake" He smiled at me as I walked backwards.

"Night, Will" My back met my door. We stared at each other in silence for a few seconds before I turned around and opened my door.

I changed out of my outfit into something way more comfortable and hopped in bed next to Lena.

Remi showed up at my house the next day. She wasn't happy like she normally was. She looked a little bit upset. Everyone left around ten this morning.

"Remi?" I asked. "Are you okay? What's wrong?"

"I just broke up with Bryce" she said quietly.

I ushered her inside and into the living room. We sat on the couch.

"Tell me what happened" I said softly.

I knew she didn't feel the same way as he did and she was worried about their relationship.

"I told him how I felt and he understood. He was very accepting of the situation."

I gave her a look of confusion with a tilted head. "Then why are you upset? Isn't that what you wanted?"

"It's just the look I saw in his eyes as we said goodbye. He looked heartbroken, Cor. He was devastated but he didn't say anything. We agreed to stay friends. It's not like it ended badly or anything." She threw her head in her hands.

This is the second time I've seen her conflicted like this. I gently rubbed her back with my left hand. I pushed her fiery red hair out of her face and behind her ear.

"Hey, it's okay Rem. This happens all the time. It's life" I assured her.

"I know, I know. I just feel terrible about it"

"I have an idea. How about we get some snacks and watch some movies to get your mind off of it?" I asked.

She nodded in return to my question. I walked over to the kitchen and left Remi sitting on the couch. I grabbed some pre-made popcorn, ruffles, animal crackers, Gatorade, and two boxes of mug cakes. I went back to the living room and dumped everything on the couch between us. "I also have some ice cream in the freezer, if that's what you want"

She laughed lightly at all the snacks.

"What do you want to watch? I vote Never Been Kissed or How to Lose a Guy in 10 Days."

"Definitely How to Lose a Guy in 10 Days and maybe Never Been Kissed after that." She answered. I nodded happily and turned on the movie.

Carter trotted down the stairs and stopped when he saw us snuggled on the couch. What really caught his eye was Remi and the fact that she was still a little bit upset.

"Are you okay?" He asked as he walked closer to her.

She nodded and looked up at him. "Yeah I just broke a guys heart so I'm eating out my guilt" She responded and motioned to all the snacks in front of us.

"You broke up with Bryce?" He asked. I know he was trying to be sympathetic.

"Yep, it wasn't working out between us. Nothing bad, it just didn't work"

He nodded and looked over at me as a look of realization crossed his face. "Coco, you do realize you're grounded, right?" He smirked.

Dad wasn't home right now. He had stuff to work on in his office and had to go grocery shopping. He wouldn't be home for hours.

"Oh shit, Carter please don't tell him." I begged my brother.

Remi looked at me with concern. Carter looked like he was seriously contemplating the situation.

"Come on. How many times did I cover for you when you snuck off to go see your girlfriends back in Dallas? Or when I told Dad that you finished your homework and let you copy off of me?"

He put his hands up in mock surrender. "Relax Coco. I won't tell him, God knows how much I actually owe you for all the crap I pulled." He smiled. "And I didn't have girlfriends back in Dallas, I had dates. There's a difference." He winked at Remi and went back upstairs.

I don't know why he came downstairs in the first place, but I don't doubt that he'll be back for whatever it was he needed.

Remi turned to me and smacked my arm.

"Ow!" I exclaimed and rubbed the spot on my arm that was just abused. "What was that for?" I pouted.

"You didn't tell me you were grounded" she scolded. "Why are you grounded?"

I found the popcorn really interesting all of a sudden. "I might have broken the one rule my dad has for us when we drink. I drove home after I had a drink. It was only a beer a few hours before I drove, but in my defense, everyone else was pretty much wasted and Cooper and I were the only ones decent enough to drive." I put my hands up in defense.

"Okay okay. Are you sure you're not going to get in trouble with me being here? I can always leave." She went to stand up but I pulled her back down to me.

"No stay here. It's fine. If he comes home and sees you here, I can always explain the situation and maybe he'll be lenient" I shrugged.

"I really don't want you to get into anymore trouble because of you"

"Remi, It's fine. Let's just watch the movie."

We watched the movie and laughed. This movie was literally one of my favorite movies of all time. After we finished this movie, we started Never Been Kissed.

"Ha, this girl is actually me" I laughed.

Remi looked at me questioningly. "You've never been kissed?"

I shook my head. "Nope, I've had one jerk of a boyfriend my freshman year then no one in my school was interested in me and I wasn't interested in anyone" I shrugged. "And I was recovering from my ACL surgery so I couldn't go anywhere without the boys or Dad driving me"

"Don't worry, unlike Josie, you'll be kissed before you're twenty-five" She smirked at me.

She turned back to the movie and we watched it.

Her phone rang while Josie was waiting at the pitcher's mound. "Shoot, it's my mom sorry"

She answered the phone and had a conversation with her mom.

"I gotta go. Tabby has a softball game that I have to go watch then take home after." She stood up and started to gather her things. "I'm sorry. I'll see you sometime soon." She blew me a kiss and I blew her a kiss back.

"It's okay, my dad will probably be back soon anyway. I love you!" I called after her as she left my house in a hurry.

I decide to clean up the big mess Remi and I made. I cleaned the mugs we made mug cakes in and put away all the snacks we ate. I made my way up to my room to chill before Dad gets home.

"Kids I'm home. Come downstairs I have some news." Dad called as he walked in the house.

I made my way downstairs as well as my brothers.

"Hey Dad" I kissed his cheek and sat on the couch.

Once everyone was sitting in the living room Dad told us the news.

"Since we have the next week off from football, we're going on a mini vacation to Port Aransas."

We all went up in cheers. We all loved the beach. We don't get to go a lot because of all the football during the summer. We normally go camping during the summer because it was faster than going to the beach. Not that we minded, we love camping too.

"Don't get too excited I haven't even told you the best part yet" Dad laughed.

We all looked at him in anticipation. I don't know what he's adding to the trip that's better than going to the beach.

"I've talked to the Erickson's and their going with us!" Dad smiled.

"What?" I jumped up in shock.

"All of them?" Coop asked.

Dad nodded. "Yeah they have family that have a couple houses on the beach that they are letting us stay at for a couple days."

"Hell yeah," Connor cheered.

"That's awesome." Carter said.

Dad gave me a pointed look. "Cora remember that you are grounded this week, but not next week. You can call Remi and tell her that she can come. I believe Grayson is coming too and Karla said that Remi can bring her brother and sister, if she their parents let them come."

"I know I'm grounded, but thank you for letting Remi come" I hugged him an ran up to my room to call Remi and tell her the news.

I can't believe we're going to Port A with Will's family and Remi gets to come. This was going to be one wild ride and I couldn't wait.

CHAPTER 18

"Ah, oh my gosh I'm so exited." I squealed. I threw my suitcase in the back of Will's truck. We decided to take his truck because there's a lot of room for luggage in the back of. The rest of us were stuffing in the back of the other two cars.

There's thirteen people coming on this trip. Our family, Will's family, Grayson, and Remi and her two siblings. Thirteen people means there's a lot of suitcases and three cars to fit them in.

We took Karla's suburban, Dad's equinox, and Will's truck. Karla, Michael, Kenzie, Grayson, Isaac, and Tabby are riding in Karla's car. Cooper, Connor and Dad were riding in Dad's car. Remi, Carter, Will and I are riding in Will's truck. Carter and Will agreed to switch out who drives.

"I know me too" Remi squealed as I helped her put her fifty pound suitcase in the bed of the truck. She also put her two siblings suitcases in the truck.

"Three days at the beach, tanning in the sun. It's literally my dream vacation and add the fact that I'm not only going with my family but also my best friends. It's amazing."

"Are you girls gonna stand there daydreaming all day or are you gonna do something to make us leave faster?" Dad joked as he came out with his suitcase. He put it in the back of his car.

I slung my arm around Remi's shoulders. "You know us Dad a bunch of slackers." I joked.

Michael and Karla came to our house next. They were only a couple minutes later than everyone else.

"Okay guys are we almost ready to hit the road?" Michael asked.

We all nodded in excitement.

"Isaac and Tabby, you're riding with Karla and Michael." Remi told her siblings. She looked at Karla. "If they're any trouble call me, okay?"

Karla waved her off. "I'm sure they'll be fine." She smiled.

"You two behave, okay? If you give Karla any trouble, I will call mom" she threatened.

Both kids nodded understandingly.

"Hey snowflake, are you excited?" Will asked from behind me.

I turned to face him and hugged him. Despite him being there for almost thirty minutes, I still hadn't seen him.

"More than you know" I smiled.

"Okay, I think that's the last of it. Everyone in the cars let's go" Dad called. Everyone hopped in their respective cars and buckled up excitedly.

Will was driving for the first three hours and Carter the next three hours. We started the road trip off strong with the four of us singing to the music Will was playing. We also talked about what we did for the Fourth of July. Which wasn't much, we just had a family cook out.

We grabbed lunch around one o'clock. We just had some Wendy's. It was a fast option to keep us on the road. We still had six more hours left until we go there.

After hour lunch, the car got quiet. The boys started talking about college football and Remi was out. The music was still playing faintly in the background. I was playing a game on my phone until it got boring and I decided to take a nap. I put my headphones in and played some music.

I was shook awake by someone. I opened my eyes to see Will in my immediate line of sight.

"We're stopping for a bathroom break. Just thought I'd let you know" he smiled at me.

I sat up. "Wait for me" I told him. I unbuckled my seat belt before I slipped on my shoes. Will did as he was told and waited just outside the car.

The boys were in line getting snacks, but I headed straight to the bathroom. After I did my business, I washed my hands and found some snacks for me. I was one of the last ones back to the cars. Carter was driving now. I'm not sure if they switched just now or they switched while I was sleeping.

"We have four more hours left in this amazing car ride, before we make it to the beautiful Port Aransas." Will announced.

We played games like I spy. We brought cards against humanity and read the funny cards. We stopped two hours later at another gas station to get snacks and go to the bathroom.

"Cora!" Kenzie called and hugged me.

"How's the trip so far, Kenz?" I asked her.

A smile took over her face. "It's amazing. Tabby and I have became such good friends and Grayson and Isaac seem to be getting along well. Gray is being so cute. He was holding my hands for more than half the drive so far." She said happily.

I grabbed some snacks and went to the register. Kenzie was just behind me.

"Hey Kenz, I'll buy yours too" I nodded my head towards the register.

"Are you sure?" She asked wearily.

"Of course Kenz. I love you and I'm buying your snacks. I will force them out of your hands" I joked.

She gave them up, but insisted that she pay me back. Of course I told her she didn't have to. The kid was like a little sister to me.

We all got back in the cars and on the road. We had two hours left and my car was buzzing with excitement. The last two hours went by extremely fast and before we knew it we were in Port Aransas.

There were lines of beautiful houses colorful houses. Soon enough our three cars pulled into the driveway of a blue gray house. Right next to it was a bright pink house. It matches the town so well and both were in walking distance of the beach.

We all piled out of the cars together. Everyone met in one big circle.

"Okay listen up. The big teens will be staying in the pink house, while the adults and four little teens will be with us in the gray house." Michael said.

"We're putting a lot of trust into you teenagers. Please don't break it." Dad looked specifically at the boys, while he said this. "Just a reminder, I'm your football coach and four of you's father."

They all threw up their hands in defense. I laughed at the four of them. I would say I'm shocked but honestly I'm not. They can be very irresponsible when left alone.

"We will cook breakfast for you, but I know you lazy teenagers don't get up until ten at times. Your on your own for lunch though" Karla said.

"You guys know the basic rules so let's not waste time going over that. Yes there are golf carts and you can pretty much drive them anywhere in town, if you have your license." Michael said.

"Okay now that all that is cleared out of the way. Meet back at the cars in an hour ready for dinner." Karla said.

Everyone grabbed their stuff out of cars and made their way to the houses.

"I can't believe we get a house all to ourselves" Remi said in disbelief. "I really hope my siblings are being good. I really hate that I'm leaving them with the adults to deal with."

"It's okay Rem, my sister and Grayson are there so they're already taking care of kids their age. Plus my mom loves them." Will assured her.

Will unlocked the door and we walked into an island retreat. It was so beachy and cute.

"Oh my gosh it's perfect" I said as I took in the house. The boys are buzzing with excitement behind me.

"Remi and I call dibs on the master bedroom!" I yelled before the boys could get to it. Remi and I deserve our own private bathroom for all our 'girly' things.

The boys groaned. Will laughed and pointed us into the direction of the rooms.

The master bedroom had a king sized bed with beach designed quilted blanket and two bedside tables. There was a brown dresser and a tv hanging in front of the bed. Remi immediately threw her stuff to the ground and jumped onto the bed.

I laughed and joined her.

"This is amazing" I sighed in content.

"We have to to get ready for dinner." Remi said as she got up and began to rummage through her suitcase.

I sighed and sat up. I didn't feel like getting ready but I knew I had to.

I grabbed my suitcase and picked out one of my outfits. It was a red cropped tank top and Tommy Hilfiger denim shorts. I paired it with white high top converse.

I took out my two Dutch braids. My long brown hair cascaded down my back. I lightly brushed it so the waves would stay intact. I grabbed the front two pieces and used a blue scrunchie to tie them together in the back. I put some mascara on my eyelashes and a light shade of blush on my cheeks.

"Damn you" Remi cursed from beside me as she still was putting on her makeup.

I giggled at her reaction. "What?" I asked.

"I hate you for being so naturally pretty. You hardly have to do anything to get ready." She growled in frustration.

"I don't want to hear it. You're so hot it's not funny. You had more than half the football team drooling over you at my house."

"They're just scared to drool over you because your dad's the coach and your brothers are on the team."

I laughed at how accurate her statement was. After at least thirty minutes and the boys nagging we were finally ready. When I said we, I meant it was mainly Remi that was taking forever.

She finally chose to wear a white cropped cami and a orangeish brown wrap around skirt. She wore her white air forces with it. Once we were ready we made our way to the living room where the rest of the boys were waiting.

"Finally took you long enough" Carter groaned as he and the boys stood up.

"Don't blame me. Blame Remi, she's the one that took a million years getting ready" I put my hands up in defense.

"let's go get food" Cooper said and rushed us out of the house. Honestly, I agreed with him right now. I was starving.

We met back by the cars with everyone. We were all pretty dressed up. Not completely fancy just more than our casual attire back home. Once everyone was there we hopped in the same cars we were in for the trip over here. We followed Michael, who was driving the suburban. Dad followed next and Will was the last one out of the drive way. We rolled the windows down and played music as we drove down the highway.

We pulled into a parking lot to a place called MacDaddy's Family Kitchen. It was a cute beachy blue place. The sun was getting lower in the sky making the restaurant and the rest of Port Aransas look beautiful.

We found a parking spot and met with the rest of our families inside.

"Hello, welcome to MacDaddy's Family Kitchen. How many for your table?" The lady at the receptionist desk asked Karla.

"Thirteen" She answered with a smile.

"Okay would you like the tables pushed together or separate tables close to each other?" The lady asked.

"All together would be great, but if you can't separate tables will be fine"

The lady looked at her ipad thing. "That will be about a fifteen to twenty minute wait for one big table. Will that be okay?" She asked.

"Yes ma'am, thank you"

"No problem," She smiled.

Karla came back over to the group and told us what was happening. Ten minutes later the lady came and got us and led us to a log table. We all sat down.

Dad sat at the head of the table. In order from left to right was Michael, Karla, Connor, me, Will, and Carter. Sitting across from Carter and going left was Cooper, Remi, Tabby, Kenzie, Grayson , and Isaac.

A waitress came by and stopped at our table.

"Hey guys, I'm Anna and I'll be your server today. What can I get y'all started off to drink." she said. She took our drink orders and didn't even write them down. "Can I get you started off on an appetizer?"

The adults shook their heads no.

"Okay I'll be back with your drinks shortly" she smiled and sauntered off.

She came back a few minutes later with all of our drinks. She gave all of our drinks to us.

"Have you decided what you wanted or do you guys need a few more minutes?"

"Can we have a few more minutes, please?" asked Micheal.

"Of course" Anna nodded before going to check on another table.

We all looked at our menus for something to eat. The only problem was the food all looked so good. I finally narrowed it down to two choices.

"What are you thinking?" Will asked from beside me.

"I can't chose between lemon pepper fish or fried chicken" I told him my choices.

He laughed lightly. "I was thinking the same thing. How about we each order one of the plates and we'll share" he offered.

"That actually sounds like a good idea, I'll get the friend chicken" I said.

"Okay then I'll get the lemon pepper fish"

Once we came to the agreement, we started talking with the rest of the table. They were talking about what we're going to do at the beach tomorrow and the boys planned to play football, unsurprisingly.

"How's your house?" I asked Kenzie and Tabby.

"It's so cute. We're in a room with two bunk beds and Gray and Isaac are sleeping on the top while Tabby and I sleep on the bigger beds" Kenzie ranted.

I was shocked to find out that Karla and Micheal let them sleep in the same room, but they're trustworthy.

Anna came back later and everyone was ready to order. We all ordered and Anna went to put the order in the kitchen. It was almost thirty minutes before we all got our food. I wasn't expecting the service to be that fast.

Let's just say that dinner was absolutely amazing. Will and I shared our food and both plates were so good. Anna came back around ten minutes after we all finished our dinner.

"Would you guys like any dessert tonight? I can recommend our peach cobbler, it's really good this time of year."

"No thank you" Karla smiled.

"Is this all one big ticket or separate?"

"Separate. I have me and that whole table as well as this one next to me" Dad motioned to Isaac who was on his left. I assumed Karla and Michael were gonna pay for Connor to make it even.

Remi looked up in shock. "Mr. B, you don't have to pay for us. My mom sent us with money for dinner" She tried to tell him.

He waved her off. "Nonsense, we were the ones who invited you and your family. Us eight please Anna" He told her.

Anna nodded and looked at Micheal. "The rest of you on a separate ticket I presume?"

"Yes ma'am" Micheal said.

Anna nodded before walking away. She came back a few minutes later and gave the tickets to the two males. After she came back with their credit cards, we were ready to go.

Remi tossed a ten dollar tip on the table followed by a couple dollars from each of us. Anna probably got at least a fifty dollar tip that night. Plus whatever the parents tipped her.

We went back to the houses and it was dark outside, but it was beautiful.

"Guys there's a hot tub at the house. We could hang out there for a while" Will suggested and we all agreed.

We all changed into our swimsuits. I wore a one shoulder black and white one piece with one side cut out of the stomach. Remi put on a bright yellow bikini with little ruffles on it.

"Cute" We said at the same time as we saw each other's swimsuits for the first time.

We both laughed at our simultaneous thoughts.

"Let's go the boys are probably waiting on us" I said. Remi agreed and we made our way out back. The boys were waiting on us as expected.

We spent the rest of the night in the hot tub. We were talking about whatever stuff came to our mind. There was a lot about school next year. I can't wait but I also never want summer to end.

CHAPTER 19

"It's time for the beach" I squealed.

The adults were packing all the food in coolers to take down to the beach. I already packed my beach bag. It had all the essentials in it ready to use. There was my sunscreen, tanning lotion, sunglasses, lip balm, my towel, an extra pair of clothes, portable charger, and baby powder.

We went out to the golf cart to take it to the beach. Dad was taking the kids, coolers, beach chairs and the umbrella in his golf cart. Micheal and Karla were taking Dad's car.

"We call the back!" Remi squealed and dragged me to the back of the six seater golf cart. I jumped in the back of the cart with Remi. Will ended up being the one who drove and Carter next to him. Cooper and Connor got the middle row.

It was a five minute drive to the beach and it was beautiful. It was a perfect day for the beach. It was breezy by the water which made it amazing.

We were the first ones out of our group to get there so we went to find a spot. It wasn't hard to find a spot. There wasn't a lot of people here yet, but it was fairly busy. We only walked around for a few minutes before we found a great spot for all of our things.

Dad wasn't quite here yet, so we had to stand our ground until he got here with all of our stuff. We started putting on sunscreen. I took off my shorts and t-shirt. My white bikini with boho stripes showed. I rubbed in what I could with sunscreen and let Remi do my back where I couldn't reach.

By the time we all got sunscreen and tanning lotion on, Dad and the kids made it with all of our stuff. Being the good children that we are, we helped set it all up. Karla and Micheal made it a few minutes later.

I made sure to drink some a water before going in the water.

"Last one to the water has to jump in the pool with their clothes on!" Remi yelled before we all fought to get to the water.

The boys were the first ones to get to the water followed shortly by Remi and I. The kids followed in after us. I'm not sure who was actually the last one there, but in that moment it didn't matter. We were having fun and the smiles on our faces showed it.

The boys began splashing us and we splashed back. We were all laughing.

"Raahh" Will grabbed my from behind and threw me into the water. I glared at him once I resurfaced.

"William" I yelled at him. He was laughing heartily.

"I'm sorry snowflake I had to" He laughed.

My glare turned playful and I slowly sneaked closer to him. I splashed him in the face. He picked me up and tickled me in retaliation.

"Okay okay truce?" I said when I couldn't take it anymore.

He set me down and put his hands up where I could see them. He gave me a skeptical glare. I put my hands to where he could see them.

"I promise" I smiled at him.

He rolled his eyes and we made a truce. We skeptically shook each others hands. I was trying so hard not to crack a smile. Will had already failed and broke into his perfect smile. One look at his smile and one broke out on my face no matter how hard I tried to keep it back. His smile was just contagious.

"Yo, Will, let's play football" Carter called from the shore as he walked to us. He threw the old football in the air and caught it again. They brought and old one so it didn't matter when it got wet.

"Hell yeah, I'm in" He smiled.

"Me too" I smiled. "Remi Come play with us and make it even" I begged her.

She looked over here. She looked like she didn't want to play with us. "I don't know, guys" She said skeptically. I think she preferred watching football rather than playing it.

"Come on Remi, you can be on my team" Carter tried to get her to play.

"Oh alright" She gave in and walked over to us.

We picked teams and it was me, Connor, and Cooper against Carter, Remi, and Will. We played for almost an hour.

"Okay guys. I need some water and I think we need to reapply sunscreen." I said as I tried to get back to our parents.

Will grabbed my hand and turned me around.

"One more play?" he pleaded as he held up one finger. The boys began to beg with him. All of them gave me puppy dog eyes.

"Okay, one more play" I agreed.

We got in position. It was their turn to have the ball. Will was obviously the quarterback and I was his opposite. There weren't many rules like real football because this was purely for our enjoyment.

Remi hiked the ball to Will and I swam around to behind him without him seeing me. I saw that he was about to throw the ball to Carter. Before he could throw the ball, I jumped on his back, essentially tackling him. This caught him by surprise and he almost fell over. He held onto me thighs so I wouldn't fall.

"Snowflake" He said in a warning tone.

"William" I replied in a innocent voice, while still on his back. I wrapped my legs around his waist and my arms around his neck to where Will was now giving me a piggy back ride.

"Did you just cause me to lose a point?" He asked.

"Maybe" I said sweetly.

In a second, he fell backwards in the water, making me fall back with him. I didn't let go of him and he came back out of the water. I squealed as I came back out of the water.

"Will" I squealed.

"Sorry snowflake that was payback." he shrugged.

I rested my chin on his shoulder. Even though I couldn't see his face, i could tell he was smiling.

"Can you take me up there?" I asked sweetly.

He let out a big over dramatic sigh. "Only because you're cute snowflake" He said.

My cheeks reddened at his statement, but thankfully he couldn't see my face.

The others already made their way up there when dad said that they had cut the watermelon. When we made it back to the parents, Will set me down on the towel.

"You kids having fun?" Michael laughed.

"Yes, Dad, I'm having a great time. Thank you very much" Will smirked as he took a seat next to his dad. Micheal threw his arm around Will's shoulders before bringing Will's face into his chest.

I grabbed two watermelon slices and happily took bites into it.

"Okay so since everyone's here. Let's talk about dinner" Karla clapped. "So I was thinking that the adults go out to dinner and you kids go out and have some fun."

"What about us?" Kenzie asked.

"You can go out with the big kids or you can stay at the house. It's up to y'all, Ken"

She nodded in understanding. She started talking to the four littles with her.

"So how does that sound to y'all?" Karla asked us teens.

"I think that sounds great, Mom" Will smiled, while he ate a piece of watermelon.

I took a bite of my watermelon and the boys answered with a yes. Remi thought it sounded great a well. They all looked at me expectantly, like I was going to be the deciding factor. I swallowed my watermelon.

"Yeah that sounds great to me" I answered in agreement with everyone else.

After eating and reapplying sunscreen, we went back into the water. We were there for hours and it was absolutely amazing. I was with a best friends and family. The smile never came off my face, unless of course it was to evilly smirk at one of the boys.

We went back to the houses around four thirty to rest a little before we got ready for dinner.

"Ugh I'm exhausted" Remi fell to the bed dramatically.

"Yeah me too" I laid down next to her in the bed.

"I say we take a quick nap before we shower." She said.

I laughed. "I would agree with you but I'm going to shower right now." I forced myself out of the bed and to my suitcase.

I grabbed my stuff out of my suitcase and went to the bathroom that was thankfully attached to our room.

After I got out of the shower, I got dressed. I picked out a white shay cinched puff sleeved smocked crop top with a pair of high waisted denim shorts. I did my simple makeup.

By the time I finished my makeup, Remi had gotten out of the shower and got dressed. I started drying my hair and Rem started on her makeup.

It took about thirty minutes but Remi and I were ready.

She was wearing a white dress that went to mid thigh with ruffled tank top sleeves.

We walked out to the living room and the boys were waiting on the couch minus Will.

"Where's Will?" I asked.

"Right behind you, snowflake." I heard from behind me.

Cooper clapped. "Great so we're ready to go. We can take the gold cart around town, right?" He asked Will.

"Yeah. I'll grab the keys." He turned around and went back to his and Carter's room.

Will came back and we all went out to the golf cart. Kenzie and the others were tired so they decided to stay instead of come with us.

"So where do you want to go?" Will asked as the six of us piled in the golf cart.

We all shrugged. We didn't know where to go.

"I saw this place, Kody's, online. It has a mini golf course and a pool table." I offered.

"We are so going there" Carter said excitedly. Everyone else cheered in agreement.

I pulled up the directions and handed them to Will. I don't think it's that far from here. Will drove to Kody's. It was a two minute drive until we pulled into the parking lot.

"Can we get a table for five please?" Connor asked as we walked up to the host station.

"Right this way" The lady smiled. We followed her to a table by the pool table. "Your server will be right with you. Have a good night"

"Thank you" I called after her as she went back to the front.

The boys immediately went to the pool table and arcade games that were in this little corner. Cooper started playing Pacman with Carter and Connor and Will were playing pool.

"Hey guys, I'm Gabe and I'll be your server tonight. What can I get you lovely ladies to drink?" He winked at Remi. Carter saw this out of the corner of his eye and he was not happy.

He marched over here and I could see this wasn't going to end nicely.

"Hey babe, did you order the drinks yet?" Carter asked as he sat next to her and threw his arm around her shoulder.

"We were just about to I wasn't sure what y'all wanted" She answered with a blush across her face. I think she was developing a crush on my dear brother, but I couldn't know for sure.

"Boys, we're ordering drinks" Carter said. The boys all walked over to us and took their seats. Will sat next to me and Connor was on my other side.

I swear the guy's face paled a little bit. We all ordered our drinks and were all talking. We were having a great time. Cooper challenged me to a pool game. Of course, I couldn't turn down an opportunity to beat my brother at something else.

The guy came back and we ordered our food. He tried to hit on me this time and the boys immediately stopped him. To say it was funny would be an understatement because it was hilarious.

For the rest of the night, we talked, we joked, we played pool and mini golf, which I dominated at by the way, and we were just being teenagers, There were no worries about college or football. We were living in the moment and that's exactly how I liked it.

CHAPTER 20

The next day we woke up and the girls all decided to go shopping. We piled into Karla's suburban and went out for the day. We left the boys at the houses to do whatever they want. I wouldn't surprise me if they went to the beach and played football all day long.

"So where are we going?" Karla asked as she looked at all of us. I got in the front because Kenzie wanted to be with Tabby.

"I think there's a lot on avenue G." They all looked at me. I have been giving directions for the entire trip. "I've done my research. Let me get out google maps."

I pulled out the directions and Karla followed them. We ended up on a road with a bunch of cute stores. Karla parked in a parking lot close to the stores.

We spent all day shopping and having fun. It was great. All day we just had us girls. No boys to take care of or entertain.

"Oh my gosh, Cor, we should should get charm bracelets." Remi suggested from the other side of the store.

"Hell yes I'm in" I ran over to her to look at the bracelets and all the charms. They were definitely an off brand pandora bracelet.

I picked out things that reminded me of how my summer has been here so far. I picked out a suitcase, a pizza slice, a football, a snowflake, a star, and a beachy charm.

Remi picked out a few and we even got a matching pizza one. We also got stopping charms so our charms won't slide around.

After a few more shops and snacks, we decided it was best to head home. We were all tired and ready to eat dinner, especially Karla. She needed to get off of her feet for a little while.

The boys were all chilling in our house. Kenzie and Tabby were immediately to the boys showing them their stuff.

"Will, Will. Look at this new hat I got" Kenz hit her brother violently. She showed him her new hat.

"It's nice, Ken" he laughed.

"Okay I think Randy and I will start on dinner now" Micheal said as he sat up from the couch.

Dad nodded in agreement. They both left to go back to the other house for dinner.

Karla and the kids left to go back to the other house. I flopped down on the couch next to Connor and Will. I rested my head on Connor's lap.

"Hey sis" he laughed.

I put my feet up on Will's and Carter's laps. My feet were on Carter's lap which he wasn't too happy about but he didn't mind that much.

Will subconsciously pulled my legs closer to his body. "Comfy there?" He laughed.

"Mhm" I mumbled in response.

"So what are y'all doing?" Remi asked as she opened the fridge.

The boys have done hardly anything according to them. They did go down to the beach to play football. Apparently, they came back and have been watching tv ever since.

"Could you grab me a sprite please?" I asked.

Remi came back and handed me a bottle of sprite. I took a long sip.

Connor was channel surfing for something to watch. I slapped him repeatedly when I saw that the Big Bang Theory was on.

Carter and Cooper groaned. "Not one of your sitcoms" Carter complained.

"Oh shut up, who doesn't love Sheldon?" I countered.

We watched the show and even if they hate to admit it, they actually thought it was funny.

"Dinner's ready" Kenzie popped her head in to tell us.

We all made a rush to get to the burgers. We were hungry teenagers. What'd you expect?

"Glad your finally here" Dad joked as we all came in through the front door.

Dads burgers are the absolute best so I'm glad we got to have them tonight. We all ate and talked. There were jokes and sarcastic remarks flying around everywhere. Karla would pretend to be offended but she would smile when everyone else looked away.

"I heard that we could have a bonfire on the beach as long as we follow the guidelines. Who wants to do that after dinner?" Michael asked.

We were all one hundred percent in. Bonfires are my favorite part of summer. Something about being around a fire with some of your best friends and family as you all joke around and spend time together just makes me happy.

Once it got dark we all rode down to the beach. It was pretty empty considering it was almost nine o'clock. I made sure to put a cardigan over my sage green tank top and shorts. Micheal and Dad started the fire as the rest of us set up the blankets and chairs.

"Hey kids, I brought a surprise." Karla said and pulled a whole bunch of sparklers out of her bag.

The four young teens' faces lit up with excitement, especially the boys. I'll never understand the teen boy urge to play with fire. Tabby and Isaac looked at Remi with questioning excitement. She nodded, but warned them to be careful. They all grabbed a couple and Grayson took the lighter.

I watched as the four of them danced around happily with the sparklers in their hands. They made intricate drawings and wrote their names with the fire.

I sighed and leaned back in content. Carter was telling the Karla and a Remi about the constellations.

"Happy, snowflake?" Will asked as he plopped down on the blanket next to me.

"How can I not be? The kids are having the time of their lives, Carter's talking about something he loves, the boys are playing football in the dark, and I'm here with you. There's no way this could get any better." I explained the scene in front of me.

He nodded in agreement. "You're right. It couldn't get any better." He reached his arm around me and pulled me closer to him. I laid my head against his chest.

I was so glad that we moved out of Dallas and moved here. I could've had anything I wanted back in Dallas and I probably would've gotten it, but I never could've gotten this experience and these people in my life if we stayed there. After all, the best things in life aren't things.

"We're going to the Zoo?" Cooper asked excitedly as he stared at Dad.

"Yeah. Everyone except Michael and Karla. She can't walk around all day again." Dad answered with a laugh as he took a bite of the breakfast casserole Karla made.

Cooper has a thing for zoos. Ever since he was a child he was in love with looking at all the different animals and cool facts about them.

"Yes" he cheered.

"We leave in a hour and a half, so y'all be ready."

We nodded and finished breakfast before going to get ready for the zoo. I think it's a three hour drive so I decided to dress somewhat comfortable. I put on a brownish pink flowy tank top and a pair of denim shorts. I put on some gold jewelry and tan sandals. I grabbed the small tan purse that I brought and put my phone, portable charger, and a charger cord in it along with some lip balm and sunglasses.

I was ready and walked out to the living room. Remi was still getting ready in our room. No one was out in the living room, which was surprising because they usually are by the time I finish getting ready. I set my stuff down on the bar and grabbed myself a sprite from the fridge.

"Ready already?" Will smirked as he was the first boy to enter the living room.

"You are too" I countered on shock.

He laughed light and shook his head. "Yeah but we're usually waiting on you and your lazy ass."

"Fair point" I shrugged. "You want one?" I asked referring to the sprite.

"No thanks snowflake I'm all good" he smiled and flopped down on the couch.

I made my way over to him and sat next to him.

"You look cute, what's the occasion?" He joked.

I punched his arm as my cheeks turn red with embarrassment. He put his hands up in defense.

"Just saying you don't dress like this back home" he smiled his perfect smile successfully making me melt in my seat.

"I was just feeling it I guess" I shrugged.

Everyone met outside and we were off. Will said goodbye to his parents.

"You want me to drive?" I asked. "You've been driving all vacation"

He sighed and gave me the keys to his truck before he hopped in the passenger seat. Carter had to get in the back with Remi and Connor, not that he minded.

After a three hour drive, we finally made it to the zoo. Cooper was buzzing with excitement like the kids were.

Dad paid for everyone to get a ticket and we found a map. The gorillas were the first animals we saw at the entrance.

Connor read the fun facts. Cooper looked like a little kid. The kids looked in awe at the gorillas. Carter, Remi, and Will watched the gorillas. I watched everyone with a smile on their faces.

Dad picked up Kenzie and pretended like he was going to throw her in the cage. She was laughing, as was everyone else when she squealed.

We decided to go right and looked at all the cool animals. It was the tropical American animals first. My favorite was the Macaw Canyon because my love of the colorful birds.

Then Indo-Australian animals as well as African. My favorite from this section was the emu.

Everyone walked on to the orangutans but I stayed to watch the emus for a little while longer. I didn't even notice Will's presence behind me until he spoke up.

"You like these ones, huh?" He asked and leaned against the railing with his forearms like I was currently in.

"Did you know they have two sets of eyelids? One is for blinking and the other keeps dust away" I said in awe.

"I didn't know that" he laughed.

"They're such underrated animals because they're ugly, but I think that's what makes them beautiful. That and the fact that kicking is their main defense." I laughed. "The emu is discarded everywhere else but in Australia. There's over 600 places in Australia named after the emu."

It's crazy how just in a different part of the world one type of animal could have such different popularity.

"I'm surprised you know those facts." Will said honestly.

I looked at him with a smile, but he was already looking over at me.

"Let's go catch up with the rest of the group" I grabbed his wrist but he pulled me back. I gave him a quizzical expression.

"I want a picture real quick." He dug his phone out of his pocket and put it in selfie mode. He held the camera up to where the emus were in the picture.

"Do you want me to take that?" A woman asked. There were little kids running around her legs. I assumed they were her kids when one used her legs to hide.

"That'd be great" Will smiled and handed her his phone.

We posed together and the lady took our picture. She handed the phone back to Will.

"You are a cute couple" she smiled at us.

I was going to say that we weren't a couple but Will cut me off.

"Thank you" he smiled before he grabbed my hand and we started back to the group.

"Why didn't you say anything?" I asked.

He shrugged. "It didn't need to be said. We're never going to see her again, not like it matters"

But it does matter to me. On the other hand, he has a fair point. We're never gonna see her again.

"You're right" I said as we found the rest of the group.

We walked through the zoo looking at all the animals and taking pictures. Smiles on everyone's faces. Grayson and Kenzie were holding hands and I took a picture of them from behind.

We stopped at the lion's pride restaurant for lunch. We all had hot dogs, but topped with different things.

I found out that Will's favorite animals was the giraffe. Fitting, huh? Tall and blonde. I chuckled under my breath at the thought.

We reached the end of the zoo. The kids and Cooper wanted to go to the mini petting zoo so they did that while the rest of us, besides dad who stayed with the kids, went to the gift shop.

We walked around and looked at all the zoo related stuff. T-shirts, stuffed animals, and more. It was crazy how much stuff they had in this store.

I was in the mood for a lemonade popsicle that I saw at the oasis cafe by the Komodo dragons at the beginning of the zoo.

I dragged Will and the others to get one with me. Will, being the gentleman he is, insisted he pay for it and would not give up. I finally gave in and let him get it for me.

After we got back to the petting zoo, the kids were done and everyone was ready to go back.

Will drove this time. We decided to get in the hot tub since it was our last day. Dad grabbed domino's pizza on the way back and we headed straight to the houses.

Will went straight to see his parents while the rest of us went to our house. We changed into our swimsuits.

I had a Dalmatian print bikini top and reddish-orange bottom. Remi had a bright coral bikini.

Everyone decided to chill at our house, because our house had a hot tub and everyone wanted to be together for the last day.

"I just wanted to say that we had such a great time with everyone this past few days. I'm so glad we got to spend our summer vacation with all of you. And thank you to the Erickson's for letting us have these houses for the past few days" Dad said as he looked around at all of us.

"Thank you for inviting us Randy" Micheal stood up and hugged my dad.

We all had pizza and a great time. We put on music and danced and ate and sat in the hot tub all night. We had a long drive ahead of us tomorrow.

CHAPTER 21

I t's been almost two weeks since we got back from vacation and I've done nothing but hang out with Remi, Lena, and the boys. Our group has gotten extremely big. It was just me and my brothers before we moved here. Now it's me, Remi, Lena, my brothers, Will, and the other five boys and summer when she gets back. She won't come back until the week before school starts. It's been a crazy summer and I couldn't be happier.

Will picked me up for some "snowflake time" as he called it. He said he wanted to just hang out with me.

"So a week until your birthday, are you excited to be seventeen?" He asked as we drove in his truck. We were in our way to get ice cream floats from Riley's. The sky was cloudy and looked like it would rain soon. I didn't mind because I loved the smell of rain.

I shrugged. "It's just a birthday. I don't want much."

"Snowflake, it's your birthday. A day to celebrate you and only you, aren't you just a tad bit excited? What do you normally do for your birthday?"

I shrugged."We never did much. The boys tried their best to make my birthday special. They make me chocolate chip pancakes and give me presents and we hang out all day. My mom was never around for our birthdays, even before my parents were divorced. They try to make it feel special, but when the one person you've wanted there your entire life never shows up, you don't feel very special" I looked down at my hands in my lap.

"Hey" he said softly as he put a hand on mine. "It's okay. I know you have had a hard time with your mom and I know you say you're over it, but you can come talk to me anytime."

I looked at him with tears in my eyes. "Thank you" I whispered and kissed his cheek softly.

A car honk brought back to reality. We were at a light that had been red and turned green. We both laughed and will drive off. I wiped my tear filled eyes.

We pulled into Riley's parking lot. It was really empty, probably due to the weather. The sun wasn't out but it was glorious outside. I took a deep breath of the rain air.

Will held the door open for me as we walked into Riley's.

"Two of your best Root beer floats please"Will asked the cashier.

"That'll be $4.20." She said with a bored look on her face. "It'll be ready shortly." She said.

Will nodded and put the extra eighty cents in the tip jar. We went to find a place to sit. The place was empty besides the few employees that are working right now. It's the first time I've seen this place without any customers. We sat at a table with a couple chairs.

"It looks gloomy in here" I pointed out to Will.

"How can that be you're in here?" He joked slightly. A red tint brushed across my face.

"I'm serious Will" I whined but a smile found its way on my face.

He just laughed in response.

"Two root beer floats" the cashier said in the same bored tone.

Will got up to grab them from the pick up area. He handed me mine and we dug in happily. We started saying dad jokes and it just kept going.

"Why do bees have sticky hair?" He asked.

"Why?" I asked already regretting it.

"Because they use honey combs" he laughs.

I laughed despite the fact that that was one of the worst dad jokes I've heard.

"Okay okay. This is one of my dad's favorites. A three legged dog walked into a bar and said I'm looking for the man who shot my paw" I laughed.

My dad always told us that one. Will laughed and nodded his head at me.

"Did you know Bruce Lee has a vegan brother? His name is Broco Lee" he said nonchalantly, which made me die even more.

"If you think your microwave is collecting data and your tv is spying on you is bad enough. The vacuum cleaner has be gathering dirt on you for years" I said.

He laughed so hard his face turned a shade of red.

"Whoever invited the the knock knock joke should get a prize?" I started again.

"What kind of prize?" Will cocked his eyebrow, unsure of where this joke was going.

"The no bell prize." I answered as the corner of my mouth twitched up.

Will laughed. He put his hands up in a mock defense. "Okay okay I think you won that one. We should get going. You need to get home before dinner, I promised your dad you would" He stood up and I followed suite.

We looked out the window and it was pouring rain. Will looked at me before turning back to his car. "I'll be right back, stay here"

Her ran to his truck and opened the door. I assumed he was bringing it over here so I didn't have to go far in the rain, which I wouldn't mind if I did it would only be for a few seconds

He turned on the truck and turned up his music all the way up and hopped back out in the rain.

"Will, what are you doing?" I asked.

"Dance with me?" He asked. He was already soaking wet and I knew the second I got out there for too long I would be too.

I shook my head and scooted back even more. "We're going to get sick" I called out to him.

"So what? Come on, snowflake, dance with me"

Just when I was about to refuse again Will came over to me and threw me over his shoulder. "No Will please stop" I squealed and hit his back with a laugh. He set me down but kept his hands firmly around my waist so I didn't run away.

"Please dance with me, snowflake?" He asked softly. Our bodies were pushed against each other. I had to lean my head back to look at him.

"Will we're going to get sick" I protested at a whisper due to our close proximity.

"If I get to dance with you, it's worth it."

My favorite song to dance to came over the radio and I couldn't help but crack a smile and dance with him. We danced together and screamed the lyrics to every song that came over the radio. He spun me around and dipped me at some points. The smile never came off our faces. We were stuck in our own little reality.

The radio host said something about a request for a slow song. All of me came over the radio and Will pulled me closer to him.

"Can I have this dance?" He leaned down and whispered in my ear.

I nodded silently. We swayed to the rhythm of the music. I sang softly under me breath. Will spun me out on the chorus and spun me back in. I giggled under my breath when I hit his body on accident. He spun me a couple times before the song was coming to an end.

Just as the last words were sung he dipped me. Our faces were so close I thought we were about to kiss.

"I should probably get you home" He whispered but didn't move from the position we were in.

"Yeah probably" I whispered.

Neither one of us made a move to leave. We sat there as the rain poured on us and looked into each others eyes. His amber eyes looked so beautiful and his dimples showed as his lips curved into a soft smile, it was perfect. The next song came on the radio, but we didn't pay attention.

After what felt like hours, in the best way, Will stood up and brought me with him.

"Let's go" he coughed awkwardly and scratched behind his head.

We both awkwardly got in the car. The awkwardness died down as we reached my house. The rain had let up but it was still drizzling.

"Thank you for this, I had a good time." I turned and smiled at him.

"No problem snowflake" He smiled at me. "I like hanging out with you"

Something bubbled in my stomach at his words. I haven't felt like this before and I don't know what it is.

I kissed his cheek before going into the house. It was useless to cover my head I was already soaking wet.

"What happened to you?" Dad asked from the kitchen.

"Will and I were caught in the rain." I explained. "I'm going to take a shower and change clothes" I pointed at the stairs, gesturing to my room and bathroom.

"Okay sweetie"

"You were with Will?" Carter asked as I got upstairs.

I looked at him questioningly. "Yeah why? Do you have a problem with that?" I asked.

"Yes last time I checked, he was my best friend not yours."

I rolled my eyes at him. "Do not pull this elementary shit on me Carter Maverick" I warned. "Because last time I checked we are both teenagers and can have the same friends. You're seventeen start acting like it. Now move out of my way so I can take a shower" I pushed past him when he didn't move.

I went to my room and got clothes and stuff ready for when I got out of the shower. I went to my bathroom and stripped myself of my soaking wet clothes. I felt warm as I stepped into the hot water of my shower.

After my shower, I went to my room and got dressed in one of Connor's old hoodies and a pair of running shorts.

I face-timed Remi to pass time before dinner.

"Hey girl what's up?" she asked at she answered the call.

"I just back from hanging out with Will" I sighed happily as I remembered what happened.

"Oh tell me everything" she perked up and clapped.

I told her about how we danced in the rain and screamed to songs that came over the radio.

"And when a slow song came on we slow danced in the rain. He spun me softly and at the end he dipped me. The song ended but we both just stayed there staring into each other's eyes."

The same feeling bubbled inside of me that did when I was talking to Will in his car. I could feel the heat rise in my cheeks.

"After that, he drove me home" I smiled, at the memory from not even an hour earlier.

"Oh you got it bad" Remi's voice pulled me out of my thoughts.

I looked at her with wide eyes. "What do you mean I got it bad? I don't have anything" I asked.

"Cor, you like Will and from what I heard he likes you too." She said slowly.

"Pffffh" I waved her off. "You're joking. Will and I are just friends." I laughed nervously.

I don't like him like that. I can't like him like that. He's my brother's best friend and Carter just got mad at me for hanging out with Will. Imagine what he'd think if I liked him. It doesn't matter because I don't like him.

"I don't like him like that. We're just friends." I said defiantly.

"Do you get nervous around him or turn into a blushing mess when he compliments you? Do you get butterflies in your stomach when you're around him or even when you think about him?"

I thought for a second and she was completely right. "Oh my god. I like him. I like Will." I groaned and fell back on my bed.

Remi's laughter could be heard from my phone.

"Shut up" I groaned but a smile made its way to my face. "That doesn't mean he likes me though."

"Does he ever hold the door open for you? Or call you beautiful?" Remi smirked.

"Well yeah but that's how he was raised." I shrugged her questions off.

"Do you ever catch him looking at you when you weren't looking? Does he ever blush when you say something?"

"That doesn't mean he likes me"

"He really cares about you. He introduced you to his grandma before the boys. You've heard from several people that he talks about you to his family. When we hang out as a group, he stays with you when he could be with his best friends."

All these things she's pointing out about him could be just us being friends. I'm sure will doesn't think of me as anything other than his best friend's sister and coach's daughter. I'm probably not even one of his best friends. Yeah we're friends but he probably pities me.

I got called down for dinner and I had to leave Remi.

There are two things I know for sure after that phone call. One, I have a crush on William Erickson. Two, he can never find out I have a crush on him.

CHAPTER 22

I woke up to the sweet smell of chocolate chip pancakes.

I got up and immediately went downstairs to the kitchen.

The boys were all standing around the kitchen in aprons. I'm not entirely sure where they got them.

Cooper's apron said 'I wear my cape backwards when I cook.' Connor's was 'all this...and I can cook.' Carter's read 'I cook as good as I look.'

He must not cook very good, I thought to myself.

"Um, where's dad?" I asked wearily as I sat down at the counter.

"He went to the store to get syrup." Cooper shrugged before doing a double take and crushing me in a hug.

The others shook their heads before hugging me too.

"Our baby sister is finally seventeen. She's just so big" Cooper cried dramatically.

I couldn't help but smile.

"Happy birthday, Coco," Carter said.

"Happy birthday to my favorite sibling," Connor said. Carter and Cooper looked at him and feigned hurt. Both put their hands over their hearts. "Did I say sibling? I meant sister" He scratched the back of his head.

"I'm your only sister you nut" I shook my head and laughed.

Dad walked in also wearing an apron but his said 'kiss the cook' a classic.

"How many people tried to kiss you with that on?" I laughed.

"Surprisingly none" he smiled and crushed me in a big hug. "Happy birthday, baby girl. I love you so so much." He kissed my head.

I looked up at him. "I love you too and I also happen to love chocolate chip pancakes"

He chuckled and put the syrup on the counter. The boys put two pancakes on my plate and I dug into the syrup.

We ate breakfast as a family. We all joked and played around. This was the best part of my birthday. There were always birthday parties with my friends and stuff, but there was nothing quite like having all your brothers and Dad cook for you.

"Coco, you get your birthday present after the boys clean up breakfast."

The boys groaned, but after one glare from Dad they all put a smile on their face, as fake as it may be.

"I'm going to get ready a little bit"

I jogged upstairs to my bathroom. I brushed my teeth and washed my face first, before I even looked at the mess that was my hair. It was thrown up in a bun, so it was out of my face.

I brushed out my hair and threw it up into another messy bun. I didn't feel like changing out of my pjs.

I jogged back downstairs. The boys each held a present for me at the bottom of the staircase. I went to the living room and sat down on the couch. I opened the one from the boys first. They said they're gifts were wrapped differently but all went together. I opened Connor's gift first.

It was a teal blue record player. It was just like the one my mom used to own before the boys broke it when we were kids. I traced my fingers over it lightly.

"It's beautiful." I smiled at the boys. "Thank you"

I opened the gifts from the other two boys. It was my two favorite albums. Midnight Memories by One Direction and Meet the Vamps by the Vamps.

I hugged all three boys at once. "Thanks, you guys really"

"You're welcome Coco. We know you were sad when we broke mom's" Connor said.

"We? You mean Cooper right?" Carter was offended.

"Hey it wasn't just me. You threw the ball" Cooper pointed at Connor.

The boys fought. "It was Carter who ducked out of the way," Connor pointed to Carter accusingly.

"Hey don't blame this on me" he put his hands up in kick surrender. "Cooper's the one who can't catch a ball" he pointed to Cooper.

I laughed as the boys argued over who's fault it was, even though it was over ten years ago.

"Okay boys she has one more present to open" Dad chuckled and handed me a box.

I unwrapped it to reveal a giant shoe box. I opened the box and there was the pair of roller skates that I had wanted for a while. They were white and had coral wheels. My face lit up.

"Thank you dad!" I squealed and tackled him in a hug. "Is there even a rink here?" I asked.

"Yep and we're going later, so go get ready."

I hopped up excitedly and took all my stuff to my room. I put the record player on as loud as it could go and hopped in the shower. I screamed to my music as I took my sweet time to get ready.

Once I was done I put on a skinny denim jumpsuit. The top was a tank top with a v-neck and the back was completely. The pants were flared at the end. It looked like I stepped right out of the 70s and I loved it. I don't wear it often but it was one of my favorite outfits.

I put on a coral headband and left my hair down.

I felt really cute. I slipped on a random pair of shoes.

"Okay let's go" I said happily as I grabbed my new skates.

The boys followed me outside. Connor decided to take his own car and Cooper went with him, which left me with Dad and Carter.

Carter generously gave me shotgun and dad took us to this skating rink.

Connor and Cooper arrived before us and I think they were already inside. Carter and Dad walked in after me.

The place was 70s themed and I loved it. I gasped as I saw Will and Remi.

"Hey guys" I breathed out and hugged my friends. "What are you guys doing here?" I asked.

"We came here for you. Oh, and before I forget Kenzie wishes she could be here, but she had soccer." Will said. "Happy birthday Snowflake" He smiled and nudged me with his elbow. My heart nearly exploded on the spot.

"Happy birthday Cora" Remi squeezed me tight.

"And that's not all," Dad smiled.

I looked at all six of them confused. "What do you mean?" I asked.

Will smiled at me and held out his hand. I wrapped my hand around his. "Right this way" He smiled. I followed him and everyone else followed us.

We turned the corner and the whole football team jumped out to surprise me.

I gasped and covered my mouth. "Happy Birthday Coco" The team shouted at the same time.

A smile took over my face. "All of you guys? Just for me?" I asked.

Darren walked up to me and gave me a hug. Will was reluctant to let go of my hand at first. "Of course we would do this for you. You're basically part of the team and that makes you family."

I awed and hugged him back. I aslo hugged the other six boys in my brother's friend group. As infuriating as they may be they can all be pretty sweet. Nick and Sam are a little much sometimes though. What the hell am I talking about? They all can be a little much sometimes.

"Thank you guys so much for coming. I didn't need all this" I gestured to the whole party around us. Not only was the roller rink 70s themed but my party was too.

Suddenly, someone put something on my face. I opened my eyes and there was a pair of sunglasses on my face. The lens was pink tinted and Remi was standing on the other side.

I took them off and took a look at them. They were a pair of pink flower sunglasses. They had beads on them that spelled out my name and flower beads.

"Thank you Remi" I smiled and realized that she had her own pair on. "They're super cute" I hugged her tight.

"Thank you and you're welcome" She hugged me.

Will came up behind us. "Let's skate" He nodded over to the rink.

I nodded and held up my brand new skates with a smile. I put them on and immediately went to the rink. All the boys and Remi joined me. Music played as we all skated together, having a fun time.

All the football team held hands and screamed the lyrics to Sara Bareilles Love Song. I laughed and linked arms with Remi and sang along with them. A few songs later, I was linked with Connor on one side and Carter on my other. Cooper was at Connor's side.

"Are you having a good time?" Connor asked.

I leaned my head on his shoulder, well as much as I could with us skating.

"Yes I am, you guys really didn't have to do this for me."

"Oh it wasn't us. Our plan was to have everyone over and have a barbecue." Carter explained.

I looked at the three boys with confusion. If it wasn't them, then who did all this for me?

I didn't even have to ask because Connor answered that question for me. "It was Will, he said that he wanted to do something for you and he didn't know what to get you so he threw you a party. Apparently he knows about your obsession with the seventies and rollerskating." He shrugged.

I looked around and saw Will on the other side of the rink. I smiled at him as he skated with some of the boys.

"I'll be right back" I told the boys and unlinked our arms. I stopped and waited for Will to reach me. He slowed to a stop as he reached me. "So I'm told you threw this entire thing just for me"

He grabbed my hand and we started skating around the rink again.

"That did indeed happen," He smiled. I swear this boy's smile will be the death of me. I don't know how he does it.

"Why?" I asked before I could stop myself. My cheeks reddened in embarrassment.

"Because I like to do special things for special people" He answered.

I stopped for a second. He can't be talking about me. I'm not special, I'm just average.

"Don't even start, Cora. Yes, you're special to me." He stopped me before I even started.

"But all I am is your best friend's younger sister, your coach's daughter. There's nothing special about me. I'm just an average girl."

"You seem to forget that you're my friend too. You're not just my best friend's sister or my coach's daughter, Cora. You are my friend and you are special to me." He looked at me seriously.

My face burned at his words. It did hurt a little when he called me his friend. I kind of hoped he thought of me more than a friend, but I'm glad I have a place in his heart, even if it's just as a friend.

"Thank you, Will, for everything. You helped me more than you know." I hugged him.

"Trust me it's my honor." He hugged me back.

"Who wants cake?" Dad called and all the boys raced to him.

Will and I hugged for a few more seconds. "We should probably go get cake," I laughed.

"Yeah" He took me by the hand and we skated towards the cake.

They all sang me happy birthday and I opened my gifts. I got one from Remi, one from Remi's parents, and one from Kenzie. Remi got me a seventeen charm for my charm bracelet.

"This is from all of us. We all chipped in and got you this" Sam handed me an envelope.

I opened the envelope and pulled out two tickets.

"No way! Two front row tickets to The Vamps?" I looked at all the boys in front of me. "Seriously? Y'all have got to be shitting me right now!"

Tommy shook his head. "Nope, we're 100 percent real," he smiled.

"I can't believe you!" I squealed and hugged him. I hugged all the other boys too.

Maybe they actually think of me as a friend.

"Seriously, you guys are amazing" I smiled. "Thank you for all the gifts. You didn't need to get me anything."

"Eh I guess you're worth it" Darren shrugged.

I pushed his shoulder and laughed. These boys were amazing, whether they knew they were or not. I really did love every one like my own family.

I was telling Remi about this morning and I showed her a picture I took of all the boys with their aprons on.

"What you up to?" Carter asked and slung his arm around Remi and then me. "Oh isn't mine just amazing?" He joked with her.

She looked up at him. "You must not cook very good" she joked.

"That's what I was thinking" I laughed at how much alike Remi and I are.

"Great minds think alike!" Remi squealed and we high fived.

"Hey!" He yelled in protest and tickled her sides.

The boys heard a song come over the speakers and before we knew it, we were getting serenaded by the entire football team. A smile never came off of my face for the rest of the day. It was the best birthday we've had in a while. I didn't even have time to think about my mother.

Chapter 23

"How was your birthday?" Lena asked me. "I'm so sorry I couldn't make it. I was too busy getting enrolled in Greenhill High School" She smirked.

"Oh my gosh no way" Connor jumped up and hugged her. She giggled and wrapped her arms around his neck for support when he spun her around.

We all burst with happiness. It was me, the boys, including Will, Remi, and Lena. We were sitting in our living room just hanging out and watching movies.

"You have got to be shitting me right now" I was the second one to hug her.

She shook her head with a smile. "I'm being one hundred percent serious"

"We're all happy you're going to be at school with us" Carter said.

"Sucks to be you losers, she's in my class" Coop stuck his tongue out at the rest of us.

Will laughed and Con smacked his chest. Con turned to Lena.

"How'd you get your parents to agree to it?" He asked. I think he was the most excited that Lena was moving to our school. They text almost nonstop and he's always smiling at her text. I can tell he really likes her, but he won't confess to it.

"Well I told them what happened at the party and that I met some amazing people that go to Greenhill and the immediately agreed to let me go there."

Connor's face paled a little bit. "Lena, you told them?" He asked.

She nodded. "We can talk about it later. Right now I just want to hang out with my new friends." she told him. He nodded in understanding.

I assume she told him already. She talks to him all the time and by the way he reacted, he definitely knew.

"And to answer your question Lena, I had a amazing birthday."

"Your present is in my car" She said as if she remembered all of a sudden. She hopped up to go get and Connor followed.

We were all talking as we waited for them to come back. She walked through the door with a wrapped box in her hands.

"I was gonna have me coming to school with you as a present but I decided to get you a little something else"

I opened the box to find a few face masks, some chocolate, a mug, and some nail polish. I grabbed the card that read, "Happy birthday to you, you deserve a day to yourself so here's a spa day in a box just for you. Happy birthday Cora. Love, Lena"

"Aww, I love it" I stood up and hugged her. "Thanks Lena"

"You're welcome Cor." She smiled and wrapped her arms around me.

"Oh yeah, I could beat you in an arm wrestle any day" Carter challenged Connor.

I rolled my eyes at their behavior. How does this happen all the time? "This happens all the time. It's pretty much a daily occurrence." I laughed lightly at Lena's shocked and slightly concerned look on her face.

The two boys set up for an arm wrestling competition on the coffee table. I laughed and sat back on the couch with an amused look. Everyone took a side and began cheering them on. Carter won and they started playing best two out of three.

Will came and sat on the couch next to me. His arm almost immediately found its way around my shoulders.

"How are you today?" he asked as we watched the scene in amusement.

I leaned my head on his shoulder. "I'm great, my best friends and I are all hanging out and no one has once mentioned football. I love it and all, but they make it seem like their only personality trait" I laughed. Although what I said was a joke, it was half true. Every time one of the boys is around they feel the need to play football.

I could see Carter slightly glaring at us from the ground. He hated when Will and I were even somewhat affectionate or friendly towards each other. Something about him being his best friend and not mine.

"I'm glad you're happy, snowflake" He smiled at me.

His smile made me feel all giddy inside. Something about him drew me in and I loved every second of it. Will made me feel like I was actually a special person. I hadn't ever felt that because of my mom. Yeah I had my brothers and my dad, who tried to make me feel special and it worked for a short period of time. After I got to bed I couldn't help but think, why didn't my mother want me? That question still haunts me to this day.

"Okay, I'm bored what do you guys want to do?" Carter hopped up from the ground where he was with the other brothers.

We decided to go outside. None of us really had anything else to do.

The girls came up to me with cheeky grins across their faces. "Don't worry about you and Will, Cor. We've got a plan" Lena said to me.

I looked to Remi to try and give me some clue as to what Lena was talking about. "We've seen the way Carter has been looking at you two. Trust us, we have this under control" She winked at me.

Coming from them two, there wasn't enough assurance in those seven words.

"Tag!" Remi screamed before taping Lena on the shoulder. I looked around in confusion as the boys started running in different directions.

Lena tagged me and ran off with the rest of them. I was running around trying to catch someone when Will, gave me a challenging look. He almost dared me to try and catch him and that's exactly what I did.

The girls somehow ended up ushering the boys inside, leaving Will and I alone outside. I see what they're doing.

"I'm going to get you Erickson" I said.

"You'd have to catch me first Barnes" he teased me.

We ran around and I chased him all throughout the yard. It wasn't until I tripped and Will caught me that we stopped running.

My breathing hitched at the lack of distance between us. Will had his arms wrapped around my waist to steady me. I looked up to his face and he was already looking down at me. My cheeks turned red and I wanted to turn my face away to hide my blush, but I couldn't. I hate how he makes blush just by looking at me.

"Are you okay?" he whispered in my ear and caused shivers to run down my spine. I couldn't articulate a response and hummed a yes as an answer.

My eyes flickered down to his perfect lips and perfect smile. I could see his eyes flicker down to my lips. Before I could stop myself, I reached up on my tippy-toes and wrapped my arms around his neck. We both leaned in until our lips met in the middle.

He picked me up by the waist and spun me around. "You have no idea how long I wanted to do that" he whispered in my ear, which caused a blush to form on my face.

"Yeah me too" I smiled at him.

He pressed another kiss to my lips, just a little peck, before my brothers came outside and we jumped away from each other.

"Hey guys, what'd we miss?" Coop said and wrapped his arms around our shoulders, which was easiest for him because he was the closest to Will height out of all of our brothers.

Will's and my faces turned red. "Nothing much, we were just talking" I said.

"You looked a little close for just talking" Carter mumbled under his breath, but I heard him. That earned him a smack to the stomach, not only by me but by Remi too.

"Well while you two were out here, we came up with an amazing idea." Lena sang happily.

"We're making a fort" Coop squealed.

"We already got the blankets and pillows ready to go, now we actually have to build it, so let's go" Remi stated and grabbed my wrist. She and Lena dragged me inside while the boys followed us inside.

It only took us half an hour, Cooper yelling, and at least three bedrooms worth of pillows and blankets but at least our fort was done.

We all got into our fort and snuggled up together. I was next to Remi and Will, but it was really everyone next to everyone. There wasn't a whole lot of space, but there was enough to for all of us.

"Oh dang it we forgot snacks." Coop frowned.

"I'll get it" Will and I said creepily at the same time. We both laughed it off.

"Don't worry snowflake, I'll get the snacks" Will offered.

"Oh it's okay I can get them" I said.

"You can both go get them" Lena suggested with a little wink in my direction. I rolled my eyes at her but we took her advice anyway.

Will and I crawled out of the fort and made our way to the kitchen, not that it was a long walk. The kitchen was right beside the living room.

We stayed silent as we pulled out various types of snacks. I grabbed some candy from my secret stash for me and the girls.

Will went to grab drinks from the fridge. What I didn't know was that he opened a bottle of water. We both walked in opposite directions facing each other causing us to run into each other. The open water bottle spilled all over the two of us and the floor.

"I'm so sorry" I apologized. "It was an accident" I grabbed a towel and weirdly began to pat down his shirt.

"Hey" he said softly and grabbed my hands. "It's okay, accidents happen."

I nodded slowly and realized we also spilled it on the floor. I bent down to dry the water off the floor. Will bent down with me with a towel of his own. He began drying the spot with me.

"Thanks" I blushed. I feel awkward ever since the kiss but he seems completely unfazed by it.

"No problem snowflake" he smiled at me. His smile alone made me weak in the knees. We stood up and put the towels on the counter next to us. "Oh and by the way, you look good in red" he smirked.

I gave him a look of confusion and he walked off with a couple of the snacks and a smirk engraved in his mouth. I looked down at my shirt and realized it was white and my red bra was proudly showing through my shirt for anyone to see.

I gasped loudly and ran upstairs to change immediately. I can't believe Will saw my bra and had the audacity to tell me I looked good in red. I mean I do and I still had my shirt on, but that's besides the point.

I took a deep breath before leaving my room and grabbing the snacks that Will missed.

"What took you so long?" Con asked.

"We spilt some water. I was just cleaning it up and changing my shirt because it got wet" I explained.

He nodded and we went on with our movie.

"Kids?" Dad asked as he walked into our house. He's been going out a lot recently. He keeps saying he's got stuff to do, so I guess he's just really busy all of a sudden.

He peeped his head in our fort to see his four children and the additional the three they brought over.

"Oh hey Will, Remi, and Lena. Would you like to stay for dinner?"

"That'd be great, Thanks Mr. B" Remi smiled.

Lena answered either pretty much the same thing.

"Of course Coach" will answered.

He smiled at the seven of us. "Great, I'll order pizza. Cheese okay with everyone or pepperoni?"

"I'm more of a pepperoni person, but I'll eat cheese" Lena said.

We all came to an agreement of cheese. Dad left to go order it and we continued our movie.

Dad came in the fort with us for a little bit during dinner. We all were making terrible jokes and laughing uncontrollably. It was nights like these I cherished the most. No one cared about the outside world, in this case the rest of the house, and we were just together. These were the days that I felt special.

Chapter 24

Will and I were just sitting on his front porch, when a dog came out of nowhere. He happily trotted up to us. He was just a puppy. He didn't look much older than six months old.

He had light tan fur with spots of whites on his nose, feet, and tail. His eyes were a clear crystal blue. The fur was on the shorter side and his ears were all perked up. His paws were big, meaning he would grow a little more.

Will stood up and looked around. There wasn't anyone in sight.

"There's no one here. Maybe he got out, check his collar," Will said.

The dog had a collar with tags. One tag had his shot records on it and the other had a single phone number. There was no name or anything on the tags.

"Oh it has a phone number." I pulled out my phone from my back pocket. "Go get him some water, I'll call the number." I told Will. He went inside to get water for the dog.

I dialed the number. It rang a few times before the person on the other side of the phone picked up.

"Hello?" They said.

"Hi, my name is Cora Barnes. I'm calling because your dog just showed up at my front door. Is-" I started.

"Keep the dog. I don't want it anymore. Keep it away from me and please don't call me again." She interrupted me.

"But ma'am your dog."

"I told you to keep it. I want nothing to do with that mutt. Have a nice day." She snapped angrily and hung up the call.

I looked down at my phone in shock. What kind of person would say that about their dog? I sat back down on the steps. The dog came and sat next to me. He looked at me happily.

"How'd the call go?" Will asked as he set down a bowl of water in between us for the dog.

The dog immediately started drinking the water. He's probably hungry too.

"It was horrible. The lady picked up and once I mentioned the dog she cut me off and told me to keep him away from her. She was all bitter and rude."

I looked down at the cute boy. He's such a sweet dog. I don't know why the lady doesn't want him.

"What are we supposed to do, Will? The owner doesn't want the dog anymore."

He shrugged. "I don't know, Cora. We can't keep it here. Mom is allergic to dogs."

"I can try to get Dad to agree to keep him, but no promises. We might have to find a family to give him away to."

Michael pulled up with Kenzie and her friend. They saw the dog and immediately ran straight to him. Micheal got out with a confused look on his face.

"Where'd you get the dog?" He asked.

"He just walked up to us when we were sitting here. We called the owner and she made it clear that she didn't want him anymore. Cora's going to see if she can keep him." Will explained to his father.

Michael nodded and bent down to pet him. "He's a cutie. Good luck getting Randy on board"

"Thanks Michael" I rolled my eyes playfully at him.

"Come on girls, we gotta get your soccer stuff, so we can go to practice" he said. The girls went inside to get their soccer stuff.

I stood up and Will stood with me.

"Do you want me to go with you? Or do you want to go alone?"

"I think I can brave it alone. If I don't make it back, tell Connor he was my favorite." I said jokingly.

He nodded seriously. "Farewell soldier" he fake saluted me and we both died laughing.

Once I stopped laughing I looked at Will. "Okay but seriously if we end up with this dog you are going pet shopping with me. I don't care if you want to or not. I will force you to come with me."

Will chuckled at my statement. "It's a date"

"Sayonara" I waved. I picked up the puppy and took him to my car. I set him in the passenger's seat before getting in the driver's seat myself.

"You better not go to the bathroom in the car" I pet his cute little head. He tilted his head at me.

I started my drive to the house. The dog seemed to like the music I played. He was wagging his tail the entire ride there.

I couldn't help but wonder how far the dog had traveled. The lady could've lived hours away for all I know. She could've lived in the next town over. Either way I bet this dog is hungry and he needs food.

I stopped by the store to get a leash, so he's not running around everywhere.

I pulled up to the house and put the car in park. I looked over at the dog. "Let's hope Dad thinks you're as cute as I do"

He followed me out of the car and I pinned the leash on his collar. I noticed that the boys' cars weren't here.

"Dad!" I called the house. "Are you home?"

"I'm in my room, I'll be out in a second" he called.

I thought about what I was going to say when he came out of his bedroom.

"What the hell is that?" He asked.

"It's a dog," I said quietly.

"I can see that Coco. What is it doing here?" He asked.

"Well you see, it came up to me and Will, when we were at his house" I started.

"Did you try to find the owner?" He asked.

I nodded and explained the story about the owner not wanting him. They probably just kicked him out with nothing.

"Can we please keep him, Dad? Will can't keep him because Karla's allergic. I really think he came to us for a reason. He could've kept walking, but he came up to me and Will. I promise, I'll train him and take care of him. I'll buy everything he needs. Dad please. Can I keep him?" I gave him puppy dog eyes.

"I don't know Coco," Dad said. The dog went up to him and rubbed him as he tried to get him to pet him. He laughed and reached down to pet him. The dog licked his face happily. "Okay we can keep him, Coco, as long as you promise to keep up with him. Clean up after him, train him, and everything a dog needs. I will pay for the vet bills for his check ups though."

I jumped up and hugged my dad. "Thank you, thank you, thank you" I squealed. "I'm going to tell Will. Thank you so much, Dad. I'm going dog shopping."

I went outside and loaded the dog back in the car. I drove straight to Will's house. He must've seen me pull up because he was outside as I got out of the car.

"Will, I get to keep him!" I yelled with excitement. "Hurry up, we have to go to the pet store!"

"Okay okay, I'm coming" he chuckled. He went back inside for a few seconds before coming out to my car. He got in the passenger seat of my car.

I drove to the mall where the pet store was. I happily jumped out of the car. The dog followed me and I grabbed his leash. Will chuckled at my excitement and got out of the car too.

We walked into the store and Will grabbed a cart. I started listing all the things I needed for my new puppy.

We went to the bed section first. There were so many different cute beds to choose from. After looking for one for a couple minutes, Will helped me choose one with a wicker basket base with a big, white, fluffy pillow attached to it.

We were on our way to the bowl section and Will asked, "Have you thought of a name yet?"

I stopped in my tracks. I hadn't even thought of a single name for him yet. "No I haven't, I feel like a terrible dog mom"

He chuckled at me for what felt like the twentieth time since we found the dog. "Not to worry, I'll help you out"

I grabbed a bowl stand that came with two bowls.

"What about Biscuit?" Will asked.

I shook my head. "Not feeling it"

As we shopped. Will and I both were shouting out names, but none of them seemed to stick.

"Rocket?" He suggested.

"No. Atlas?" I shook my own head to that one.

We made it to the toy aisle. I knew this is where I'd most likely spend the most money. I saw a bone shaped wicker basket for his toys and I couldn't resist getting it. I got some squeaker toys, some balls, and a tug of war rope. I forced myself out of the aisle before I could spend any more money on toys.

Will and I walked around the store looking at random things. I got him a new collar and an ID tag to put his name and my number on it.

"Apollo?" Will suggested.

"It's cute, but I don't think it's quite right"

We looked around for a little longer and I saw the cutest red bandanna. I picked it up and showed it to the dog. His tail wagged with excitement. Was he thinking it was a toy? Most likely but it gave me the cutest idea for a name.

I turned to Will with a smile on his face. "What about Bandit?"

"That's a great name" He smiled.

I bent down to the dog. "Hello, Bandit" I pet his head. He wagged his tail and kissed my face. "I think he likes it" I smiled up at Will. He was already smiling down at me.

"Yeah me too"

I stood up. "Okay the last thing on the list is a crate" I said.

"I think they're over here" Will pointed to a part of the store. I followed him to where the crates are supposed to be.

Since he was supposed to be a little bigger we got a bigger crate. Will carried the crate to the register and I had everything else in the basket.

"Did you find everything just fine today?" The girl asked. She looked up and saw Will, which instantly put a smile on her face. "Hey Will"

"Hi Jackie. I didn't know you worked here."

She nodded as she continued scanning items. "Yeah, I started this summer with Mason. I thought Karla was allergic to dogs," she said.

"She is. This is actually my friend's dog. Jackie, this is Cora. Snowflake, this is Jackie." Will introduced us.

I don't know how to feel when he calls me his friend. We're more than friends at this point, but we're not dating. Friends don't kiss each other. I don't know what we are at this point.

"Nice to meet you Jackie" I smiled kindly at her.

"Right back at you, Cora. So what's the bundle of fur's name?"

"Um Bandit."

"He's a cutie. Would you like to get his tag engraved? We do it here for sixteen-ninety-nine." She held up the tag and collar.

I nodded. "Yeah, that'd be great," I answered.

She handed me a form to fill out and a pen. I filled out the form as she scanned the rest of my items. I handed her back the form.

"Okay, that'll be $108.85. Your tag will be ready to pick up in about thirty minutes. You'll get a text telling you when it's ready." She smiled at me as I paid with my card.

"Okay that sound great, thank you"

Will was already loading up the stuff in the cart. I helped him with the rest of the stuff.

"Thank you Jackie, tell Mason I said hi" He waved at her.

"I will" She promised and waved back at him.

We packed all the stuff in the car. Will got in the driver's seat this time and I got in the passenger seat.

"We have thirty minutes before we have to pick up the tag. What do you want to do?" He asked.

I shrugged. I don't know what to do. We can't take Bandit in many places and I don't want to leave him in the car for long.

"We can go to Riley's to get ice cream floats. We can get them to go so we can eat them in the car with Bandit."

"Okay."

We went to Riley's and ordered ice cream floats. I got a big red float and Will got the classic root beer float.

"Thank you for coming with me for this." I said as I took a bite of my float.

"It's no problem, I feel partly responsible. He showed up at my house. I feel like a dad or something" She shrugged it off.

If I'm Bandit's mom and Will feels like Bandit's dad, what does that make us?

Chapter 25

"Down set hut" I called and pretended like someone hiked it to me. I ran with the ball right at Will.

"You'll never get me, Erickson" I taunted.

"That's what you think, Barnes" he smirked at me.

I tried to juke him out and failed as he tackled me. We were both laughing as he laid basically on top of me. We both sobered up and looked each other in the eyes. His amber eyes mesmerized me.

He leaned in to kiss me and our lips met. He pulled away. "We can't" he sat up and turned his head away from me.

"What's wrong?" I sat up too and looked at Will.

"You're my best friend's little sister..."

I looked at him in shock. "That's all you think of me as. The annoying little sister of your best friends. Here I am thinking that I'm your friend and maybe something more. Well I guess not." I yelled and walked away in anger.

"Cora! That's not what I meant!" He followed me. He grabbed my wrist as I was in the middle of the street. "You didn't let me finish"

I stayed silent, letting him finish whatever he was about to say.

"Cora, you are my best friend's little sister and because of that I can't just kiss you when we're not dating. I don't want to lead you on and keep kissing you without committing to you. You deserve better than that. I owe you and your brothers that. So I guess what I'm saying is will you...would you...like to go to...to dinner with me...like on a date?" He cutely stumbled over his words.

"Yes, of course I would" I smiled and reached up to kiss his cheek. "I'm sorry for lashing out on you. I should've let you finish" I apologized.

"Don't be. I understand I shouldn't have started the conversation like that."

My phone rang and I had to answer it. It was Dad.

"Hello?" I asked.

"Cora Maeve Barnes, you need to get home as soon as possible." He yelled into the phone.

My eyebrows furrowed in confusion. "What's wrong?" I asked.

"Your dog is what's wrong. He just tore up my shoe"

I tried my hardest not to laugh. "Okay, Dad I'll be home soon. I'm at Will's right now."

"As soon as possible. Bye Coco" he reminded me.

"Love you Dad" I smiled and hung up the phone call. I began laughing as soon as the phone was away from my face.

"What?" Will smiled at me.

"Bandit is in trouble. I have to go home but I'll see you soon" I told him.

"I'll pick you up at seven" he smiled.

"I'll see you at seven then" I smiled at him. He wrapped his arms around me for a hug.

A car honked and caused us to break apart. A blush covered both of our faces as we moved out of the way.

"Sorry, Mr. Henderson" Wills waved at him.

We looked at each other and burst into laughter.

"Bye Will" I said as I got into the car.

"Bye snowflake" he smiled at me and waved as I drove off.

It took a few minutes to get from Will's house to mine.

"Dad?" I asked as I opened the door. Bandit came running to greet me. I bent down and pet his head. "Hey buddy" I smiled at him.

"That dog chewed my shoe" dad said as he walked in the living room with a chewed up dress shoe. He doesn't normally wear his dress shoes unless he has some sort of special event and as far as I'm concerned he doesn't have one.

"Why your dress shoes? Did he get into your closet?" I asked. There was no way for Bandit to open his door unless Dad left it open.

"No, I had them out. I was about to put them on and he stole it from me and chewed it up."

"Where are you going? You never wear your dress shoes unless there's a special event." I pointed out.

"I have a dinner with some of the faculty members at the school and I was supposed to dress nice but I guess I'll wear tennis shoes." He sighed. "Co, you have to get that dog under control. Punish him or something."

"Okay, I will. I'm going out with Will tonight. He's picking me up at seven" I told him.

"Picking you up, like as a date? Or as a friend?" He interrogated.

My cheeks burned red. "It might be as a date, but please don't tell the boys anything. I don't want them to make a big deal out of it"

"I won't say anything Coco. The boys are upstairs. Connor's in his room with Lena and I think the other two are in their room"

"Lena's here?" I questioned and my face lit up. I guess I didn't notice he car outside or Connor picked her up. She could help me with my outfit.

I ran up to Connor's room and opened the door without knocking. Lena was on top of a shirtless Connor as they were making out. I shrieked and covered my eyes from the scene.

Connor groaned. "Coco, you should really learn how to knock."

"We'll excuse me I didn't know my brother and friend would be up here making babies" I sassed back. "I need to steal Lena until seven." I grabbed her wrist.

"You can't steal my girlfriend" he pouted.

"Boo hoo so sad" I said sarcastically and dragged her out of his room and into mine.

I pushed her on my bed.

"Start talking. When did you and Connor become a thing? Why haven't I found out?"

"Please don't be mad. He asked me out last night, but we've been talking for a little while. I know he's your brother and I'm your friend but I really like him Cora"

I laughed lightly. "I'm not mad Len. I saw this coming ever since we've met you in the ferris wheel. I'm actually happy y'all are together. I just wanted the tea."

She let out a breath of relief I didn't know she was holding. "Okay great, now what's the big emergency that I had to be dragged away from Connor for?"

"I have a date" I blurted out.

She immediately had a smile on her face and stood up. "With who?" She asked with a knowing smirk.

"It's with Will he asked me out today when I was at his house. He's picking me up at seven and I need help" I said frantically.

"I got you boo"

It took a little while but I think we finally found a cute outfit. It was a light yellow cropped tank top with a tie in the front and a pair of denim shorts. I opted out of sandals and put on my trusty white high top converse.

Lena picked out some silver jewelry for me to wear and I grabbed my favorite pair of stud earrings.

I let Lena do my makeup, but I told her not to do a lot. I think all she did was mascara, blush, eyeshadow, and a touch of lip gloss. She even braided two strands of hair from the front and tied them together in the back. My heart was wavy from when I decided to curl it yesterday from boredom.

"And we're done" Lena said as she put down the last brush.

"How are we doing on time?" I asked.

"Seven minutes until your boy arrives" she smirked at me. "Speaking of your boy, bandit is so adorable" she squealed.

Bandit waddled over to her at the sound of his name. He wagged his tail and begged to be pet by Lena, which she happily obliged.

The doorbell rang and I looked at the time. It was only six fifty-five. He was five minutes early. I just hope the boys don't come down here.

Lena wiggled eyebrows at me and walked off to Connor's room. Dad answered the door and I could see him glaring at a very nervous looking Will.

"Dad? What are you doing?" I asked.

"Just reminding Will here that I'm his coach and if he breaks my baby girl's heart I can make his life a living hell" he smiled and clapped Will on the back.

"Okay we're going to go now, bye dad"

"Where are you going?" Carter asked as he made an appearance behind us.

"I'm taking Cora on a date" Will spoke up. Carter looked at his best friend in shock.

"And you didn't think to ask me or even tell me about it?" Carter growled in anger. He was obviously upset. "I thought I told you that I didn't want you dating my best friends" he snapped at me.

"Carter" dad warned.

"Excuse me, I don't see how this is my fault. You're not in charge of who I get to date. Will makes me feel special, more special than I have felt since Mom left and I'm going on a date with him whether you like it or not" I blew up. I turned around to Will and grabbed his hand. "Let's go" I said softly.

Will opened the door for me and I climbed into the passenger seat of his truck. He got in the drivers side and pulled out of the driveway.

He set his hand on top mine on the center console. "I'm sorry things got so out of hand. I didn't know he was going to react like that." He apologized.

"It's okay. He's always been overprotective about who I date, but ever since we moved and met you and the guys it's been crazy." I said. "Let's forget about it and have an amazing date."

"You look beautiful, by the way" he told me. Of course my cheeks turned red.

"Thank you and you look handsome.Where are we going?" I asked excitedly.

"First, we're going to go to Riley's and get some ice cream floats and then I have a surprise for you." He smiled.

I looked over at him. How did I get lucky enough to even go on a date with him?

"Thank you Will"

"You don't have to thank me snowflake, I'll always treat you right. That's a promise" he brought my hand to his lips and kissed it softly as he pulled into Riley's parking lot.

He opened all the door for me and was the perfect gentleman as always. He ordered and paid for my float.

"Do you want to eat in here or go to the surprise?" He asked.

"What do you want? It can't be all about me, it's our date"

"I vote let's go to the surprise and eat in the car." He was so excited about our date and I don't think either of us stopped smiling.

"Okay then I'm down"

He lead me back out to the car and started driving somewhere. I wasn't really paying attention to where we were going. We were playing some of our favorite songs and singing to them. He pulled into the parking lot of the park.

"What are we doing here?" I asked as I slowly unbuckled my seatbelt.

"You'll see" he said, before hopping out of the car and opening the door for me. "Milady" he offered me his hand which I gladly accepted and giggled. He grabbed something out of his backseat. It was a picnic basket.

"Aww you made me a picnic. Will that's so cute" I smiled up at him.

"Not as cute as you" he said like it was nothing.

My face burned. Why did he have to be so cute?

"I can't take all the credit, Poppy helped me out a little. She made her southern belle sweet tea just for you. She doesn't do that for just anyone, you know?" he set out the blanket and the basket.

I sat down next to him as he set out all the food. There was sandwiches, grapes, strawberries, watermelon and almonds.

"Welcome to Will's kitchen the five star restaurant, as you can see there's a great variety of foods we have today" he joked.

"Will this is amazing, thank you" I reached over him and kissed his cheek.

"The most amazing part is that I get to spend it with you"

For the next hour, we ate the food and had the best sweet tea I've had in my whole life. Apparently, Poppy won't pass down the recipe until she knows she's on death row.

"Snowflake, I have a question to ask you." Will said out of nowhere.

I perked up instantly. "Anything for you Will."

"Will you be my girlfriend?" He asked.

"Of course I will. A million times yes" I squealed and tackled Will in a hug. "This better be the only time I see you get tackled, Erickson." I teased.

"Only for you Barnes" he smiled with his perfect smile and caused me to melt on the spot. I can't believe William Erickson is my boyfriend. I don't deserve him.

CHAPTER 26

Will and I told everyone we were dating the next day. Of course Remi and Lena were super excited. Coop and Con were a little overprotective but trusted him. Dad was happy and overprotective and set ground rules, like any dad would. Carter was upset that his best friend was dating his sister but he got over it. Overall, I think everyone was happy for us.

"Do you wanna go to laser tag?" Will asked as he drove me through town. The windows were down and my hair was in a ponytail so it didn't get messy.

"I've been here for almost three months and I didn't know there was a laser tag here?" I asked in shock. I love laser tag.

He laughed. "Yeah it's at the arcade."

"Let's go, let's go, let's go!" I jumped up and down as much as I could with my seat belt restraining me. I hit Will on the arm several times.

He pushed me off of him. "Hey, don't punch the driver. You could kill us"

"Take me to laser tag!" I demanded like a child who wanted ice cream.

He glanced at me with a smile and returned his gaze back to the road. "What's the magic word?" He asked in a fake condescending manner.

"Pwease" I batted my eyelashes at him with my puppy dog eyes.

"Actually, that's not it. It's more of a phrase"

"Cora is the best?" I guessed.

He shook his head. "Why would I make the magic word a lie?" He said.

I put my hand dramatically over my heart. "Hey! That's not nice" I protested.

I could see his small smile from his side profile. "If it makes you feel any better, you only missed one word" He took my hand off of my chest and interlocked our fingers. His thumb caressed the back of my hand.

I swear this boy will be the death of me.

"Sorry, I meant to say awesomest"

"I don't think awesomest is a word" He laughed and ended with a smile.

That stupid perfect smile, that I've grown to love.

"It is!" I argued. He shook his head and smiled over at me. "Hey eyes on the road mister" I chastised him and turned his head with my free hand. I promise this boy will be the death of me one way or another.

"You still haven't guessed the magic word" He taunted.

"Carter is the best?"

He shook his head.

"Connor?" He shook his head. "Cooper?" Another head shake. "Coach?" Again, a head shake. "Darren?" Nope. "Nick?" Nada.

I pretended to be deep in thought. I gasped as if I had an idea come to mind. "Is it...you?" I asked dramatically.

He rolled his eyes playfully, but a smile overtook his face. "Wow turns out you're not as dumb as you look" He joked.

I let go of his hand and smacked him in the chest. "Hey, that's offensive!" I crossed my arms and jutted out my bottom lip.

We came up on a red light and he turned to me. He reached over to grab my hands but I kept them firm, crossed over my chest.

"I'm sorry" This time it was his turn to give me the puppy dog eyes. "Snowflake?" He asked.

I turned my head in the other direction. I noticed the light changed colors. I pointed to the light wordlessly. I obviously wasn't mad at him. I just felt like messing with him a little. I hoped he knew I was joking.

A couple of seconds of silence occurred before he put the car in park and turned his entire body to face me.

"Sunshine? I'm sorry, are you going to forgive me?" He asked.

I shook my head with a pouty lip.

"We're here" he smirked.

My face lit up in excitement and quickly unbuckled my seatbelt and jumped out of the car. He laughed and followed my lead.

"Do you forgive me now?" He asked. I wrapped my arms around his torso.

"Of course. Now let's go." I grabbed his hand and took off into the building.

Will being the best boyfriend ever, paid for my ticket.

The laser tag was free for all. The place wasn't really crowded. Will and I as well as a few children were the only ones in there. The guy explained the rules. We had ten minutes to go around shooting people. Will and I went separate directions.

Will and I shot at each other in our own little world. We didn't care about all the little kids around shooting at us. Out of nowhere, I was pushed up against a wall by Will.

"Hey sunshine," He smirked and kissed me. He'd been calling me that since we started dating. He said it's because I'm his little ray of sun and I can make him happy no matter what.

I melted into the kiss. We naturally broke apart. I didn't even notice the giant evil smirk forming on his lips. He shot me before running away and evil laughing.

"William Erickson!" I chastised. I rolled my eyes at his dorky self. I ran after him to shoot him.

It wasn't much longer that the game was over and Will so obviously won.

"You are a dork" I said as we walked out of the laser tag area and into the main arcade.

"Maybe" he said and wrapped his arms around me from behind and rested his chin on my head. "But I'm your dork" he quickly kissed my cheek and popped back up to me head. "What's next?" He asked and motion the arcade.

"Air hockey. Definitely air hockey" I answered and pulled him that way.

He were playing for a while but Will wouldn't give up until he beat me at least once.

"Babe, I've won seven times already, just give up." I whined.

"No I will beat you at least once. I'm not going to have my girlfriend show me up." He grumbled.

"Aww is somebody's masculinity being threatened?" I teased.

He grumbled a shut up and we began the next game.

"Hey guys what's up?" A familiar voice said and caught me off guard.

I turned to see Sam and Darren walking up to us with Aubrey on Darren's shoulders and Aaron walking next to Sam.

"Cora! Look at me! I'm on Dare bear's shoulders!" Aubrey squealed as she bounced up and down.

I giggled at her. "I can see that"

I heard the sound go off of the game when someone made a point. I looked over at Will, who had the striker in his hand and a sheepish smile on his face.

"Hey, that's cheating!" I argued.

"Sorry babe, you were talking." He smirked at me.

I rolled my eyes and shook my head. "William Erickson you are impossible." I couldn't help but smile.

"Babe?" Sam questioned.

"Wait are you two dating?" Darren basically shouted.

Will walked around the table and wrapped his arms around me from behind. I leaned into him.

"Yes" I answered him. "He asked me out on Thursday and I said yes"

"Congrats guys" Sam laughed. "We knew you guys would end up together. It was bound to happen sooner or later"

"Sammy, Sammy, I wanna go over there" Aaron grabbed Sam's hand and pointed into another direction of the arcade.

"Looks like we're outta here, see you guys later" Darren said.

The four of them walked away waving. I took Will's hand in mine. I started tracing his fingers and messing around with them casually. Next, we went to skee-ball, which I also beat him.

We were here for the next hour playing various arcade games. I might have beaten him at pretty much everything. He was a sore loser, but his dorkiness made up for it.

"I have to get home, Dad told me that I had to be at dinner tonight and he had to tell us something important." I told him.

"Then, I guess I'm driving you home" He took my hand in his and led me out to his truck. He opened the door for me and let me get in.

"Thank you sir" I kissed his cheek before he shut the door and got in his seat.

I started to fiddle with my hands. I didn't know what was so important that Dad had to tell us. Usually if he had something to tell us over dinner, then it was something big.

I was pulled out of my thoughts as Will pulled up to my house. He must've noticed my fiddling hands because before I made a move to open the door, Will put a hand on my hands. I looked up at him.

"Hey don't worry, I'm sure everything is going to be okay" He assured me.

"It's just last time he said that he told us we were moving to Greenhill. Honestly, I'm kind of scared as to what he might say. What if it's something bad?"

"Cora, I'm sure everything is going to be fine. Moving here was good news, maybe this will be too"

"Yeah maybe, I guess I have to go now" I said.

"Goodbye snowflake" we both reached over the console for a goodbye kiss, but we didn't want to stop.

He deepened the kiss by cupping my cheek and pulling me closer. I dove my hands into his blonde hair. We broke away, but we stayed close to each other. Neither one of us wanted to stop.

"Do I have to go?" I complained.

"Yes you do" he gave me a quick kiss and unbuckled my seat belt for me. He got out of the car and jogged to the other side to open my door.

"You seriously don't have to open my door all the time. I'm a big girl I can handle it."

"Yeah but you secretly love it. Plus I'm your boyfriend, it's my job" he said as he walked me up to my front door.

I shook my head at my boyfriend. "Bye Will" I smiled at him.

"Bye sunshine." He gave me one last kiss and let me go inside. I watched as he walked to his truck.

"Dad I'm home" I called but when I turned the corner he was there in the kitchen with an unknown woman. "Oh hi I wasn't aware we were having company."

"Hey Coco, this is Harper. She's gonna have dinner with us tonight" Dad said before he turned back to the dinner he was cooking.

"Hi I'm Harper Ellis. You must be, Cora. Randy has talked so much about you" she said as she reached out a hand to me. She had just been cutting some corn and green beans.

She had beautiful dark brown hair and soft facial features. Her eyes were blue. She was a very pretty woman.

"I'm Cora, but you already knew that" I smiled and took her invitation to show her hand.

"It's nice to meet you Cora" she smiled at me. She had a pretty smile.

The boys all came in from their run and all stopped when they saw Harper standing there.

"Hey boys this is Harper. Harper, these are my boys Connor, Cooper, and Carter. Then of course you already met Cora." He addressed Harper then turned to the boys. "Dinner will be ready soon, go get in the shower"

The all headed upstairs. I was left with dad and Harper.

"Coco, can you set the table please?" Dad asked me.

"Yeah of course." I said and grabbed all the plates from the cabinet and forks and knifes from the drawer.

The table was set, dinner was almost ready and the boys were mostly out of the shower. Dad made homemade chicken fried steak and buttered corn, green beans and a roll.

We all sat down for dinner and there were so many conversations going around.

"Cora, what do you like to do in your free time?" Harper asked me.

"Well, I like spending a lot of time with my friends and boyfriend, but when I'm not doing that I usually watch Friends or the Big Bang Theory." I shrugged. My life isn't very interesting

"I love those sitcoms" she said.

"Yeah me too" I smiled.

Dinner was almost over and I couldn't help but wonder what the big news was. Harper was over and she was great. I like her a lot.

Dad cleared his throat. "So kids, I have some news for y'all. Harper and I are dating." He placed his hand on hers and squeezed gently.

A smile took over my face. This made so much more sense. I'm glad that he's back to dating. It took him years after Mom left to date someone again and even after his last heart break he's back and trying again. He hadn't dated anyone in five years.

"You're what?" Carter demanded as he stood up from his seat.

"Carter, Harper and I are dating." He said again.

"What about Mom? Do you even care about her anymore?" He yelled. "She doesn't deserve this. How would she feel if she knew the you had another woman?"

"Your mother left this family long ago. She made her choice and I'm making mine. We've been divorced for ten years, Carter. It's time to move on." Dad said.

"You're just giving up on her." growled and turned in his feet, leaving the rest of us down here.

Dad sighed and put his face in his hands.

"Dad, we're happy that you and Harper are dating. Carter's just upset at the world right now. He'll figure it out eventually." I stood up and cleaned my plate off in the kitchen, before putting it in the dishwasher.

I kissed Dad's head and hugged him. "It was nice to meet you Harper." I hugged her. "I'm going to talk to Will, in my room. Knock if you need me."

"Okay, Coco. I'll come see you before I go to bed."

I nodded and headed upstairs to call Will.

CHAPTER 27

"Hey Dad, can I use your credit card today? The girls and I are going school shopping today and I need money." I asked as I plopped down on the couch next to him and Harper.

"As long as you don't spend all my money on clothes and stuff you don't need." He answered with a laugh. He pulled out his wallet and handed me his credit card.

"Great thanks Dad" I kissed his cheek and ran back up to my room to get ready.

The boys were all at Cole's, but I had my girls date planned all week so I opted out.

I put on my black ripped denim shorts and a black and white leopard print tank top. I paired it with my white air forces and simple jewelry and I was ready. I left my hair down.

After I sprayed my perfume, I heard the door open and Dad calling me from downstairs. The girls were in their way up to my room.

They busted in with excitement. Bandit jumped up off my bed to greet them. They happily obliged to his begging for pets.

"Are you ready to go shopping?" Remi squealed as she jumped on my bed.

I swiped chapstick across my lips and grabbed my wallet and phone. "Okay I'm ready let's go"

We walked downstairs. Bandit followed at our ankles.

"Wait who's driving?" Lena asked as we reached the bottom of the stairs.

"We only have Dad's car here so I vote one of you two" I said. The boys took their cars to Cole's house.

"I'll drive" Remi said and pulled her keys out of her purse.

I smiled over at Dad and Harper cuddled on the couch together. I walked over and hugged and kissed Dad. "Bye Dad, we're going shopping for school stuff. I think we're going to grab lunch first though. I don't really know how long we're going to be gone, but I guess we'll be back soon. I've already fed Bandy this morning and I should be here in time for his second feeding"

"Okay. We're having the Erickson's over for dinner, be back before then please" he said. "And don't spend all my money on clothes, school stuff only please"

"You got it, I love you Dad" I hugged him one last time.

"I love you too, Coco" He laughed.

I hugged Harper too. "Bye Harper, I'll see you later I guess"

"Bye Cora" She smiled at me.

The girls and I headed out to Remi's car. Lena got in the back, I got in the passenger seat, and Remi obviously got in the driver's seat. I immediately grabbed the AUX and began to play music for the three of us to jam to as we made our way to Riley's.

"Aren't you guys excited for school? I personally can't wait." Lena said from the back.

"I just don't want school to be over" Remi admitted. "This has been one of the best summers I've ever had. I met Cor and her brothers, I became friends with half of the football team, I met Lena, and I had a vacation that I could never forget. I just don't want it all to end."

"But think of all the things we'll gain when school starts." I started. "We'll still be friends with all the boys, we might sit with them at lunch, there'll be pep rallies, Friday night lights, victory parties, and let's not forget that we will see each other everyday and get to have Friday night sleepovers." I listed all the things good about the fall.

They both nodded in agreement. "You're right, maybe it won't be so bad after all"

"Okay but is everything good about fall, football season to you" Lena joked.

We laughed and I shrugged my shoulders. "That's how we roll" I said as Remi pulled into Riley's parking lot. I realized that some of the boys' cars are here, including Will's truck. They must've come for lunch.

We all walked into the restaurant and the boys were all sitting in the corner booth. None of them noticed us as we walked in. I saw the perfect opportunity to scare the hell out of Coop. I put an evil smile on my face as I walked over to the boys. Will and a few other boys saw me, but I put my finger to my mouth, hoping they got the hint.

Coop still had his back to me when I came right up behind him. I grabbed his shoulders and screamed in his ear. He jumped up from his seat and screamed like a little girl. We all busted into laughter. Coop glared over at me.

"Cora Maeve Barnes you scared the ever loving shit out of me"
He growled with a hand over his heart. His face was bright red.

"Sorry Coop all is fair in love and war" I shrugged. Will scooched
his way out of the booth.

He wrapped his arms around me and lightly kissed my head. "Hey
darling."

"Hey babe" I reached up and pressed a quick kiss to kiss lips. It
wasn't long enough to satisfy me, but my brothers and their friends
were here. No one wanted to see us kiss right now. I turned to the
table and ultimately my brothers.

"I thought y'all were going to Cole's?" I said interrogatively.

"We got bored and hungry so we came here" Connor shrugged.

"You do know, y'all have to be home by dinner, right?" I asked the
boys. Sometimes they don't listen and end up not having any idea
what's going on.

They assured me that they know we're having dinner with the
Erickson's tonight and they'll be there on time.

"Cor, we got you chilly cheese fries and a root beer" Lena announced as she walked over to me and the boys.

"Thanks guys" I said.

Connor was the next to get out of the booth. "Hey babe" He said
before crashing his lips on Lena's without a care in the world who
was watching.

"Hey baby" She smiled as they pulled away.

"Ugh y'all are gross." Remi stated and stuck her tongue out in
disgust. I pretended to gag and vomit.

She rolled her eyes at us.

"We've got to get going," Cole said.

All the guys all nodded in agreement and started to get up and grab their drinks. They said their goodbyes and left Riley's.

"Looks like we're out of here" Will kissed my cheek. "Bye snowflake" he smiled at me.

"Bye Will" I waved at him. "I'll see you tonight" I smiled.

He blew me a kiss and left with all the other boys. I shook my head at him as he almost ran into the door when he was walking out. He was a dork, but he was my dork nonetheless.

The girls and I quickly ate so we could go to the store to get our school shopping done. We spent a total of thirty minutes eating. We really couldn't wait to go shopping.

I was really excited when we left the house, but the closer we get to it the more I think about how school is going to affect my relationships with my friends and boyfriend. This summer has been a dream and I don't want school to be the nightmare that wakes me up. A knot curled up in my stomach just thinking about it.

"Cora" Remi said and pulled me out of my thoughts.

"Huh?"

"I said we got here. Are you okay? You look a little pale" She worried and put a hand up to my face.

I took her hand off of me and gave her a small reassuring smile. "I'm fine. I was just lost in thought. Let's go shopping"

"That sounds good to me" Lena said and hopped out of Remi's car.

Remi looked worried but we followed Lena out of the car. Remi and Lena pulled me into the store and into the school section. They squealed with excitement and grabbed a shopping cart.

For the next hour, we talked about school, what we would wear on the first day, the teachers, and pretty much everything that comes with starting school.

"I just feel bad for the class that has Mrs. Atkins. She's so strict and if she doesn't like you she calls you out for everything." Remi shuddered at the thought.

Why did that name sound so familiar?

"I hope I don't have her class" Lena said.

"You probably won't. She's a sophomore and junior English teacher. Not many people like her."

I just realized why her name sounded familiar and I stopped in my tracks. "Wait, you mean she could be my English teacher?" I asked, fearful of the answer.

Remi nodded slowly. "Yeah, but she'll probably like you. You're nice and I don't think anyone could hate you" she waved me off.

"I think it might be too late for that." They both looked at me in confusion. "One day I was with Will at the store, we were just messing around and she got all angry at Will because he 'wasn't showing proper behavior in public'" I air quoted. "I got so mad and I told her in so many words to f off."

"You what?" Lena laughed.

"You are literally my hero" Remi laughed.

"She's going to hate me now. I should've kept my mouth shut. Now she'll hate me and I'll probably fail English class" I groaned.

Remi laughed at me. "She doesn't fail people just because she hates them. She's just really hard on them. Don't worry it's not the end of the world. She probably won't even recognize you"

We were there for almost another thirty minutes before we checked out and went back to my house. The girls both had to go once we got there, but we had fun for the day anyway. I waved goodbye as I walked inside. The boys' cars were here as well as Will's.

As soon as I walked in the door, Kenzie and Will fought their way to me. Kenzie won and got to hug me first. I laughed and gave her a big hug. I haven't seen her in a while.

"Hey Kenz" I smiled.

"I missed you, Cor. You've spent too much time with my brother and not enough with me" She complained.

"Don't blame me, blame Will. He's the one who hasn't taken me to see you"

She turned to punch Will in the arm.

"Ken, don't punch your brother" Micheal chastised from the living room.

She mumbled something under her breath and followed her dad. Will hugged me without a second to lose. I laughed and wrapped my arms around his neck. He picked me up and spun me around. He kissed me softly. I loved it when he greeted me like this.

"Hey" He said softly as he gently placed me back on the floor.

"Hi" I giggled. "Wanna bring my school supplies to my room?" I asked after I decided to be lazy and let my boyfriend do all the work.

He nodded and grabbed the majority of the bags from the store while I grabbed a few. We hauled the bags up to my room.

"Where do you want them?" He asked.

I nodded over to my bed and set them there. He sat there himself. I put the bags I had in my hand on the bed. Before I had the chance to move, Will grabbed me by the hand and pulled me into him.

I giggled as I fell into him and he laid back on the bed. "Will" I squealed.

He crashed his lips into mine and cupped his hand on my cheek. I kissed him back passionately. He pressed me into him with a hand into the small of my back.

"Will, our families are downstairs, we have to go socialize and eat dinner" I giggled and kissed him one more time before I climbed off of him.

He stood up with me. "Just one more?" He asked with puppy dog eyes.

I reached up and kissed him. "You're a dork" I rolled my eyes at him.

A whine pulled me away from him and at Bandit's crate. I just realized he was in here all locked up. No wonder he didn't greet me at the door like he normally did. Why is he in here? He's great around people and he loves everybody here.

I walked back downstairs with Will, confusion evident on my face.

"Dad, why is Bandy locked in my room?" I asked.

I walked into the kitchen and Harper was there holding a little girl. She looked a lot like her. I assumed this was her daughter.

"Cora, this is Harper's daughter Skylar"

"Hi Skylar, I'm Cora" I cooed at the child. She looked like she was around four years old.

She looked at me in confusion. She probably didn't know what was happening.

"H-hi" She waved at me.

"Dinner's ready" Dad called and we all went to the table together.

I sat next to Will and Kenzie. The dinner was amazing. Dad made burgers and everybody thought they were amazing as they should. Dad's burgers were the best on the planet and no one could convince me otherwise.

After dinner, all the kids decided to go to the loft and watch a movie. The silence brought the thoughts of earlier to my mind. Soon enough my mind was filled with what ifs and worries about school.

"We need to talk" Will whispered in my ear. He slowly stood up and held out his hand for me.

I took his hand with my mind racing and wondering what it could be about. We walked to my room.

"Door open" Connor warned. Neither of us touched the door and he brought me to sit on my bed.

"I can tell you're worried about something. You've been really quiet since dinner." Will said and pressed a kiss on my cheek. "Talk to me, Snowflake. What's wrong?"

"I'm worried about school. I don't want summer to end. It's been the best summer ever and I don't want it to ever stop."

"I don't want it to either, but life goes on." he smiled. "That's not it, is it?"

"Will, you're going to be a senior and I'll be a junior. We won't have most of the same classes. We won't see each other as much. It's not like summer where we can see each other whenever we want. We'll hardly see each other" I ranted.

"And what about everyone else? Or Bandit? He's going to be alone all day everyday for a week. What if something bad happens to him and I won't be here?"

Will took my hand is his and rubbed it comfortingly. "Cora, snowflake, sunshine, marshmallow, babe, darling, love, I will always have time for you. I will see you everyday at school and after school and at football practice. I'll take you on dates every weekend, if that's what it takes. I promise I will try my hardest to make this relationship work. As for Bandit, he'll be fine. He'll get used to it eventually."

I looked at him. "How did I get so damn lucky to have you?" I smiled.

"I think it's the other way around babe" he smiled and kissed me. He cupped my cheek and deepened the kiss.

We pulled away and kept our foreheads touching. "I promise to never let you feel alone, or unappreciated. To me, you are the most important person and I never want to make you feel otherwise, okay?"

I nodded and pressed a soft kiss on his lips. "I don't want to go back out there" I admitted.

"Me either" He laid back on my bed and motioned for me to lay with him. I laid back and he wrapped his arms around me and we stayed there for the rest of the night, or at least until he left.

Chapter 28

I walked down the stairs to find the kitchen and living room empty, which was a little weird for the Barnes family on a Friday morning. Dad had already gone to work by now but the boys were normally up and getting breakfast by now. I opened the cabinet and grabbed a bowl and a box of cereal from the pantry. I poured the cereal into the bowl.

I heard someone walk down the stairs and turned to see it was carter. I made my way to the fridge to get milk.

"Good morning" I said cheerily to Carter.

He didn't say anything and walked to the fridge at the same time I did. Just as I reached out to grab the milk, he swiped it and took a swig out of the milk. He screwed the lid back on and put it back in the fridge.

"Excuse me, you did not just do that Carter Maverick." I glared at him.

"I didn't do anything" He grumbled and started to make some toast.

"You literally just drank out of the milk I was just about to grab"
I tried to stay calm.

He shrugged and continued to make his toast. I snatched the
toast out of his hands and took a bite out of it. He looked at me
like I had grown another head.

"What the hell is your problem?" He growled at me.

"What is my problem? What is YOUR problem? I haven't done
anything wrong and you come in acting all grumpy and stole the
milk from me." I snapped.

"I can think of a few things you've done wrong" He grumbled.

"Oh yeah? Name one" I challenged with my arms crossed as I
gave him a look.

"You're dating my best friend, that I specifically told you not to
date."

I groaned and threw my head back. "That's what you're upset
about? Carter, Will and I are dating, deal with it. He likes me and
I like him, the only problem is you. I don't see you getting all mad
at Will about this. So leave me alone"

I was about to take my bowl of cereal upstairs to eat in my room.
Carter had successfully pissed me off.

"It's not just that, Cora. The night you and Will went on your first
date you said that Will makes you feel more special than you have
felt since Mom left. What's wrong with us, huh? Your family? We
try so hard for you. We know that it still bothers you and we try
to make you feel special. Our lives revolve around you, because
we care. All it takes is Will and suddenly he makes you feel like
everything is perfect again" He said in a softer tone.

I turned around and almost dropped my bowl. "That's what it
is? Car, I'm sorry about that. You know you and the boys make me

feel like the most important girl in the world. I'm really grateful for that, I really am, but whenever I'm with you I think about how things used to be when Mom was around. When I'm with Will, all my thoughts are about him and with him" I set my bowl on the counter next to me.

"And I'm sorry if I ever made you or anyone else in the family feel like they treat me bad or I don't want to be around them or anything like that. It's just that some memories are best kept hidden." Tears started to brim my eyes.

"Coco, we love you and we don't necessarily like having those memories either, but we're a family and if one of us is hurting we all are. I know it seems like we've moved on by now and that we should. I mean it's been ten years, you'd figure we would by now, but I can guarantee that everyone thinks about it sometimes and we all hate it. We're a family and we stick together and I'm sorry I've been such a shitty brother" He said, his voice thick.

"You are not a shitty brother" I choked out a laugh and wrapped my arms around him. "I love you Car"

"I love you too Coco" He said and squeezed me tight before placing a kiss on my head. "It's too early for this shit and I'm hungry" he pushed away from me and turned to his bitten piece of toast and started to make another one.

"There's the Carter Barnes I know and love" I teased and took a seat at the counter and ate my cereal.

The other boys came in and grabbed Pop Tarts a little bit later. "So what's everyone's plans for today?" I asked. Of course I knew they had football practice, but I wondered what was happening after that.

"Football" Coop shrugged.

"I'm taking Lena to therapy." Connor said. We all looked at him for clarification. "After she told her parents what happened, they agreed that she could go to a new school if she went to therapy. Cole is beside himself because he can't go, but I promised him I'd take her"

"So is Cole okay with the two of you dating?" I asked.

"Yeah he's cool. He knows I'm better than the last douchebag and trusts me." he shrugged.

I really wanted to do something tonight with everybody. It's the end of summer, school starts in a week and I wanted to hang out at least one more time before school starts.

"Will said something about a movie night in the park. The whole town pretty much comes and watches a movie in the park. I think they're playing a dog movie" Carter suggested.

"Is everyone going?" I asked.

"Yeah, I think all the guys are. You could ask Remi and Lena, if they want to come too. The movie won't start until it's dark enough to see the screen." he answered.

I nodded happily. Now I have all day to wait and do nothing. "I think I'm gonna go to practice with y'all. Not going to work out today, though."

"Wow, I'm exhausted" Will sighed and sat next to me.

I giggled. "Don't let my dad hear you say that. Go get in the shower and we can hang out at my house with Bandit."

"I'll agree with that statement" He smiled over at me. He kissed me and I ran my hand through his sweaty head of hair.

"You taste like sweat, go shower" I pushed him off the bench.

"See you in a minute, sunshine" he smiled and made his way to the locker rooms.

Dad sat next to me a second later. "Hey Coco"

"Hey dad" I said and laid my head on his shoulder. "Will's coming over, is that okay?" I asked.

"As long as I don't have to see you lip lock the entire time like you were a few seconds ago and if you stay in your room, keep the door open" He said.

"Dad!" I whined and playfully shoved his shoulder.

He laughed. "What? It's true" He threw his hands up in defense. "Harper and Skylar are coming over too"

I crossed my arms and stuck my tongue out at him. "Hypocrite" I grumbled.

He gasped and his jaw dropped. "What did you just call me?" He was appalled.

"Nothing" I giggled. "I don't know what you're talking about" I tried to keep a straight face but a smile found its way to my face and my lips curled up in happiness. I tried to scooch away from him down the bench.

"I don't think so" He smirked and grabbed me and began to tickle my sides.

"No! Dad!" I squealed and tried to squirm out of his grip. "Stop!" I laughed and I couldn't breathe.

"Coach" Someone called from the locker rooms.

Dad sighed and stopped tickling me. He stood up and I took the opportunity to jump on his back. He shook his head and laughed but still supported my legs and carried me away. He dropped me off when he saw Will waiting for me at the doors of the locker room.

"Bye, Dad. I'll see you at home" I kissed his cheek and went with Will.

"Bye Coco" He called after me.

We started walking to Will's car. "Race you" He said before we both started running to his truck. He made it there first and I pouted as we got into the truck. We buckled and he started the car.

"Aw are you pouting?" He teased and leaned over the center console where his face was inches away from mine. I wasn't sure how his seat belt allowed him to move so close.

"Yes" I pouted and crossed my arms. I was facing forward. If I were to turn my head left, my face would be almost against his.

He turned my head to face him and crashed his lips into mine. I kissed him back for a second before we both pulled away.

"That make you happy?" He teased.

I shook my head and smirked a little. "Maybe you should try again"

He kissed me again and pulled back.

"That's better" I giggled.

He shook his head and started to back out of the parking lot. He drove me home and when we got there nobody was there. Dad and the boys still hadn't got back from practice. Bandit greeted us as we walked into the house.

"Look Bandy, I brought your dad" I said as I reached down and pet his head as I do every time I come home.

"Hey buddy" Will said and pet Bandit.

"Come on, we have the house to ourselves for a little bit" I smirked and dragged Will to the living room.

"And what did you have in mind?" He asked.

I shrugged "Nothing in particular" I reached up and kissed him.

He happily kissed me back and picked me up. I wrapped my legs around his waist and he sat down on the couch. I adjusted my body to where I straddled him. My hands went his hair and his stayed planted on my lower back, rubbing circles. He licked my bottom lip for entrance to my mouth, which I gave him.

He reached one hand up and cupped my cheek. He used this to pull me closer to him. He broke our lips and attached them to my neck as they left wet kisses. I moved my neck to give him more access. He trailed the kisses all the way down to my collarbone. I suppressed a moan as he began sucking, leaving a sensation I have never felt before. It felt amazing.

"Will-" I tried to stop him but my body enjoyed the trail of burning skin he left as he moved to the other side of my neck. I played with his blonde locks as he played with my neck.

I moaned as he got to a sensitive area. He began his hickey process one more time. His hands traveled to my thighs as he gently rubbed them.

"Will, my dad will be home soon" I warned him.

"I don't care" He mumbled against my skin. I loved the feeling of his lips against my skin.

"Then kiss me again" I mumbled. He brought his lips back to meet mine.

The door opened causing me to jump off of Will and sit next to him. He threw his arm over my shoulders, successfully hiding my hickeys.

"Hey kiddo, what have y'all been up to?" Dad asked as he walked further into the house.

"Not much, we barely just got here. We were playing with Bandit for a minute" I said the first thing that came to my mind. Bandit's head popped up from the middle of the living room at the mention of his name.

He nodded like he actually believed me. "Mhm, that's why your lips are red and there are hickeys on your neck."

Will and I both opened our mouths to defend ourselves. Dad cut us off with his hands.

"You are both old enough to make your own decisions, but be safe. If you hurt my daughter or I find out your pressuring her into something she's not ready for, I think you can imagine what's going to happen to you"

"I would never do that, Coach. I respect and care about your daughter and I couldn't live with myself if I did something to hurt her" Will said.

"Don't worry, Will, I trust you more than any guy I know. It's just a warning, son" He said before walking upstairs to his room.

I stood up and reached my hand for Will to grab. He took it and stood up from the couch. "Let's go to my room" I said. "We can watch a movie or something"

Will and I stayed in my room and watched The Blind Side. He stayed until I had to get dressed for the movie. I changed into a pair of comfortable denim shorts and Will's hoodie, that I stole from him. I made sure to cover my hickeys before we left, even though the hoodie covers them. I wanted to be safe.

"Hey, that's mine" He pointed at the hoodie.

I laughed. "Your point?"

"Don't worry it looks better on you anyway." He kissed me gently and we headed downstairs.

The boys were in the kitchen popping popcorn for the movie. I think it's bring your own snacks and beverage. This is a community thing and I'm kind of excited.

We got everything and headed out to the cars. I was with Will. We headed to the park. Everyone else was going to meet us there. Remi and Lena are coming together and I guess the rest of the boys are either coming together or with their families.

The park was packed with people and their blankets and some even brought pillows. Kids were running around and playing while they waited for the movie to start.

"Hey guys" Will said to Darren and Sam. They were not shockingly together with Sam's family. Each of them had a kid on their shoulders.

"Hey" They answered.

"Can we go play?" Aubrey asked Sam as she bent down to see his face.

"Wanda?" He questioned. She nodded and the two ran off to play with their friends at the park. "Can I go with Cora and Will?" He asked her again.

Wanda smiled over at him and us. "Of course you can, go be with your friends"

He kissed her cheek and we went to find the rest of the guys. We found a spot big enough for all of us. Harper and Skylar were here with Dad but they were sitting somewhere else.

The guys all showed up and the girls as well. We all sat together and talked before the movie started.

"Look, the movie's starting" Remi called and everyone around us noticed it as well.

It turned out the movie was A Dog's Purpose. I've seen the movie a couple times and I loved it.

The movie played and we were all sitting comfortably.

"I never want to stop making memories with you" Will whispered as I laid my head on his chest.

"Good because you're not allowed to" I smiled at him.

"And that's perfectly fine with me" He kissed my head and squeezed his arm around me.

I smiled in content and put my eyes back on the screen. We had one week until school started. I can't wait, but I'm also terrified. I don't even know what to expect. I've been to a big school my whole life. All I know is I have the best people with me through it all.

Chapter 29

That week passed by like seconds. I didn't want it to end, but sadly it had to. All good things come to an end, right?

On the bright side, I get to see my boyfriend and best friends more than a couple days of the week. My best friend and brother are in my grade and we have a ton of classes together. I even have some classes with Lena and Will.

"Come on Cora, we have to get to school." Will rubbed my back.

I groaned and flipped over.

"Come on snowflake" He urged me and sat on my bed.

"Do I get cuddles first?" I asked, like a little kid with puppy dog eyes and a cute pout.

He rolled his eyes playfully but laid down next to me anyway. I spent no time climbing on top of him and laying my head on his chest. He wrapped his arms around my torso and his hands laid on my back, rubbing it soothingly. Every now and then he would kiss my forehead and rest his head back on mine.

It took all I could to not fall back asleep. The beat of his heart mesmerized me and I was at peace. He was my peace.

"As much as I love this, Coco, you really need to get ready for school. I just happen to know that your outfit is the cutest and you need to show it off to everyone."

"No" I pouted and clung tighter to him.

"No kisses until you get up and get ready," He said.

I jumped up in protest and quickly grabbed my clothes that I put out last night. Will might have helped me pick it out. It was a blue plaid mini skirt and a thin, white long sleeve shirt. I paired it with my white air force 1's.

I pushed him out of my room and changed out of his sweats, that I stole, and into actual clothes. I quickly went to the bathroom and put on some mascara and blush. I brushed my teeth and hair. I french braided the top half of my hair into two braids. After one last look in the mirror, I hopped downstairs for my kiss. Bandy followed at my feet.

What? Motivation is motivation.

I saw Will and jumped on his back, with the help of the couch. He was caught off guard but caught me anyway. I kissed his cheek.

"See, that wasn't that bad was it?" He laughed.

"It was terrible," I pouted. He sat me on the counter before he turned around and stood between my legs. His hands were on either side of me. I was a little bit taller than him now. "Do I get what I was promised?" I asked and wrapped my arms around his neck.

"Oh you mean this?" He asked before he kissed me.

I kissed him back happily.

"Okay, okay, break it up" Dad said as he walked into the kitchen covering his eyes with a smile on his face. Bandit went over to him for attention, which he got.

Will and I broke apart, and I looked at Dad with a sheepish smile.

"Good morning sir" Will sucked up to my dad, while he scratched the back of his head. His smile matched mine.

"Yeah yeah, I can still make you run, you know?" He waved him off.

"Noted" Will cleared his throat.

I opened and closed my hands, gesturing like a little kid wanting to be picked up. He picked me up and lifted me off the counter.

"So what's for breakfast?" I turned to Dad.

"I'm not cooking. I have to leave right now, I'll cook tomorrow though" He kissed my head. "I'll see you later, okay? Please make sure the boys are up before you leave and feed Bandit. I'm sorry about breakfast"

"Don't worry Coach, I'll take her to get breakfast" Will chimed in.

Dad pointed at Will. "You got him. What do you need me for?" He looked around for his keys. I picked them up off the counter and handed them to him. "Take care of my girl, Will"

"I will, sir" He answered and wrapped his arms around me.

Dad walked out of the door.

"Where were we?" I smirked.

"Right about here" He answered before leaning down to kiss me.

We cut the kiss off at the same time.

"I think we need to wake up your brothers," He whispered.

I groaned. "Those two take forever to get up."

He took my hand and led me upstairs to Carter and Cooper's room. I knocked before going in, not like they could hear me. I turned on the light. I heard the groans of the two boys, meaning they were at least halfway awake. Bandit busted through the door and jumped on their beds. He's always good at waking people up.

"It's the first day of school, boys. You have to wake up." I opened the blinds and the sun was right at their window.

"No," Carter grumbled.

Cooper was up at the reminder of the first day of school. He's so excited to his senior year at the school with him and his football team.

"Yeah let's go!" He cheered and jumped on Carter's bed, like a little kid.

I laughed as Carter pushed him off his bed and tried to cover his face with a blanket.

"Looks like my job here is done. Coop, if he doesn't get up in the next two minutes pour water on him." I smirked. As if it was a miracle, or a little blackmail, Carter jumped up.

"Okay okay, I'm up."

"Me and Will are out of here. Get to school on time or I'm dead, or more accurately you are" I smiled sweetly and grabbed Will's hand.

I led him out of their room and into mine to get my backpack and phone.

"Are you sure we can't skip school and stay here all day?" I stood right in front of Will and pouted.

He cupped both sides of my face and leaned down to be even with my face. "As much as I would absolutely love that, we can't. We both know that your dad would kill me then resurrect me and make me run until I puke and then your brothers would beat me to death."

I laughed knowing that ninety-nine percent of that was correct. "I say we take the risk." I smirked and pulled him down to my bed with me.

We both laughed as he landed on top of me. I bit my lip to try and stop my laughter.

Will groaned. "I really hate when you do that, you know?"

"Do you now?" I smirked.

He nodded. "Oh yeah, you're being all cute and sweet and it's making me want to kiss you."

"Is that so?" I smirked and crashed my lips into his. He kissed me back but not for long.

I pouted when he pulled away.

"I love you, but we have to get to school and breakfast."

Love? He loves me? Do I love him? I've known him for a little over three months. We only started dating two weeks ago. Can you fall in love with someone in only three months? After dating for only two weeks?

I took one look into his amber eyes, perfect smile and cute dimples and immediately knew the answer. I had fallen for this boy and I had fallen hard.

He sat up and got off my bed. "How do you feel about donuts?" He reached his hand out for me to take.

"I think donuts sound amazing" I smiled and took his hand. I fed Bandit and made sure he had fresh water. After I had everything I needed, I left the house. Will opened the door for me as always.

He drove me to the donut shop and bought me donuts. He really was the best boyfriend ever. We ate and sang as Will drove me to school.

He parked the car in the parking lot of the school. A knot formed in the pit of my stomach. Suddenly, I wasn't too excited to go to school or to even see my friends.

What if none of the teachers like me? What if there's assigned seating and I don't get to sit with my friends? What if I get lost or something?

"Hey, it'll be okay." Will said and rested his hand on top of mine. "The first day at a new school is always nerveracking, but you'll have me, the boys, the girls, and your dad all here to have your back. It's Lena's first day too"

Just listening to his voice calmed me. He reached over and gave me a quick kiss before getting out of his truck. He came over to my side and opened the door for me. He took my hand and we walked into school together.

Once I saw the boys all standing in the middle of the hallway talking, my body calmed itself. It was just like any other day at school. I don't know what I was so nervous about.

"Hey guys" I said.

"Coco!" Nick said and hugged me.

"Hey Nick" I laughed.

Will and the guys did the bro hug things. Remi and Lena showed up not long after Will and I did. I of course hugged them immediately and we fell into our own conversation.

"Where are Cooper and Carter?" Cole asked me.

"They should be here soon, they were waking up when Will and I left this morning" I shrugged and answered his question.

The first bell rang and some of us dispersed to go to our classes. Will was one of them.

"Have a good day, snowflake" He kissed my cheek. "I should see you third period in Trig"

"Bye babe, love you" I said without thinking. It was true but it wasn't exactly how I wanted to tell him for the first time.

"Love you too" He smiled and went off into the direction of his first class.

The girls both looked at me with wide eyes and knowing grins.

I looked at them in confusion. "What?" I asked them. I started walking to our first class. Remi and I had our first class together and Lena's was on the way there.

"You and Will just said I love you to each other" Remi pointed out like it hadn't happened just five seconds ago.

"Yeah so what?" I shrugged.

"That's big, Cora. Keep up" Lena said. "When was the first time you said it?"

I stopped. "Uh just then?" I said, but it sounded like more of a question. "Look, I didn't mean for it to slip out, it just did. That doesn't mean I don't love him because I do. He told me he loved me this morning and I really didn't plan to tell him in passing"

They both started squealing and jumping around.

"You two are just so adorable, I can't" Lena gushed.

"I want what you two have" Remi said.

I gave her a knowing look. "You could if you fessed up to my brother"

"I don't know what you're talking about" She denied and continued walking.

Lena gave me a questioning glance. I told her that I'd tell her later.

Lena went off to her class and Remi and I kept going to ours. The school wasn't that big and our classes weren't that far apart. It was already so much smaller than my old school and easier to get from class to class.

"Good morning Remi" The teacher said as we entered the room. "And you are Cora, I presume?" She asked, looking at her roster. I must've been the only new student in this class.

"Yes ma'am" I answered politely.

She nodded at me. "Take a seat wherever you'd like" She told me and I followed Remi to a spot in the middle of the classroom.

The door opened and Tommy walked into the classroom. He waved at us and made his way over. "Hey girls, I didn't know you had this class. We could've walked together." He took the seat behind me.

"Tommy, you weren't even here five minutes ago when we walked down here" I said and Remi laughed.

"I take my time, Coco" He said.

I rolled my eyes playfully at him. "Do you guys have football practice today?" I asked.

"Your dad's the coach, your brothers and boyfriend are on the team and you don't know?" He laughed at the irony.

"Of course I know, Tommy, that's why I'm asking you" I said sarcastically and rolled my eyes playfully at him.

"Yes, Cora, we do have practice today. Are you coming?"

I shrugged. "Thinking about it. Will and I are getting floats after."

The bell rang and we all turned to face the teacher. More students had come in when we were talking with Tommy.

"Hello everyone. Welcome back to school. I'm Mrs. Cook for those of you who don't know me. A little bit about me is I have three girls Katherine, Annabelle, and Madeline. Katherine is enlisted in the military, Annabelle is in vet school, and Madeline is a senior at Baylor university. Cora since you're new, would you like to share something about yourself?" She asked me.

I stood up, though I wasn't sure if she wanted me to or not. "I'm Cora Barnes. I live with my three brothers, my dad, and my dog, Bandit. I moved here at the end of May and my dad is the football coach here" I said.

Tommy whooped at the mention of my dad. I sat back down and some of the other students introduced themselves.

The next four classes went by quick and it was time for lunch. Lena, Remi, and I walked together.

"Cheer signups! Cheer signups!" A girl called with a clipboard in her hand.

"We should try out for cheer together" Lena suggested. "All the boys play football, so it's only fitting we try out for cheer"

We were unsure about it at first but we all decided to try out for the fun of it. The three of us signed up. I saw Summer's name was already on the list.

"Practice is everyday after school this week until five and tryouts are on Friday" the girl told us and handed us all a flyer.

"Thank you" I said as we walked to lunch.

We sat at a table with all the boys. There was barely enough room for all of us at one table. Every seat was filled.

"What's this?" Will asked, referring to my cheer flyer.

"Cheer tryouts. Me and the girls are trying out. We thought it'd be fun." I shrugged.

"Good luck" he kissed my cheek.

"Thank you" I smiled and began eating my lunch.

Chapter 30

We walked into his house hand in hand. We've been dating almost a month and it still seems crazy when he holds my hand and does everything in his power to make me smile.

"Mom, I'm home and Cora's here too" he called out.

"Come in the living room" she called back.

Will and I walked to the living room. There was an old lady, who I assumed was Will's grandma from the other side of the family.

"Hi Nona, I didn't know you were in town." Will smiled.

The lady stood up and reached out her arms to hug Will. Will let go of my hand and leaned over to hug her. It seemed hard for him considering he had to be at least a foot taller than her. It was honestly kind of cute and funny to see him bend down to hug his grandma.

Karla cleared her throat and nodded her head over to me.

"Nona," Will started and grabbed my hand to bring me closer to them. "This is my girlfriend, Cora. Cora, this is my other grandma Nona."

"Nice to meet you, ma'am" I smiled and went to shake her hand. She pulled me in for a hug instead.

"I've heard a lot about you, Cora. It's nice to finally meet you" She held me at her arms length and smiled at me.

I smiled at her.

"I trust Will has been treating you right?" She questioned with a raised eyebrow.

I laughed lightly. "Yes ma'am. He's been amazing, honestly." I assured her.

"He better. He's been raised to know better" she looked at him. "I approve of her" she told Will before going back to sit with Karla.

"Let's go up to my room." He took me by the hand once more. He kissed Karla and his Nona on the cheek and we went upstairs.

He hopped on his bed and laid down.

"I like her" I admitted as I crawled up on his bed and laid my head on his chest.

He wrapped his arms around my torso and pulled me on top of him. I kept my head on his chest and absentmindedly played with the ends of his hair. He gently rubbed my back.

"Good, because I think she likes you too" His voice vibrated through his chest.

"Are you excited for the baby?" I asked him.

Karla was due anytime now. It could be in two minutes or two weeks. We're all waiting anxiously to see him.

Will took a deep breath. "I don't know, Cor. Don't get me wrong, I'm freaking ecstatic. I know this baby will have every opportunity in life with us and no one will ever give up on him. I'm just scared."

I sat up and looked him in the eye. "Scared? Of what?" I asked.

"I don't know. I'm scared that I'm going to be a terrible big brother. There's almost a nineteen year difference between us. What if I'm nothing like everyone expects me to be? What if he ends up hating me because I'm going to be at college for four years?"

"Babe," I put a hand on his face. He melted into it. "I promise you, you're going to be a great big brother. He will love you, no matter the age gap, no matter how far away you are. You are amazing with Kenz. You are a great big brother and no one expects any more than that" I told him.

He grabbed my hand and pressed a kiss gently on my palm. "Thank you," he whispered. His lips grazed my palm as he spoke before he pressed another kiss to my hand.

"Anytime you need me, I'll be there. I don't care if it's two in the afternoon, or two in the morning." I said and kissed his forehead and laid my back on his chest.

"Thank you snowflake" He whispered and kissed my head.

"Have you talked to Carter recently? I know y'all live together, but he really hasn't been answering me. It's been a while since I've seen him outside of football." Will asked.

I almost visibly winced at the topic. Carter had been a lot to handle recently. He'd been fine most of the summer. Sure he was a pain in the ass, but this was another level.

"I don't know what's wrong with him Will. He stays up in his room all the time. Hardly comes out for dinner. He slams doors and yells. He seems so angry at the world and I don't even know why. He won't talk to anyone. He yelled at Dad this morning. If you know this boy like I do, then you know he doesn't yell at Dad or anyone really. If he's angry, he hides away or talks it out. Him and Dad had a screaming match this morning"

"Maybe he's just going through something and he doesn't want to talk. He's a teenager. We all get a little angry and distant sometimes" Will shrugged.

"Yeah but not our family. Ever since mom left, we talk. We don't leave each other, not even if it's to our rooms"

He kissed my head reassuringly. "I bet he's fine. He'll come to y'all when he's ready"

I sighed "You're right"

"So when do you find out who made the team?" He changed the conversation.

"Wednesday. They're posting it during lunch. I'm kind of nervous. I know we only tried out for fun, but what if one or two of us make it. I'd feel so bad if I made it and and one of them didn't." I worried.

"It'll be fine. I'm sure you all three made it. Besides if one of you didn't, they'd be supportive of you no matter what. I'm proud of you no matter the outcome"

"You always know what to say"

"It's a gift" he smirked.

I laughed and hit him lightly. "Oh so humble about it too" I joked.

I looked up at him and him down at me. "I love you Will" I whispered.

"I love you too Cora" he whispered back and kissed me.

"Hey Will" Karla said and knocked twice before opening his door. "Nona and I are going to the store for dinner. We'll be back soon. Cora, you're more than welcome to stay for dinner if you'd like"

"Thank you Karla. I might just take you up on that offer." I smiled.

She laughed lightly. "You kids have fun. Ken is at Gray's house. She shouldn't be back before I get home but she might. Bye"

"Bye mama" he called as she walked out of his room and shut the door. "Do you want to watch a movie?" He asked me.

"I kind of just want to stay right here" I admitted.

"And that's perfectly fine with me" he kissed my head and continued to rub my back. ***"I can't believe we find out if we made the cheer team today. I'm so excited" Lena squealed as we walked to first period.

"I know I'm so excited, but really nervous" Remi gushed.

I laughed at the two of them. Honestly I don't care if I made the team or not, but I would be really happy if all four of us got to do it together.

"Guys that's not until lunch. We still have four hours"

They both groaned. "Four dreadfully long hours" Lena said and leaned against Remi.

"Way to be a party pooper" Remi joked with me.

Lena separated into her class and Remi and I went to ours. Mrs. Cook was already in there. She greeted us and we took our normal seats.

This girl I've seen a couple times in the hallway came and sat next to us. "You're Will's girlfriend, right? And Carter Barnes' sister?" She asked me.

I nodded. "Yeah that's me. Can I help you?" I was unsure of what she wanted or why she was talking to me.

"Um so this is kind of awkward, but I was wondering if you could help me. So I kind of have a crush on your brother, Carter that is. I was just wondering if he was single or if you could help me get to know him or something." She rambled.

I could here Remi's breath hitch in her throat from behind me.

"Um well technically he is single, but he has someone else in mind when it comes to that. Sorry, but I really can't help you" I told her.

"Oh well thank you anyway." She said quickly and basically ran off.

Remi rolled her eyes and pretended like she didn't care that someone wanted to date Carter. "Who does he like? Is he talking to someone?" Remi asked.

"Don't like him, huh?" I smirked at my best friend.

"Shut up" she grumbled and kicked my chair. I laughed and shook my head.

The next two periods went by quite slow. I just wanted to see my boyfriend again.

"Hi Mr. Pittman" Summer said as we entered the classroom.

"Hi Summer, how are you today?" He asked her.

"We'll find out after lunch when the cheer team gets posted." She smiled.

"Good luck with that." He said and went back to doing whatever he was doing before.

I sat down in my normal seat next to Will. "Hey" I said.

He looked up for the first time. "Hey" he said softly and turned back to his phone. He was normally really talkative when we get to this class.

"Are you okay? You seem quiet" I asked.

"Mom was just emitted into the hospital for the baby. There were some complications. As far as I've heard, everything's fine. Mom and the baby are fine, but she might have to go into an emergency c-section." He explained.

"What are you doing here? You should be with Karla and Michael."

I was shocked to hear that he wasn't there. His family is everything to him.

"I have to be here for school and football. You're dad said we have to be at the practices all week if we want to play this week. Mom told me not to worry and stay at school."

"Go be with your family. I'll talk to my dad. I promise." I set my hand on his arm.

"Are you sure? I really want to play this week and Mom would be really upset if she found out I skipped and couldn't play." He worried.

"Yes, you need to be with your family, Will. Dad will understand." I kissed his cheek.

He stood up and kissed me before gathering his stuff and whispered a thank you. He explained to Mr. Pittman that he had a family emergency and he was free to go.

Summer looked at me with a confused look. This class we had assigned seating. Luckily, I got seated next to Will, but Summer and Darren got seated on the other side of the room.

"I'll tell you later" I mouthed to her. She nodded and Mr. Pittman started today's lesson.

I tried to text Will for an update during Spanish class but Mrs. Hogan took up my phone. She didn't believe me when I told her I had an emergency that I had to get updated on and she wouldn't give me my phone back. It wasn't like I was missing the lesson. I was paying attention, but I was texting Will for updates.

She was my last class before lunch. I needed my phone. I needed to know what was happening with Karla and the baby.

"Señora Hogan please. I wasn't wasting time on my phone. I was simply checking up with updates for a family emergency. Please, I need to know what's happening." I begged her.

She sighed. I was going on into both of our lunch times and she didn't seem so thrilled. She opened her desk drawer and handed me my phone. "Very well, señorita. If you are ever on your phone in my class again, I will not give it up so willingly. Now get to lunch" she pointed to her door.

The girls met me outside of my class. "What took you so long? They already posted the list" Lena groaned.

"I got my phone taken away." They all looked at me weird. It was kind of out of characteristic for me. "I'll tell you at lunch. Let's go"

We made our way to the cafeteria, which was buzzing with excitement. I saw a few girls with tears in their eyes. I was honestly more nervous own than I had been since the tryout.

We decided to all look at the same time, so no one felt left out or anything.

Greenhill High Cheer Team

Cora Barnes

Remiah Burton-Ruiz

Eliza Clark

Selena Coleman

Lucy Cooper

Briana Gates

Isla John

Summer Morris

Holly Newman

Evelyn Stratford

Addison Terrel

Daphne Web

We all squealed with excitement. "We all made it" Lena squealed.

We happily made our way to the table with all of the boys.

"You guys are looking at four of the cheer team members." I said as I sat down in my regular spot.

"You guys made it?" Sam asked and I nodded.

"Congrats guys" Darren said.

"We never doubted you for a second." Cooper smile over at us.

Carter gave him an incredulous look. "Didn't you say just yesterday that you didn't think they would make it?"

Cooper punched him in the arm, but Carter just laughed. "Where's Will? I figured he was with you" he asked.

"Something happened with Karla and the baby. They're fine, but she might need an emergency c-section. He went to be at the hospital with them"

"What about practice? He knows the rules." Cole asked. "We need him for the game."

I shrugged. "Hopefully Dad'll be lenient about this family emergency. Don't worry guys I'll talk to him. How could he say no to this face?" I joked and pointed to my face.

Chapter 31

"It's Game day!" Coop screamed as he came into my room and jumped on my bed. Bandy barked as Coop almost landed on him. I groaned and threw him off of me. I sat up to see half of the football team in my room.

I quickly covered my body in my blanket, fearful that they would see something.

"Cooper Mason Barnes, get these guys out of my room this instant." I growled. He looked at me and turned as pale as a ghost.

He swallowed hard. "Sorry coco" he kissed my cheek before he ushered the guys out of my room. He was getting shit from all the guys for being scared of his sister.

Will was the only one that stayed behind and I relaxed. "Do I get my morning cuddles?" I asked.

"Every morning, snowflake" he said and climbed into bed with me. I took my normal position on top of him as he stroked my hair.

I started getting in the habit of getting my stuff together the night before so I could have time for this every morning. He kissed my head and ran his fingers up and down my back.

"I love you Snowflake." He told me.

"I love you babe"

He stopped rubbing my back and I sighed. It was time for me to get ready. I really didn't want to get up but if I didn't I'd be late.

"Do we have to? We could skip school and stay here" I suggested.

Will laughed. "You say that every morning, sunshine, and every morning you get the same answer."

"I would love to but you know we can't" I said for him as I climbed off of him and grabbed my clothes for today. Since I was on the cheer team, I had to wear my uniform all day to school.

I changed into my uniform and put my hair up in a half up, half down with the bow facing the front. I did my regular make up, but added red lipstick.

"Isn't that different?" Will asked as I came out of the bathroom.

"We're all doing it." I informed him and started to head down-stairs. His hand wrapped around mine and pulled me back to him.

I looked at him with a cocked eyebrow. "Would you do the honors of wearing this for good luck?" He handed me his letterman jacket.

My eyes lit up in surprise. "Seriously? Of course I would" I squealed and immediately put my arms through the holes.

"Thank you" he kissed my cheek and headed to breakfast. Dad was feeding pretty much everyone that was here. I don't know why they were all here, but they were.

We all ate as fast as we could to get to school in time.

"Coco, you ready?" Connor asked and tossed his keys in the air.

It's a tradition for all the Barnes kids to drive to school together on game day. I just forgot to tell Will that. He gave us a look of confusion.

"Sorry babe. It's tradition and I forgot to tell you" I said sheepishly.

He smiled at me and washed all my worries away. "It's okay, love" he assured me. I kissed his cheek, leaving a lipstick mark and running out to meet with the boys.

We drove to school screaming to songs and laughing at the stupid shit Coop came up with.

Will and I met at the front of the school to walk in together. He intertwined our hands together as he walked to meet up with the rest of the group.

"It's kind of cliché." He said out of nowhere.

"What is?" I giggled. He stopped and we faced each other.

"Star quarterback and cheerleader." He smirked.

"You know me Erickson." I said and wrapped my arms around his neck. "My life is full of clichés" I smirked and reached up and kissed him.

"That's enough of that" Dad's voice cut in. Will and I pulled away sheepishly and turned to face him.

"Hey Dad, what are you doing here?" I asked as my cheeks turned red and I put on my best adorable smile for my dad.

He laughed. "I work here. What are you doing here?" He interrogated.

"Going to class, coach" Will answered quickly.

"Ah good answer Will" he laughed and clapped him on the back. "You kids have a bit of time before first period. A little advice Will, if you wanna play tomorrow maybe don't kiss my daughter in front of me." He threatened.

"Dad!" I chastised. "Don't worry babe he's just joking." I rolled my eyes playfully at him.

"All fun and games here Will. I can't wait to watch you play tomorrow" Dad smiled. "Oh and Will, you got a little something there." He pointed to his lips before wandering off.

I nudged Will with my elbow. "Come on, everyone's waiting" I smiled.

He reached down and stole a quick kiss before he interlocked our hands again and we walked into the school together.

The day could not have gone any slower. Why did the teachers have to give so much work for the weekend? Especially Mrs. Atkins and I'm convinced she gave me extra work just because she hates me.

"Ugh that was so dreadfully long" I groaned as I walked up to Will. He was rummaging through his locker, looking for something.

"I agree" he said before he turned to me. He stopped and stared at me for a second with adoring eyes. My face heated at the gesture.

"What?" I asked shyly.

"You just look so good in my jacket" he said awestruck.

My face burned happily. "Thank you" I smiled at him. I don't know how a simple compliment turns me into a blushing mess but that's the affect that Will has on me.

He turned back to his locker and found what he was looking for. He closed his locker and reached his hand out to hold mine, which I gladly accepted.

The two of us walked to his car and he drove me to the football field.

"What number are you?" I asked to fill the silence.

"Sixteen. It's my lucky number. I won my first football game on the sixteenth. I was also born on the sixteenth. So it's kind of special. When I met you, you were sixteen, so that works out for me." He smiled over at me.

My heart skipped a beat and my cheeks turned the color of my uniform. This boy will be the death of me, I swear.

"Number sixteen on the field, but number one in my heart" I told him as I played with his fingers.

He parked at the field and looked over at me. He was silent as he leaned in and kissed me. I kissed back. He rested his hand on my cheek and stroked it ever so slightly. I think he really was trying to kill me.

"I love you" he whispered against my lips. The corners of my mouth twitched up into a smile.

"Not as much as I love you" I whispered back. He stroked my cheek a few more times before he pulled away.

I giggled as I saw his face, or more accurately his lips. They had red lipstick all over them. He shot me a look.

"You have lipstick all over your mouth" I laughed and tried to wipe some of it away. "You might have to convince everyone you just got a rash" I teased. I licked my thumb and wiped away some of the lipstick. We used a napkin to get the rest off. His lips were now red from rubbing them so much.

"I think I liked it better when it was all over" I giggled.

"I've got to get ready for football before your dad kills me, but I'll see you later okay?" He kissed my cheek before getting out of his truck and running to the locker rooms.

I got out of his truck and made sure it was locked before I went to the bathroom to reapply my lipstick. While I was in there, a couple cheerleaders from the other team got there. We were playing our rivals, Woodside High. They were the Broncos.

I was about to walk out when I heard Lena's name come from the stalls.

"Did you hear that that slut Selena goes to school here? I knew that she would downgrade after that whole thing with Adrien. She's such a slut. Can you believe she tried to pin the whole thing on him? She told everybody he raped her." Some girl said.

I stopped in my tracks. Lena is not one to lie about something like that. Is this what happened with her and Cole?

"If you ask me, she did it for attention" another girl said.

"No, she did it so she would have a reason to break up with him and get with that cousin of hers" The first girl sneered as they came out of the stalls.

They looked at me like I was crazy. I shut my mouth and walked out of there. I didn't need to start a fight. This is supposed to be a good day and I'm not about to let those girls ruin it.

The game was starting soon and the boys were warming up on the field. I found the girls stretching on the sidelines.

"You look like you just saw a ghost, are you good?" Lena asked with a smile on her face. She's okay. For all I know, those girls are talking about some stupid rumor or even another girl.

"Yeah, I'm fine. Let's get stretching" I smiled and sat down on the grass, so we could stretch together.

We all cheered when the boys ran out onto the field together. Will, Cooper, and Carter walked to the middle of the field with Nick, Darren, Tommy, Sam, and Cole walking together behind them, for the coin flip. Only one guy from the other team walked up to their side.

The whole school was in the stands cheering on our boys as the announcer reported that we got the ball first. They came back to the rest of the team cheering and hyping up for the game. I ran over to the huddle to wish the boys good luck.

"Y'all better win this game for me, or I'll be very disappointed in you guys" I teased.

"Coco, so glad you're here" Nick smiled over at me.

"I just wanted to say good luck to all my boys." I said looking around at everyone. Connor was even here. They allowed him to be on the sidelines with the team because he was the son of the coach. "So good luck everyone" I said.

"Thanks Coco" Dad smiled. "Would you like to do the honors and break us out?"

I put my hand in the middle and all the guys put their hands on top of mine. "Bloodhounds on three! One, two, three!"

"Bloodhounds!" Everyone joined in with me. I smiled as the boys took the field.

Will gave me a good luck kiss and ran out onto the field with everyone else. I smiled at the dork of a boyfriend I have. That boy will seriously be the death of me and I'll let him. I gave Dad a good luck kiss and went to be with everyone else.

"We're about to put up a stunt and you're flying" Remi informed me.

"Me? Flying?" My jaw dropped.

"Lena's the tallest so she's the backspot and Sum and me are the strongest bases. You are the smallest. You fly" Remi told me.

I have only flown once before in practice. It wasn't terrible, but I was just getting the hang of it. After I agreed, we sat up and I loaded into the stunt. I looked at the other two stunt groups who were doing the same thing.

Lena counted us off and they dipped and I stood up. We started the cheer and I felt free. It's like I was weightless and flying. The fans in front of us cheered along and the football team behind us played the game.

They popped me off and the smile stayed on my face. "I loved that. I can't wait to do that again"

"I knew you'd get the hang of it" Daphne smiled next to me. She was the flyer in the stunt group next to us.

"Thanks Daph" I said.

The game went on and I tried not to yell at the refs when they made a crappy call. I was in my cheer uniform and I couldn't yell at them like I wanted to.

After the first half, we did a cheer with some stunts before we took a break. I saw Kenzie in the stands and went up there to say hello. She was here with Grayson and his family. I was introduced to his mom and dad. Sadly I had to leave soon for the second half of the game.

I explained the game to the cheerleaders that didn't understand everything that was happening. It was kind of funny, when they asked me a question. I tried to explain it without all the football terms and in normal terms.

We won the game and the cheerleaders rushed the fields to congratulate the football boys.

I was looking for Will when I was grabbed by the waist and turned into someone's body. I knew who it was instantly. I smiled up at him.

"You did great" I said.

"Not as great as you, snowflake. Maybe you finally found your sport"

"I'm not sure I'd count cheer as a sport, but I did like it a lot" I smiled.

He reached down and kissed me. We pulled apart before it became a make out session in front of everyone. We went to find the group but they were dispersed with their families and my family was nowhere to be seen in the crown of people. We found Lena talking to a guy from the other team. He was the same guy that was at the coin flip.

"Hey Lena" I called out to her, but she didn't hear me. Once I got closer I could see the tear streaks on her face and fear in her eyes. This guy was not friendly. A wash of concern immediately took over my face.

"G-Go away," She told the guy weakly.

I stepped in front of her and looked the guy in the eye. Something about him seemed familiar.

"Is something wrong?" I asked sharply. Something was obviously wrong.

"I'm just being friendly." He remarked.

"I don't know what your definition of friendly is but that definitely is not it. If I were you I would get out of here and go back to your team." I growled protectively.

He shot his hands up in defense as a smirk cracked on his face. "Don't get your thong in a twist, sweetheart, she likes it"

"Don't call her sweetheart" Will growled next to me. I stopped him with my arm.

"As I said before your definition of things is screwed up, get the hell away from my friend or I will beat your ass"

His eyebrow shot up with surprise and interest. I mentally gagged. "You're a feisty one, aren't you?" He took a step closer to me, but I didn't back down. "I like feisty" He smirked.

I hit him with my right hook. "I warned you"

He raised his fist to punch me, but stopped when Lena spoke up behind me. "Adrien stop" She yelled. "I'm the one you're here for, just leave her out of it."

He looked over at her in shock. "Oh so now you speak up. You're a worthless little bitch and you always will be."

Will straightened up beside me ready to come in if needed.

The boys came running up to us. Their faces were laced with worry. Connor went straight to Lena and stood between her and Adrien.

"Call her a bitch again I dare you" Connor said in a low voice. He's scary when he's angry. He wouldn't let anything happen to any of us, especially Lena.

The boys were all scary silent and stiff ready to kick this kids ass.

"Is there a problem over here?" Dad's voice boomed as he walked over here with the other coach.

The boys all looked at Adrien and gave him the choice. "Everything's fine" He said forcefully and walked off to the direction of his bus. His coach followed.

The boys all visibly relaxed and I went straight to Lena, who collapsed into my arms. Her body racked with sobs. I rubbed her back soothingly. It was then I realized what those girls said was true, well at least halfway.

Connor tried to console her but she backed away from him. He looked at her with a world of hurt in his eyes.

"I'm sorry" She said, before she ran away.

"Don't take it personally, Con, she's been through a lot and it all just flashed back to her" I told him. "Let her be alone for a little bit, she'll talk when she's ready"

CHAPTER 32

I threw the ball for Bandit. He ran happily through the grass and grabbed the ball before he brought it back to me. I threw it again and he went through the same cycle over and over again. It was his favorite thing to do. That and play with the frisbee.

"He's getting really good at that" Will stated. He had his arms wrapped around my stomach as he stood behind me.

"Yeah he is" I admitted and leaned back into Will's touch. I smiled as our dog came running back to us with the ball in his mouth and his own doggy smile. "I want some snow cones. Do you think they still have them even though it's the end of August?"

"It's pretty hot today, they might still have them. I'll go check for you." He kissed my cheek before walking off in the direction of where the snow cone cart usually is. I felt exposed without his arms around me. I've grown quite accustomed to having them around me.

Bandy dropped the ball next to me and I picked it up before throwing it again. I laughed as he went to catch it but it bounced off the ground to hit him in the face before he got a hold of it.

I kept throwing the ball for Bandit until Will came back with two snow cones. "I got you a cotton candy" He said and handed me my snow cone. There was an obvious bite taken out of it.

"Did you take a bite of my snow cone, William?" I asked in a fake stern voice.

"I got hungry on the walk over here" He teased.

"You have your own, dork" I rolled my eyes playfully at him. I hooked Bandit back on his leash. Will, Bandit, and I started to walk around the park. Will and I ate our snow cones.

"I can't believe tomorrow, I will have been dating you for a whole month" Will said casually.

I looked at him with wide eyes. "Tomorrow is the twenty-ninth already?" I asked and looked at my phone for confirmation. It was in fact the twenty-eighth.

"I guess time flies when you love someone" He joked.

"It really does" I smiled and leaned into him.

We stayed out at the park until we finished our snow cones then decided to head home. We walked in and the boys were all gone, including Dad. It was getting close to dinner, they were probably all out on their evening run.

Will and I sat on the couch facing each other with our arms rested on the back. Our faces were only a couple inches away from each other. Bandit took his spot at our feet. I reached over and ran my fingers through his hair. He closed his eyes in content and let my finger brush through his locks of beautiful blonde hair.

"I can't believe it's already been a month since we started dating. I mean it seems like yesterday, I opened the door to see you standing on my front porch, asking if you were at the right place" I chuckled at the memory.

"You just counted a month, snowflake, I'm looking forward to counting years with you" He smiled at me.

My heart melted at his words and my face turned red. "How do you do that?" I asked.

"Do what?" He chuckled.

"Make my heart melt by the littlest of gestures or words. You make me into a blushing mess and you hardly even do anything. It's not fair" I pouted but a smile escaped my lips.

"You're cute" He mumbled. If possible my face burned even more. I felt like a sunburnt tomato right now.

Remi and I stood in the middle of the courtyard talking before class started. We normally met with everyone inside but it was beautiful and Remi needed something from her car.

"Oh hey Drew" Remi smiled at Drew, one of the football players, as he walked up to us in the courtyard.

"Hey ladies" He sent us a wink as he approached.

"So Remi, are you coming to the game this week?" He flirted with my best friend.

"Of course. I kind of have to being a cheerleader and all" She smiled.

"Right" he smiled.

She probably didn't notice that he was flirting with her. She had her sights on someone a little different.

"There's an afterparty and you're invited so is Coco" he looked over at me. He was one of the guys I definitely didn't like calling me Coco.

"Don't you have to win before you get a victory party?" I said sarcastically.

"Are you suggesting we won't?" He challenged me.

I threw my hands up in defense.

Drew flirted with Remi. I saw a seething Carter walking this way. He reached us and without a word punched Drew in the face.

"Carter" I yelled, scolding. I looked over at Remi as her hand flew over her mouth as a gasp escaped. I slightly pushed Remi behind me.

"What the hell man?" Drew yelled, holding his jaw.

This drew a crowd.

"You know exactly what that was for," Carter yelled at Drew.

"Forgive me for talking to Remi, I didn't know that talking to her was fucking off limits" Drew sneered. This sent Carter off the edge and he punched him again. Drew knew exactly what he was doing.

Drew knew what was coming and fought back this time.

More students circled around as the fight progressed. I saw most of the people had their phones out, most likely filming the fight. Remi and I were both screaming at Carter to stop. I would break it up but I didn't want to get hurt.

Will and Nick pushed through the crowd and broke up the fight. Will pulled Carter back and Nick kept Drew back.

Will looked at me and silently asked if I was hurt. I shook my head in response.

"What the hell is wrong with you?" I yelled at Carter.

"It's none of your business, Cora. Just stay the fuck out of it" He yelled.

I took a step back in shock. He never cusses at me like that. Sure, we cuss and discuss a lot of stuff, but never like that. My blood boiled. I could tell he knew he messed up.

I stepped one step closer than I was before. I didn't care that there was a crowd. I was angry and he was going to regret it. "I don't know what crawled up your ass and died, but it's annoying the hell out of me. You are always angry at everything, you yelled at Dad, you never come out of your room anymore. Not to mention you just got into a fight. I don't know what's gotten into you but I am sick of it."

"You seem to forget that I never wanted to come here in the first place. I never wanted to leave Dallas and come to this stupid town. In case you haven't noticed, I hate it here and I want to go home" He ran his hand through his hair in frustration.

"This is our home, Carter. There was nothing for us back in Dallas and this place has some of the best people we've ever met. They're our family, Carter. We're not going back to Dallas so suck it up and get over it"

The crowd around us was silent. The boys were standing in the middle with us now. Cooper also stood silently to the side.

"You're not Mom" He yelled.

My jaw dropped. I was speechless. "You're right, I'm not Mom. She left us. I would never leave you or anyone else, not the way she did" I said in a normal voice. I didn't necessarily want the entire school knowing about our family issues.

"Yeah, well at least she tried to come back. She tried to reconnect."

What was he talking about? She never reached out to us once.

"Carter? What are you not telling me?"

"What's going on here?" Dad and the vice-principal broke up the circle.

"Everyone back to class," Mr. Powell said.

The crowd separated and went to their classes.

Dad looked at me, Carter, Drew, Will, Nick, and Cooper. Remi left when my dad and Mr. Powell broke everyone up.

"You six, my office now" Mr. Powell said angrily.

We all did what he said obediently.

Dad followed with a disappointed look on his face. This group was his team and his children. He had every right to be angry.

We all told Mr. Powell what happened and Drew, Will and Nick were all released. Carter, Cooper and I were left to face our father.

"Do you mind leaving for a moment Joe? I think this is a family matter" Dad asked.

Mr. Powell left before letting us use his office.

"What happened? I know it was more than a dumb fight between Drew and Carter. Coop?"

Cooper was always a daddy's boy. He always cracked when Dad pushed him, but he couldn't say much.

"Honestly, Dad, I don't really know what happened. I'm almost as clueless as you" He shrugged. It was one of the only times he was serious.

Dad nodded understandingly. "Then perhaps you two can actually tell me what happened" He leaned on Mr. Powell's desk and stared us down with his arms crossed.

"Carter and I had a little disagreement."

"A little disagreement?" Dad laughed humorlessly. "Is that another word for a screaming match in front of the entire school?"

It's not like I meant for this to happen; everything just kind of slipped out. It was months of pent up anger and annoyance speaking.

"Sorry, it just sort of happened" I tried to explain.

"It just happened? That's all you got?" Dad questioned in annoyance. He never talked to us like this. I could tell a wave of emotions was hitting him all at once.

"For months I had to put up with Carter and his terrible attitude. I was annoyed and upset and it just all spilled out at once." I argued and threw my hands around.

Dad looked at Carter for an explanation. Carter stayed silent and looked at his feet.

"He brought up Mom," I whispered.

Dad's eyes widened. He looked at Carter again. He held a blank expression. I couldn't tell if he was angry or disappointed or something else entirely.

"I was going to meet up with her in Dallas," he started. His eyes held a gaze at his feet. "Then you decided to move us across the state. We've been talking the weeks leading up to the move. We finally decided to meet up. Suddenly we're moving six hours away." He explained angrily.

"Why didn't you say anything?" He asked blandly. Just like his expression his voice held no emotions.

"Because I didn't know how you would react and Mom didn't want me to tell you."

"That's because your mother was a pathological liar and drug addict. I didn't want you kids to be around her. She didn't want me to know because she was scared I would take you away from her again." Dad explained in a quiet voice.

We all looked at him.

"Wait so you lied to us for half of our lives and you're calling her a liar, when all this time the liar really was you. You told us she left when in reality you took us and left her." Carter stood up in anger.

"No, your mother left for weeks at a time. She left you. I was left with four kids under the age of ten and I couldn't handle you waiting for her and wondering if she would ever come back. I couldn't see my children go through that, so I took you away from her. Before she left the last time, she told me she wouldn't be back for a long time, much longer than any other time. I told her that she shouldn't bother returning." Dad's voice was thick.

For the first time in a long time, I saw my father cry. Tears welled up in my eyes, at the sight. This was hard on him. It was hard on everyone. I jumped up and hugged my dad. Cooper joined in and after a few minutes so did Carter.

"What are we gonna tell Connor?" Cooper wondered aloud.

"We are going to have a family meeting tonight and I'll explain everything" Dad answered.

CHAPTER 33

"Now that the equation involves only a single function of a single angle, your next task is to solve for that function value. To do that, you want to solve-" Mr. Pittman was interrupted by the door being opened. It was Dad who opened the door. I looked curiously over at him and Mr. Pittman. They had a silent conversation.

"Coco, Will" Dad said, effectively getting our attention. "Bring your stuff" he said beckoning us with his pointer finger.

We looked at each other in confusion before packing up and heading out of the classroom. I gave Summer a confused look as I walked out with Will.

"Dad? Is everything okay?" I asked. My voiced was laced with worry.

"Karla just went into labor. Michael called to get Will out of school. Cora, you're staying here, but you don't have to go back to trig. I just wanted to tell you what was going on and it was easier to explain that I needed both of you. Class is almost over anyway.

Will, I mean this in the nicest way possible but get the hell out of here." Dad smiled.

Will's face lit up with excitement but I could tell he was a little worried, especially after the scare last week. I gave him a hug and kissed his cheek. "It'll be fine. I'll come see you later. Text me updates"

"I will, love you" he kissed me quickly before running out of the doors and to his truck.

I looked at Dad excitedly and the bell rang. Students came pouring out of the classrooms. Dad walked off to go teach his history class but not before placing a kiss to my head.

"So what's up?" Summer asked as her and Darren held hands walking up to me.

"Karla went into labor, Will's going to the hospital"

"Yay that's so exciting" Summer said, excitement laced her voice.

"I know right" I squealed. "I have to get to Psych, see you at lunch" I waved them bye and went to Ms. Chan's psychology class.

I was constantly checking my phone for updates on Karla. Everything seemed to be doing okay right now. I haven't heard anything from Will since he told me he made it to the hospital. There's probably nothing to update me on anyway.

My phone dinged and I instantly grabbed it to look at the text.

Everything is good. I'll call you at lunch

Will texted me. I let out a breath of relief I didn't know I was holding. Everything is fine. The scare last week not only scared Will but it also scared me.

I walked to lunch with Remi and Lena. Summer was with her boyfriend today.

"Where's Will? I haven't seen him since second period. He missed fourth and fifth" Lena asked.

"Karla went into labor so he went to the hospital. He's supposed to call for an update any minute" I explained.

Speaking of the devil, my phone rang and Will's contact picture flashed across the screen. I smiled and answered the call.

"Hey babe" I said in a chipper voice.

"Hey snowflake"

"What's happening?"

"Nothing major. We're still just waiting, I'm about to grab lunch, do you want me to bring you something? I have to go pick up Kenz anyway. She had a test she couldn't skip."

I stopped in the middle of the hallway. The girls stopped and looked at me in confusion I motioned for them to continue without me. "Are you sure? You really don't have to."

"Yes, I'm bringing Kenz a shake from Riley's because she couldn't come earlier and I love you. Burger or Chili cheese fries?" He insisted.

"Burger, lettuce and tomatoes, no pickles, unless you want me to die"

I heard him chuckle on the other side of the phone. "Well there goes my plan for the day" he joked. "Okay, I'm pulling into Riley's. I'll be there soon. Love you"

"Love you too" I said with a smile and he hung up the phone.

I walked into the cafeteria and instead of going to the lunch line, like I normally do, I went to the table with everyone else.

My brothers looked at me with confusion written across their faces. They never liked when I skipped a meal, intentionally or not. I sat down next to Remi in my normal spot.

"Why aren't you going to get food?" Carter interrogated.

"Calm down Will's bringing me lunch when he picks up Kenz in a couple minutes." They looked at me still confused.

"Karla went into labor this morning and he's been at the hospital. Kenzie had a test that she couldn't skip so he's picking her up now and bringing me lunch." I explained for what felt like the thirtieth time today.

They all nodded in understanding and burst with excitement about baby Erickson coming soon. I, for one, am excited to hold a baby. They're just so precious.

"Here you go babe" Wills voice said from behind me and plopped a Riley's to-go bag in front of me along with a drink.

"Thanks Will" I reached up and kissed his cheek.

"I have to go but I'll see you later, okay?" He said and hugged me.

"Bye love you"

"Love you more" he kissed my cheek and left us again.

"What are we chopped liver?" Nick joked as Will walked away.

We all laughed with him. Conversation fell easily over the table. I dug into my burger that Will had just brought me. I checked for pickles before I took a bite. Ever since the allergic reaction I had when I first got here, I made sure to look at every burger I ate for pickles.

After lunch, Remi, Nick, Sam, and I walked to AP US History taught by none other than my father.

"Hey Dad" I hugged him and he kissed my cheek before I sat in my normal seat.

"Hey, Mr. B" Remi said and hugged him as well before taking her seat next to me.

The boys just waved at him as they took their seats behind us. Dad took roll and started on today's lesson about the Civil War.

His class went by fast and before I knew it the class was over and it was time to go to English class with Mrs. Atkins. If I haven't mentioned it before, she hates me. In my defense, she shouldn't have been all teacherly during the summer. Just because you don't have a life, doesn't mean your students don't too.

"Good afternoon, Mrs. Atkins" I tried to suck up to her.

"Hello, Miss Barnes" her voice monotone.

Remi giggled next to me. "Why do you even keep trying? She's not going to warm up to you, if you annoy the shit out of her."

I groaned and hit my head on my desk in front of me. "I don't even know" I answered honestly.

My phone dinged. I looked to see Will texting me.

She's going into the delivery room

I'm so nervous

I laughed and texted him back assuring him that it'll all be okay. I couldn't contain my excitement. I'm so excited for their family and Will's going to be such a great big brother. Kenzie is going to be a good big sister.

I quickly texted Dad and the boys to update them, in case no one else did.

"Miss Barnes, is there something on your phone more important than my lesson?" Mrs. Atkins' authoritative voice called out from the front of the room.

I quickly snapped my phone down. "No ma'am, I just had a family thing, but I'm done with that now" I answered with a weak smile.

It took all she could not to roll her eyes at me and she continued her lesson, that I had missed at least the first five minutes of.

I looked over a Remi which I shouldn't have because we almost burst into laughter in the middle of class. I tried my hardest not to look at Remi for the rest of class. Thankfully next period is study hall and I wouldn't have a teacher on my ass about my phone being out.

The rest of the day went by pretty quickly and the boys had practice after school. I had to watch and do homework since Remi had to go home right away and there wasn't cheer practice or anything today.

My phone rang and I saw that Will was face timing me. I answered instantly.

"Hey babe" I said.

"Hey" He whispered. He was dark but I could still see the smile on his face. "Mom and the baby are sleeping right now" He said as he walked across the hospital room.

He flipped the camera to face the little baby in the bassinet. He was so small and precious.

"Oh my gosh" I covered my mouth with a gasp. "He's so precious" I awed at him. It's amazing how tiny he is.

"Cora, this is Ryan. Ryan this is Cora, she's my girlfriend" he whispered to the baby.

"Ryan?" I asked Will as he turned the camera back to him.

Will nodded.

"I can't wait to see him in person." I gushed. "He's just so darn precious."

"I can't wait either. Well I've got to go, but I love you and I'll see you tomorrow" He blew me a kiss.

"I love you too, Will." I giggled and bit my lip to stop so I could properly say bye.

He groaned and threw his head back. "Great now I want to kiss you. How could you do this to me?" He teased.

"I'm sorry. I just wanted to say goodbye to you properly, excuse me for wanting to be a good girlfriend" I laughed.

"Okay well then I promise tomorrow I will kiss the shit out of you when I see you and I won't care who sees"

I laughed at his dorkiness.

"Goodbye snowflake." He covered his eyes with his hand playfully.

I laughed and blew him a kiss. "Bye babe, I'll see you tomorrow"

We hung up, by now practice was pretty much over and they were all talking about the game tomorrow and how they're going to prepare. I know Will is probably going to be here because he wouldn't miss a game for the world, but that would mean his family would miss the second game in a row.

It was Saturday before we could go over to the Erickson's to see Ryan for the first time. We knocked on the door and Will answered. I immediately wrapped my arms around his torso. He chuckled and hugged me back.

"Hello to you too, snowflake" He chuckled. "Y'all come on in Ryan just woke up. He's in the living room with everyone else" The boys all went to the living room but I stayed attached to Will.

"Kiss me" I whispered.

"I'm hurt you even had to tell me" He joked and leaned down to give me a kiss. We pulled a part a couple of seconds later.

We wrapped our hands around each other and went into the living room. Dad was talking to Micheal, the boys were surrounding the baby that Karla was holding, and Poppy was sitting to the side.

"Hi Poppy, I didn't know you were here" I greeted her with a hug.

"Hi darling. I see you listened to my advice, huh?" She winked at me. She referred to the time I met her and she told me to date Will. It's crazy to think that just a couple months ago I thought that Will and I were just friends. Evidently, everyone knew but us.

I couldn't help but chuckle at her. "Of course, thank you Poppy" I smiled from ear to ear.

I turned to the boys and Karla. "Okay, I think it's my turn now" I said with a grin. I couldn't help it I wanted to hold the baby so bad.

Karla handed him off to me gently and I made sure that I held him correctly. My heart exploded the second I had him in my arms. I slowly sat with him.

"Oh my goodness, Isn't he just the most precious thing in the world?" I cooed. I felt the couch dip next to me and looked to see Will next to me. He laid his chin on my shoulder and leaned my head against his. "Just look at him. I could hold him all day long."

"I can't wait for this one day. You know, have kids and start a family? I hope it'll be with you Cora. I want to spend the rest of my life with you." he whispered in my ear and kissed my cheek.

I froze for a second, He wants to have a family with me? We're only seventeen and he's already thinking of our future together. We've only been dating a month, but I know there's a part of me that wants that too.

"I love you Cora Maeve Barnes"

"I love you to William Orion Erickson" I whispered to him and pressed a kiss to his cheek. I laid my head back against his and smiled at the little baby in my arms.

Epilogue

I turned up the music as Will drove me to his house. I began to sing along with the song playing. I didn't miss the constant glances Will made towards me. He smiled over at me before he looked back to the road.

"What?" I giggled.

"You're just really cute when you sing" He told me with the cutest smile ever. I loved when he smiled at me like that when he complimented me.

My cheeks turned pink at the compliment. "Thank you babe" I smiled at him. I sang to the radio again as we turned to his street. He pulled into his driveway and I noticed his parent's cars were not in the driveway. They didn't normally park in the garage.

"Are your parents not home?" I asked him as he opened the truck door for me.

He shook his head at me. "I thought I told you they were at Kenzie's soccer game tonight. I think they're going out to eat with the team after."

"Ryan too?" I asked.

"Yeah" He unlocked the house door and let me in. He shut the door behind us and locked it.

I was walking to the living room when Will grabbed my wrist and pulled me back into his chest. I steadied myself with my hands against his chest. I looked up at him to say something but he beat me to it when he crashed his lips against mine. He caught me by surprise and I wrapped my arms around his neck.

He deepened the kiss with his hands on my cheeks. He gently rubbed my cheekbones. I moved my hands down to his lower back. He grabbed me by the waist and led me over to the door before pinning me up against it. My hands found their way to his hair.

My stomach was swarmed with butterflies as he detached his lips from mine and made his way down my neck. I tried to suppress a moan when he got to a sensitive spot but I failed. I could feel him smirked against my skin before his lips began to torture the spot as his hands caressed my hips.

Having enough of not kissing him, I forced his lips back up to mine. We kissed until we needed a breath.

"What was that for?" I asked him as I was still pinned against the door and his hands were still rubbing gentle circles in my hips.

"Just because I love you" He answered and kissed my nose. I swear he was trying to make my heart explode. "I have to go make dinner. There's more comfortable clothes in my room, if you want those instead. You can also pick whatever movie you want us to watch."

I nodded slightly. He kissed me one more time and went into the kitchen.

I went upstairs and found one of Will's hoodies and his smallest pair of sweats. I changed out of my jeans and red smocked crop top and into the hoodie and sweats. I had to roll the sweats up a couple times but they worked enough. I left my clothes in a controlled pile on the floor. I, of course, made sure they weren't sitting in the middle of the floor.

I walked back down stairs to the kitchen to see Will humming to himself while making something on the stove. I smiled as he swayed his body in beat with his humming.

"What are you making?" I asked as I walked behind him and wrapped my arms around his torso and pressed my cheek to his back. "It smells amazing"

"Pizzadillas. Will Erickson special for someone special" He answered. "They're almost ready"

I reached up on my tippy toes to give him a kiss on the cheek. "Thank you" I whispered into his ear.

"Anything for you darling" He whispered back.

I leaned back against the counter and watched silently as he made us dinner. Once it was done, he washed the dishes as he waited for it to cool off. He made us a plate to share and carried it into the living room for us. I followed and sat down. He grabbed a blanket and threw it at my face.

I giggled and draped it over my legs. I opened it for Will to get under too with the food.

"Have you picked out a movie?" He asked me.

"I was thinking Remember the Titans" I said.

"Then that's what we're watching" He pressed a kiss to my temple and turned on Remember the Titans.

We snuggled together, ate our pizzadillas, and watched a movie. This was literally the best date ever. I couldn't ask for anything else. My boyfriend showered me with more love than I deserve and that's why I love him.

After we finished eating, we moved into a more comfortable position. I was laying in between his legs on his chest. He rubbed my back and I raked my hand through his golden locks.

"I love you" I whispered to him.

"I love you" He whispered back and kissed my head.

As we continued watching movies, my eyes got heavier and heavier. I tried to keep myself from falling asleep, but I couldn't keep my eyes open any longer.

I felt something shift under me. It took me a second to open my eyes and register what was happening around me. I saw Will trying to move from under me.

"I'm sorry sunshine, I didn't mean to wake you" He whispered.

I got up from my position on top of Will and looked around. I checked my phone and saw that it was ten thirty at night.

"I need to get home" I grumbled.

"Why don't you just stay here?" Will asked. "It's late and my parents won't care"

"Yeah, but my brothers will."

"Then we can tell them you fell asleep here and they won't question anything." I gave him an incredulous look. "After we assure them nothing happened." Will stood up. "Come on let's get to bed" He reached out both of his hands to me. I took them and he led me up to his bedroom.

As we were walking up the stairs we met Karla in the hallway.

"Oh Cora, you're up. I just told your dad that you fell asleep here and you were probably going to stay here. I'll call him back if you want to go home" she offered.

"I'm okay here as long as it's okay with you" I answered.

She gave me a smile and a hug. "Of course I'm okay with it sweetie. Goodnight" She kissed my head and Will's cheek.

Will led me the rest of his way to his room and we both got in his bed. Will wrapped his arms around me and held me close to him. I loved the feeling of his arms around me. I could die in this position and be completely happy.